MATTHEW PRITCHARD worked as a journalist in Spain for ten years, mainly for the ex-pat press, but also for UK nationals (at which he has some good connections). He grew up in a house filled with gas masks, military helmets, swords and rifles and has possessed a lifelong interest in WWII ever since. Together with his father and uncle, he has amassed a sizeable collection of memoirs and memorabilia contemporary to the period.

BROKEN ARROW

Also by Matthew Pritchard

BROKEN ARROW

Matthew Pritchard

SALT

CROMER

PUBLISHED BY SALT
12 Norwich Road, Cromer, Norfolk NR27 0AX United Kingdom

Printed in Great Britain by Clays Ltd, St Ives plc

Typeset in Sabon 10/13

ISBN 978 1 78463 040 9 paperback

1 3 5 7 9 8 6 4 2

To all those who are honest, open and willing

BROKEN ARROW

PROLOGUE

Gabriel Varela was released from the Cantabrian prison on June 29th, 2012. That same morning, he took a bus south across Spain and spent most of the fourteen-hour journey staring through the window, thinking of Esme. When he arrived in Almería, he went straight to the derelict lock-up where his gear was stored and rummaged until he found the box that held his M65 jacket and his punch dagger, the black stainless steel one with the four-inch, double-edged blade and the T-shaped handle.

Then he set to work.

He already knew in which order he would kill the men: long nights lying awake in his prison cell had given him all the time he needed to decide. But before he began dispensing justice he needed to plan how best to do it: he could not risk killing one of the men and having the others flee.

His preparations took six weeks, during which he followed and watched each man in turn, memorising his routines and learning his secrets. Then, one night in late August, he loaded shovel, pickaxe, compass and map into his car and drove to the Tabernas Desert.

It took him eight hours to locate the flat boulder that covered the grave and another ninety minutes to exhume the corpse and unwrap its linen shroud. Although the dead man had lain in desert soil for seven years, his remains had not putrefied; instead, all the moisture had been sucked from the corpse's flesh, reducing it to a wizened root of a thing clad in dusty clothing.

Varela searched the corpse's pockets until he found the leather wallet he knew would be there. He undid the clasp of the wallet and checked that the plastic identity card inside was still legible. Then he replaced it in the pocket, wrapped the corpse in a tarpaulin and carried it to his car.

He was surprised by how little the remains weighed. Then he thought of Esme and of how little she had weighed at the end. His expression hardened.

He was going to make the selfish pricks pay for what they'd done to her. Gabriel Varela would make sure of that, or he would die trying.

PART ONE

LA RECOGIDA

1

IT WAS MIDDAY and things were getting ugly inside the Last Chance Saloon.

The press had been waiting for more than an hour and tempers were beginning to fray. Each time the saloon's batwing doors squeaked inwards, thirty heads turned in unison to see if the Guardia Civil spokesperson had *finally* arrived and the news briefing could get going. Each time they were disappointed, the grumbling grew louder. Cynics had started muttering that there was no dead body, that Sixto Escobar had planned the whole thing as a publicity stunt.

Danny Sanchez wasn't worried, though.

He'd used the back entrance to the Little Arizona Western Theme Park and had seen officers from the Scenes of Crime unit out at the Indian village, unfolding a body bag and stretching incident tape between a pair of teepees. Whether the reality of the situation would match the sensationalist tone of the press release circulated by Escobar that same morning – *Butchered Body Found at Top Tourist Draw* – remained to be seen. So far, the existence of the dead body was the only fact Danny had been able to confirm. He still had no idea what the murder weapon might have been, the victim's age

5

or why a corpse should have been dumped on the outskirts of a fake western frontier town in the middle of Europe's only desert. The one time he'd managed to get close enough to Sixto Escobar to pose questions, the answers had been irritatingly circumspect.

Whatever the truth of the situation, it was obvious that Escobar had determined to make the most of his moment in the spotlight. The Guardia Civil had ordered the theme park to be closed down for the day, but an unlikely assortment of costumed staff-members – bandidos, cowboys, can-can girls, Confederate soldiers – lurked in the few areas of the saloon not already taken over by the invading reporters.

And, of course, the self-styled "Sheriff of Little Arizona" was there, doing all his shtick for the cameras, resplendent in white Stetson and tailcoat, cowboy boots and silver sheriff's badge. Escobar probably thought the get-up made him look like John Wayne, but with his jowly peasant face and short, dumpy body the overall effect was closer to Boss Hogg.

Danny looked at his watch and hooked a finger under the collar of his T-shirt, trying to get some air to his chest. It was the wrong type of weather to be standing inside a crowded clapboard building with minimal air con. It must have been 35°C outside.

The batwing doors squeaked and all heads turned expectantly, but it was only Escobar's PA, looking even more hassled than when she'd left thirty minutes earlier. She crossed the room, shaking her head. Escobar blew air as he listened to her and lifted his Stetson to mop his brow, revealing a sunburnt pate surrounded by a horseshoe of frizzy hair. Then he stepped up onto the stage. The discontented muttering in the saloon died, leaving only the jangle of Escobar's spurs as he walked to the front of the stage, huckster's smile spread wide across his face.

'My friends,' he said, 'I've just been informed the authorities have now been unavoidably detained. I appreciate the patience you've all shown so why don't we just go ahead and start without them?'

The reporters looked at each other and rolled their eyes. A young stringer for *El Mundo* stood. 'What questions can you answer? We were promised an official statement. Where the hell is the Guardia Civil?'

'Which part of *unavoidably detained* do you need me to explain to you?' Escobar said in a jocular tone that didn't match the look in his eyes. Some of the journalists laughed. The stringer sat down, his face reddening.

'However,' Escobar continued, hooking thumbs beneath the lapels of his tailcoat, 'the good news is that the Guardia has authorised me to answer your questions. Now, I think you all know the basics of the situation from the press release, so why don't we just go straight to the Q&A?'

Danny exchanged a look with another reporter. The Guardia had authorised Escobar to answer questions? That was bullshit and everyone knew it – you only had to see the sudden panicked expression on the PA's face to realise that – but what could they do? They had deadlines to meet, and now they had wasted most of the morning at Little Arizona they had to write something – a fact of which Sixto Escobar was probably very much aware.

The reporters fell into sullen silence as microphones and

digital recorders were placed on a table in front of the stage. Danny rested his notepad atop the saloon's pianola. The Q&A began.

'Who found the dead man?' a radio journalist asked.

Escobar pushed the brim of his Stetson back. 'I did. It's my habit to begin each day with a moment of solitude at our Indian village. As you'll probably know, every one of the teepees there was hand-crafted by descendants of the Lakota tribe, so there is a spirituality to the place that –'

'Get on with it,' someone shouted.

'– I find most restful,' Escobar continued, without missing a beat.

'What time did you find the body?'

'At 07:48 on the dot. Ever since our reptile house received a new alligator – bringing the total number of 'gators to four, might I add, every one of which is capable of killing a grown man – we have to start work here early.'

'Exactly where on the Indian village was the body found?'

'Close to the entrance. The poor bastard was tied to a wagon wheel with rope.'

A ripple of excitement flowed through the room as the reporters began whispering to each other. Tied to a wagon wheel? What did that mean? A gangland killing was the quickly formed consensus of opinion: either a drug deal gone wrong, or a punishment execution.

'Can you speculate on how he was killed?' Danny said.

'I think he'd been stabbed. There was dried blood on the front of his clothing.'

'You *think* he'd been stabbed? Why'd you describe the body as being "butchered", then?'

Escobar fixed his dark eyes on Danny. 'Butchers use knives, don't they, wiseass?'

Danny went to ask more, but stopped when Escobar's PA hurried onto the stage, looking vexed, and whispered something into Escobar's ear. He made placatory gestures, but when he turned back to the reporters his smile had lost some of its sparkle.

Danny could guess why: Escobar had said too much. The Guardia weren't going to thank him for holding a press conference in the first place, but revealing specifics of the dead man's condition could really land him in hot water.

Sure enough, the press conference meandered after that, with Sixto providing increasingly long-winded answers that were short on specifics and heavy on the blatant promotion of Little Arizona. Danny had heard enough. He left the saloon and went to sit on the wooden walkway outside.

The Little Arizona Western Theme Park occupied a twenty-five acre enclosure in the centre of Almería's Tabernas Desert. The park consisted of a wooden fort, an Indian village and a frontier town of seventy buildings divided into four streets, most of which were leftovers from Sixties' film productions, back when the desert's arid hills and arroyos provided the backdrop for hundreds of Spaghetti Westerns. All of the clichés were covered: there was a bank with thick stucco walls, a sheriff's office with barred windows and a town square with watering troughs and a gallows.

Danny lit a cigarette and watched as an ambulance drove along the dusty central street. He wanted to speak to Sixto Escobar alone, but he couldn't do that until the other reporters had departed. The minutes ticked by as Danny smoked and watched the shadows of clouds slip across the slopes of the nearby Sierra Alhamilla.

Sixto Escobar looked very pleased with himself when the grumbling press pack departed ten minutes later. It was nearly 12:30 and his performance was guaranteed a slot on the lunchtime news. As the television crews packed away their kit, Danny went back inside the saloon and watched Escobar climb the wooden stairs that led to his upstairs office. When the last of the reporters had departed, Danny followed him.

'Whoever you are, I'm not here,' Escobar said when Danny knocked.

'It's Danny, Sixto. From the English newspaper.'

'What do you want?'

'I want to see the photos.'

A three-beat pause. Then came Sixto's voice, cautious now: 'Photos of what?'

'The photos you took out at the Indian village while you were waiting for the Guardia to arrive. I'm guessing they're of the dead body.'

'Who told you I took photos?'

'I spoke to the cowboy you had out on the slip road giving directions.'

'Pepe?' A key rattled in the lock and the office door swung inwards. 'What did that bastard tell you?' Escobar said, motioning for Danny to come inside.

The air in the office had a hot, stale scent to it, more reminiscent of a bedroom than an office. The wooden walls were decorated with farmyard implements and posters of long-forgotten Westerns. Huge piles of paperwork covered the desk, and a plastic box on the floor held mounds of unopened mail.

Escobar dropped heavily into the padded director's chair behind the desk. When he was seated, there was something distinctly frog-like about the width of his mouth and the way his big, jowly face seemed to rise up out of his shoulders.

'You know you're not supposed to smoke indoors on business premises anymore, don't you?' Danny said, when Escobar clipped the end from a huge cigar and lit it. 'I could sue you.'

Escobar sneered and puffed at his cigar. 'What can I say? It's the Wild West. Now tell me what you want. I'm a busy man.'

'You've got photos of the dead body.'

Escobar rolled the cigar between his lips. 'Perhaps.'

'Your cowboy down on the gate seemed quite sure about it.'

'All right, let's say I did take a few shots of the dead man. What's it to you?'

'I want to see them.'

'How much is it worth to you?'

'I don't pay bribes to get information.'

Sixto laughed. 'If I've learned one thing in life, son, it's that *everyone* has their price. But it's not your money that I want.'

'What do you want then?'

'A full-page article in Sureste News. Tell people how much things have improved here. Tell them about the new alligator at the zoo. You're the paper's chief reporter – you can arrange it.'

'Why don't you just buy some advertising?'

The sneer returned to Escobar's face. 'Did you say buy? Mother of God, I can't afford to buy myself a damned drink and you're talking about advertising.' He grabbed a fistful of paperwork and shook it despairingly. 'Look at this. Nothing but goddamn overheads. You know how much it costs to feed four alligators? Or to heat snake tanks? It ain't cheap, let me tell you. And now I got that lot of vultures out there . . .' – he waved in the general direction of the park – '. . . whining about unpaid wages. They should be thankful they've even got jobs. Do you know how much alimony that whore of an ex-wife is screwing me for?'

'You're breaking my heart, Sixto.'

Escobar folded his hands on his gut. 'If you want to see the photos, that's fine. But first tell me when and where the article about me will appear.'

'I might be able to do something later in the month. But only a half-page. And I can't write anything that's obvious advertising.'

Escobar extended a sweat-damp, fleshy hand and they shook on it. Then he took a laptop from a desk drawer and turned it towards Danny. He rested his cowboy boots on the edge of the desk as Danny began clicking through the images on the screen.

The first photo showed the dead man sitting in an upright position against a wagon wheel. He was dressed in a blue hooded sweatshirt and jeans, the hood pulled up to obscure the face. The fabric of the sweatshirt looked dusty and stiff, the way clothing does when it has been buried, and a dark stain around the area of the heart was clearly visible. Loops of rope tied under the armpits kept the corpse from flopping forwards. Danny frowned as he noticed the corpse's hands: the skin on them was dark and withered and looked almost like jerky. Danny peered more closely.

'Those hands are nearly skeletal. This guy's been dead for months, Sixto. Maybe years.'

'So?'

'Your press release described a "butchered" body.'

Escobar smiled, revealing yellowed teeth.

'So I sexed the story up a little to create some interest. What does it matter? You don't think the Press would have trawled all the way out here if they'd known the poor bastard was mummified, do you?'

'Well, I certainly wouldn't have,' Danny said with a wry smile. You had to hand it to him: Sixto Escobar definitely had *cojones*.

'Anyway, what do you care?' Escobar said. 'You're the only one now that knows the truth. Sell it as an exclusive and make everyone else look dumb. I thought you journos loved doing that.'

Danny lit a cigarette and continued clicking through the photos.

'Why do you think the corpse is tied to a wagon wheel?' he said. 'What does that mean?'

Sixto puffed his cigar as he considered the matter. 'It means whoever put him there is a sick bastard.'

'But what's the significance of that precise spot? Tied to a wagon wheel at the entrance to the Indian village?'

Sixto steepled his fingertips. 'Someone was wandering around my theme park last night with a semi-skeletal corpse, and you're worried about why he tied it to a wagon wheel. What's it matter? The guy was probably on drugs.'

'It has to mean something. If not, why'd he take the trouble to do it?'

The faintest of frowns creased Escobar's brow. Then he shook his head. 'If you want to play guessing games about what motivated this psycho, that's up to you. But don't go trying to link it to me. That body out there is probably some *moro* that got himself lost in the desert and died of exposure. Someone found him and decided to play a prank. You've seen what the desert does to dead bodies, it turns them into leather. They can last for years out there.'

Danny flicked back and forth between the images as they spoke. There were a dozen photos in all, taken from different angles. And taken on two different cameras, Danny realised: the first set of images had a grainy, blurred quality to it that the second set lacked.

'Why are there two sets of photos?' Danny said.

'One of my workers took some photos as well. Those are the grainy ones.'

Danny chewed his lip as he flicked through the photos. He'd been a reporter for twenty years now, and instinct told him something was wrong.

'How did you know it was a man?' he said, after he'd looked at all the photos.

'What do you mean?'

'Everyone's been talking about "a dead man". It said so on the press release.'

'Yeah. So what?'

Danny pointed towards the screen, at the corpse's hooded face and the semi-skeletal hands. 'How did you know, though? There's nothing to distinguish whether it's male or female. As it is, I imagine the forensics will have to determine the sex by looking at the bone structure.'

Escobar became suddenly thoughtful. 'Patricio told me it was a man.'

'So how did Patricio know? And does that mean Patricio found the body?'

Sixto waved his hand irritably. 'Yes, all right, you've found me out. Patricio and his son, Tolo, found the body. Then they told me, and I phoned it through to the Guardia.'

'Why didn't we get to speak to them at the press conference?'

'You don't think I'd let those two bozos up on stage, do you? I pay them to shovel horse-shit, not do publicity.'

Danny squinted as something else in the photos caught his attention. He flicked back and forth between the images.

'This one was taken by Patricio, yeah?' he said, turning the laptop so that Escobar could see the screen as well. 'So this one – your one – was taken later on. Is that right?'

Escobar nodded.

'Something's been taken out of the sweatshirt pocket,' Danny said, indicating a distinct bulge amid the blue fabric of the sweatshirt that was missing in the later set of images. Escobar looked back and forth between the two sets of photos, his face darkening. Then he stood up and stalked out of the room. Danny followed.

Escobar headed downstairs, passing through the saloon and out onto the dirt road that led past the general store and stagecoach offices and down towards the stables. He walked to the back of the building and kicked the door open with the tip of his cowboy boot.

A big, dark man with watery eyes was tipping horse feed into buckets. He took one look at the expression on Escobar's face and began walking backwards away from him. Horses skittered behind the stable doors.

'Where is it, Tolo?' Escobar said.

Tolo was a big man, but there was a slow, childlike look to his face. He flinched when Escobar shouted, then made as if to shrug. His shoulders moved about a centimetre before Escobar buried his fist in Tolo's stomach. Tolo staggered backwards and fell heavily into a pile of straw.

A second man emerged from a nearby stable. When he saw what was happening he tried to run for it. Escobar froze him with a snarl.

'Where is it, Patricio, you dumb bastard?'

'Where's what?'

Patricio was a snaggle-toothed wisp of a man. Escobar crossed the stable-house and jabbed a finger into his bony chest.

'Whatever it was you took from the pocket of Sleeping Beauty out there. And if either of you waste my time denying it, I'm going to tie you to the back of my 4x4 and drag you out into the desert. What was it?'

The father was kneeling beside his son, a skinny arm wrapped around Tolo's heaving shoulders. 'Don't hit him no more,' he said. 'It was a wallet.'

'¡Me cago en Dios!' Escobar said through gritted teeth. 'Where is it now? Don't look at him. Answer me.'

'We threw it away'.

'Why?'

The two men exchanged nervous looks. 'Because we took money from it,' Patricio said in a whisper.

Escobar swore properly this time, the type of fast, fluid

outburst to which the Spanish language is so well suited. Patricio and Tolo cowered. Danny took a step backwards, too, as Escobar kicked a bucket across the stables, his face flushed a furious shade of red.

When he'd calmed down, he turned to Patricio and bellowed, 'What are you waiting for? Go and get it.'

They waited five minutes. When Patricio returned, he slunk into the stable-house like a beaten dog and handed the wallet to Escobar, mumbling an apology. Escobar told him to shut up.

The wallet had obviously been retrieved from a bin somewhere: a lump of something viscous, yellow and organic was stuck to the outside. Escobar cleaned it off with a handful of straw then opened the wallet out. The leather was stiff and dry.

'This is how they knew he was a man,' he said, fishing a plastic DNI, the Spanish identity card, from within the wallet and handing it to Danny. Escobar turned towards Patricio and told him to replace the money. Sixto reeled as Patricio handed him the stiff banknotes.

'¡*Joder*! the stuff stinks. And you were planning on trying to spend this, were you, Einstein?'

Danny blew dust and sand away from the DNI and looked at the name on the identity card: Hector Castillo Mendez. The ID card had a passport photo, bottom right. Castillo was late thirties in the photo. He had a sallow face, thick, dark eyebrows and wore spectacles. Danny thought there was something vaguely academic about the man's appearance. And vaguely familiar, too, he realised, without knowing why.

'Do you recognise this guy, Sixto?' Danny said, holding up the ID card.

Escobar was on the phone to his PA. He covered the mobile with a hand. 'How many times do I need to tell you, this is nothing to do with me? Now, give me that DNI back so I can –'

Sixto Escobar stopped dead as he focused on the identity card and got his first good look at the photo it held. For a moment he gaped and his eyes bulged, as if something half-seen and horrible had come suddenly into focus.

Then every drop of colour drained from his florid face.

2

Iт was mid-afternoon now, and the only thing moving in Almería city was the heat-haze. Danny was sitting in a bar on the *Avenida de Federico Garcia Lorca*, drinking iced coffee and yawning. He felt tired, but it had nothing to do with the stifling heat. Danny had been working every hour God sent for nearly eight months.

It had begun at the start of the year, when someone at the newspaper chain's head office had decided to reduce the staff at Sureste News to just Danny and three others, all of whom were to be employed on a freelance basis, which meant they lost out on paid holiday and sick pay. On top of that, the newspaper's editor, William Fouldes, had gone on sick leave around the same time and never returned.

The only positive factor about the situation was that Danny no longer felt obliged to bring his stories to Sureste News first. Previously, he and his photographer friend, Paco Pino, had always published the exclusives they sold to the national press under the pseudonym Alan Smithee, but as soon as Danny was forced to go freelance, he had begun using his own name.

Still, at least Danny had a job. That was a luxury one in three Spaniards had not enjoyed since the economic crash, and the experts said things were going to get a lot worse before they got better. Danny couldn't really see how that was possible: the Spanish economy was on its knees and the situation in Almería was already catastrophic. At the local job centre the queue was 300 strong two hours before the place even opened.

Danny finished his coffee and went outside to smoke a cigarette, wincing as he stepped into the afternoon heat.

Sixto Escobar had recognised Hector Castillo's image on the identity card, Danny was sure of it. Christ, the way Escobar had reacted, it was as if he'd seen a ghost. And that made it doubly interesting, because in all the years Danny had known the man it was the first time Sixto Escobar had ever lost his poker face.

Danny first met Escobar back in 2006, when a friend of a friend put some work Danny's way translating promotional material for Little Arizona. Danny had spent an entire week translating reams of Escobar's misspelt hyperbole into English, but had only ever received half of the agreed fee – and that after months of hassle.

The experience shouldn't really have come as a surprise, because everyone knew that Sixto Escobar was crooked. But what interested Danny now was whether Escobar was so crooked that it might have led someone to dump a dead body at his theme park.

Naturally, Sixto had denied any knowledge of this Hector Castillo. Moments after looking at the photo on the DNI card, Escobar had hurried away, claiming he needed to speak to the Guardia Civil. Danny had followed, but Escobar had ignored all his questions and become surly when pressed. The last Danny had seen of Escobar, he'd been heading office-wards with the urgent gait of someone desperate to make a phone call.

That was why Danny had spent the last hour on his laptop, looking up everything he could find on the man.

Sixto Escobar was forty-seven years old, the only son of a politician from Las Jarapas, a small town in the north of the province of Almería. Sixto had started out as the owner of a company that specialised in earth moving, pipe laying and foundations and had made a fortune in the construction boom at the turn of the century, although the exact source of his millions had always been a bone of contention. Sixto's version was that he'd earned them through hard graft and sharp-eyed business acumen; his detractors pointed to Papa Escobar's thirteen-year tenure as Las Jarapas's councillor for town planning and the juicy public works contracts he had put his son's way.

Escobar had purchased Little Arizona in 2000. Back then, it had likely been an impulse vanity purchase, but since the economic crash had destroyed Spain's construction market the theme park had become Escobar's principal business concern. Rumour had it that things weren't going too well at Little Arizona, thanks in part to the theme park's bigger and better rivals – places like Texas Hollywood, Western Leone and Oasys – and in part to the vicious divorce Escobar had been through a few years earlier.

Danny finished his cigarette, went back inside the bar and ordered another iced-coffee. Despite his being the only customer, the music in the bar was so loud he had to shout in order to make himself heard. Things like that reminded Danny he wasn't actually from Spain: despite having a Spanish mother and a fluent grasp of the language, his tolerance for noise was about fifteen decibels lower than a pure bred Spaniard's.

Danny took the new coffee back to his table and opened

his laptop again. This time he turned his attention to Hector Castillo.

That was when the story really began to pique his interest.

A simple internet search of the man's name revealed a number of articles describing Castillo's disappearance in March of 2005, although in this case "disappearance" was really a euphemism for "body never found", as there seemed to be little doubt that Castillo had met a violent end. Witnesses reported hearing a muffled groan close to the alleyway where he was last seen, and a pool of blood matching Castillo's blood group type was found in the same place.

Danny remembered covering the case: that was why the man's photo had seemed familiar. The case had baffled the media at the time, as Castillo's personal life was squeaky clean: he was a hard-working member of a scientific research facility and a teetotal, church-going bachelor to boot, well-liked by colleagues and neighbours. As with most mysterious disappearances, the story had drawn a lot of attention for a few days and then interest had waned.

Danny looked at the photos of Castillo that accompanied the articles. He was sallow-faced with soft, watery eyes and had a faint, diffident smile that revealed a slight overbite. He looked wholesome and healthy, the type that had bran for breakfast and went for lunchtime swims.

Danny frowned when he noticed a description of the clothing Castillo had been wearing on the night of his disappearance: jeans and a blue hooded top. He thought about the photos he'd seen of the corpse at Little Arizona. The clothing was the same.

That meant Castillo's body had likely been buried for seven

years somewhere in the Tabernas Desert: corpses left in desert soil do not rot, they wither and mummify – something to do with the lack of microbes in the soil means that the normal process of putrefaction cannot occur. But why go back after so long, dig the poor sod up and dump him on Sixto Escobar? It had to mean something, Danny decided. It was a message.

Danny sipped coffee as he scribbled theories into his notepad and decided how to move his article forward. He would need to speak to people who had known Castillo and ask them whether any links existed between the man and Escobar. The online articles mentioned Castillo's mother, but a few phone calls revealed she was now dead, and that Castillo had no siblings. Danny's first port of call was therefore the scientific research centre Castillo had worked for, MWGP.

MWGP was a Hispano/German outfit that conducted research on solar power, industrial agriculture and the effects of pesticides, among other things. Danny rang the telephone number displayed on the company's website and asked the secretary to put him through to the person that handled its press relations, who turned out to be a man named Antonio Saez. The telephone crackled. Then a male voice speaking Spanish said, 'Who is this? What do you want?'

Danny explained. Or rather he tried to. As soon as he mentioned Hector Castillo's name, Saez cut him off.

'What the devil do you want to know about poor Hector? I've nothing to say on the matter. Do you hear me? Absolutely nothing.'

'So you wouldn't be interested to know that Hector's body was found out in the Tabernas Desert today?'

Saez hesitated. Danny could hear the man thinking, so he said, 'Answer a few questions for me, Señor Saez, and I'll be happy to tell you everything I know.'

'OK. But I'm not prepared to answer anything that constitutes speculation on Hector's disappearance. That particular dead horse has already been sufficiently flogged.'

'Did you know Hector?'

'Yes. We worked together.'

'What was he like?'

'He was a quiet man. He minded his own business and did what he was told.' The way Saez said this, it sounded like he considered those the highest virtues anyone could possess.

'Did Hector have any interests?'

'Science.'

'Apart from science, I mean.'

'Donkeys.'

'As in the animal?'

'I'm unaware of the appellation being used to describe anything else.'

Danny's pen paused momentarily. Right, it was like that, was it? That would be the last time he underarm bowled to Señor Saez.

'How did this interest manifest itself?' Danny said.

'Hector volunteered weekends at a donkey sanctuary.'

'Do you have a telephone number for the sanctuary?'

'No.'

'Did Hector have any friends? Or a girlfriend?'

'Hector's private life was his own business.'

'But surely he must have mentioned some – '

'I am not prepared to be interrogated by you. I don't hold

with the way modern journalists feel they have a right to go trampling through people's privacy.'

'Did Hector know a man named Sixto Escobar?'

'I've no idea. Who is he?'

'He runs the Little Arizona theme park.'

'Why on earth would Hector consort with someone like that? Now, I've answered your questions. Tell me what the devil is going on with Hector.'

Danny explained what had happened that morning at Little Arizona. Saez listened, then cut him off again.

'Do you mean to say that the Guardia Civil have not formally identified the body?'

'Not as far as I know.'

'Then we have nothing more to discuss. And let me say how deeply I despise this speculative brand of journalism. You people disgust me.'

The line crackled and went dead.

Danny put his phone down and swirled the ice cubes in his coffee, hoping that whoever had put Antonio Saez in charge of press relations never got to handle anything dangerous.

3

DANNY DROVE A battered maroon 2004 Escort, the only thing he'd been able to afford after his previous car was written off and the insurance company diddled him. The car's interior was like an oven. Danny took a bulging address book from the glove compartment and walked back across the road so that he could stand in the shade. The address book was stuffed with so many business cards and scraps of paper that Danny had to strap the thing together with elastic bands. He kept meaning to copy the numbers into the book but never seemed to get around to it.

He was looking for the telephone numbers of local donkey sanctuaries. Danny knew there weren't many in the province – unwanted animals had a tough time of it in Andalusia – and the chances were that, during the decade he had worked in Spain, Danny had spoken to someone from the place at which Hector Castillo used to volunteer.

He struck lucky on the third call. A chirpy-sounding Dutchwoman named Anja answered. Some of the chirp left her voice when Danny mentioned Hector Castillo.

'So sad,' she said in accented Spanish. 'I wonder if we'll ever know what happened.'

Danny said nothing about the body at Little Arizona. He asked if he could come out and speak to her about her memories of Hector. Anja said sure, he should swing by about six, once they'd given the donkeys their evening feed.

The climate in Almería was near perfect for nine months of the year: crisp, clear sunshine and mild temperatures, marred only by the occasional day of rain and the high winds of winter.

June, July and August were a different story. The temperatures skyrocketed, normally hitting the mid-to-high thirties every day. That was OK if all you had to do was sit beside a hotel pool and drink ice-cold lager, but trying to work was hell. Between 12:00 and 17:00 the streets were practically a no-go area unless you were headed towards the beach, a place Danny never visited if he could help it: with his pale skin, paunch and skinny legs, swimming trunks had never been a good look.

Danny killed time wandering through a local shopping centre. This was pretty much his life in summer, wandering from one air conditioned environment to another until it cooled enough for him to go home and cross out another day on the countdown he was keeping to the start of autumn and the end of the infernal heat.

At five-thirty, Danny set off for the donkey sanctuary, a twenty-minute drive into the rural areas north of Almería. Three months of relentless sun had left the mountain slopes around the city a uniform grey-ochre colour, but the rest of the countryside was in full bloom: orange and olive trees, date palms, jacarandas. The heat haze shimmered above the asphalt as Danny drove.

The donkey sanctuary was at the end of a pot-holed road lined with scruffy palms and prickly pear cacti. The metal gates were closed.

Danny got out of his car, shook the gates and heard a padlock and chain rattle on the other side. He shouted a greeting and rattled the gates again. Then he beeped the horn of his car.

No answer.

He pulled himself up on one of the gates and peered over. The donkey sanctuary consisted of an enclosed two-acre plot of land with a stable block on the left and a small Andalusian bungalow on the right. The knackered old Citroën parked outside it made Danny's car look like a Ferrari. Three donkeys stood in the shade of a grey-barked willow tree, flicking their tails at the flies that clouded around them. The hot, dry air smelt of straw and donkey fur.

A chain link fence delineated the edge of the property. Danny walked along it until he could see the windows on the side of the bungalow. He cupped his hands and shouted.

Still no answer.

He was about to head back to his car when he saw the blinds in one of the windows part just a fraction. He wasn't sure he'd actually seen anyone there, but the sudden jerk of movement as the vertical slat swung back into place was unmistakeable.

Since the police had fined Danny for talking on his mobile while driving he made a point of turning the thing off whenever he got in the car. When he turned the phone back on, he saw someone had left him a message at 17:48.

It was from the Dutch woman, Anja, speaking in English and sounding tense and nervous. 'Mr Sanchez, I'm afraid I won't be able to talk to you today. Or any day, in fact. I'm afraid I really can't discuss Hector Castillo with you so I'd appreciate it if . . .' Her voice faltered and she said, 'Look, I'm sorry, but I really can't see you, so please don't come.'

Danny replayed the message, listening in confusion. What the hell did that mean?

Danny looked towards the house, then went back to the gate and climbed over. He dropped to the ground and headed for the bungalow, picking his way through sundried dung and buckets of water.

'Anja, it's Danny from the newspaper,' he said, rapping loudly on the door of the bungalow. 'We spoke on the phone about an hour ago.'

There was no response, but Danny was certain there was someone in there: as a reporter you got to recognise that strange hush caused by people standing behind doors, hoping visitors would go away.

Danny phoned Anja's number. A muffled ring-tone sounded inside the house. He cupped his hands and shouted through the door, 'I can hear your mobile phone ringing inside. Come on out and let's talk. I promise I don't bite.'

Danny lit a cigarette and began kicking stones across the yard, raising little clouds of bone-white dust. Long seconds passed, then he heard the door bolt slide back.

'What are you doing?' Anja's Dutch accented voice said in English. 'Go away.'

She started to close the door, but was prevented when Danny inserted his desert boot.

'Hey, not so fast. I've come all the way out here. The least you could do is tell me what the hell's going on.'

The door pressed harder on his foot, hard enough to make Danny wince. Then the pressure was released as a second woman pushed Anja aside and opened it again. She motioned Danny inside.

Anja was a slender willow of a woman in her sixties with one of those scrunched up, leathery faces that occur when skin meant for cooler climes spends decades under the Spanish sun. The other woman, the one who had let Danny in, was younger and had a short, stocky frame. Her head was shaved to a crew cut from which swung a long, beaded rat's tail of hair that hung from the back of her head. She introduced herself as Sabrina.

When Danny stepped inside, Anja said something in Dutch. Sabrina threw her hands up in exasperation and they began arguing. Danny got the impression they were continuing an argument that had started before his arrival.

'I don't mean to interrupt, ladies,' he said, 'but I'd like to know what's going on. Then you can both argue to your hearts' content.'

Anja lit a roll-up. 'I can't talk to you. I don't see that is so very difficult to understand.'

Danny softened his voice. He'd get nowhere browbeating the woman.

'Anja, try to see things from my perspective. An hour ago we had a perfectly pleasant telephone conversation and you invited me out here. Now, you won't even open the door to me. What the hell has happened? Why can't you speak to me?'

Anja sniffed, on the verge of tears. Sabrina said in English, 'Go on, tell him.'

'It was the lawyer,' Anja said in a low voice. 'He told me not to speak to you.'

'You say "the lawyer" like I'm supposed to know who the hell that is.'

'The lawyer in charge of Hector's estate.'

Danny's frown deepened. 'Why would Hector's lawyer tell you not to speak to me? And, more importantly, what do you care what Hector's damned lawyer thinks anyway?'

Sabrina nodded. 'That is precisely what I told her,' she said. 'Who does this lawyer bastard think he is phoning people up and making threats?'

Danny started to ask another question, but the two women switched back to Dutch suddenly, shouting at each other until Anja burst into tears. Sabrina rolled her eyes, then sat next to Anja and put her arm around her shoulders with such easy familiarity Danny realised they must be either sisters or lovers. They stayed this way for a minute. Then Anja turned moist eyes towards Danny.

'I remember you,' she said. 'It was at a protest meeting for a dog charity. You wrote an article. It really helped them.'

'Well, I could use a little of your help now, Anja, because I am struggling to understand any of this.'

Anja dried her eyes and rolled a cigarette, pulling the tobacco from a leather pouch. She inhaled smoke and blew it out in a long exhale. 'The lawyer said I wasn't to speak to you because of the money Hector left us in his will. Apparently there's some clause about . . . I don't know, non-disclosure. Anyway, I'm not allowed to talk to the press about Hector. Or something like that.'

'Who is this lawyer?'

Anja's face clouded at memory of him. 'His name is Gomez, Sebastian Gomez. He handled things when Hector died.'

'And when did he phone you?'

'About ten minutes after you did.'

'And he knew I was coming here?'

'Yes.'

'So he mentioned me by name?'

Anja thought about this. 'No. But he said if any journalists were to contact me, I was to tell them nothing about Hector or I would . . . invalidate something or other. It's the money I'm really worried about. There's no way we could repay 12,000 euros. It would ruin us.'

Danny frowned, assuming he'd misheard.

'Sorry, how much did you say?'

'Hector Castillo left us 12,000 euros in his will. Or rather, that was what we settled for in the end. I think the actual sum in the will was 30,000 euros, but because Hector was never officially declared dead we could have had to wait decades to receive the full sum.'

'Are you sure it was 30,000 euros? That's a lot of money to leave to donkeys. No offence intended.'

She nodded. 'Hector's mother changed lawyer when Hector disappeared and started using this Gomez fellow. It was Hector's previous lawyer that contacted us. He'd already seen the will and he knew how much money we were due.'

'Offer you a no win, no fee deal, did he?'

'Yes. We settled out of court in the end for 12,000 euros. That's what paid for all of the improvements to these facilities.'

'Pardon me for being blunt, but where the hell did Hector get so much money?'

'Well, he had a job at a science research place.'

'They don't pay that much. In fact, I'd be surprised if they paid more than 25,000 euros a year for a position like Hector's.'

Sabrina said, 'He did consultancy work, as well. For a development company, I think.'

'Development as in buildings?'

'Yes. They did a lot of work in the north of the province, building houses for the English.'

'What was a research scientist doing working for a development company? And was it anything to do with a man named Sixto Escobar?'

'The name's not familiar,' Sabrina said. 'I don't actually even remember the name of the company, either.'

Sabrina was going to say more, but Anja put a hand on her arm, looking worried. Sabrina said, 'Would you excuse us for a moment?' and led Anja into the kitchen, where they began talking in low voices.

When Sabrina came back into the living room, she was pulling the tops from three green bottles of Alhambra 1925. She handed one of the beers to Danny and said, 'Anja is still uncertain, but I'm not. Let this lawyer bastard go screw himself. I will tell you everything you want to know.'

'Amen to that,' Danny said, chinking bottles with Sabrina. 'Why don't you start by telling me a bit about this Sebastian Gomez fellow . . .'

4

THE PROVINCE OF Almería has two regional winds. The *levante* sweeps in from the eastern seaboard and brings with it rain and fierce storms. But tonight, when Danny got back to Almería city, it was the *poniente* blowing, the hot dry African wind that comes in across the Alboran Sea.

At the end of the Paseo de Almería the sun was setting, a big Andalusian sunset full of pink, red and gold, the clouds turning to charcoal as the sun sank beneath the horizon. Danny turned his face to the breeze as it swept along the street, rustling leaves in the rounded crowns of the bay trees.

As much as Danny hated the heat, he had to admit there was something about summer nights in Spain. The air seemed magically charged, as if all the energy sapped during the day began to rise from the ground, making everything seem more special and alive somehow. You could go out at one in the morning in Almería and still find the whole city awake. In the older neighbourhoods people dragged mattresses onto the pavement outside their houses and slept there. Danny had seen photos of Almería from the 1960s, when entire streets had been turned into outdoor dormitories.

It was nine o'clock now and Danny's final call of the day was at nine-thirty, covering a short film festival. Danny felt tired but he was sick of drinking coffee, so he stopped at a bar and ordered a beer and a plate of *ensaladilla rusa*. He sat on the terrace and reviewed the notes he had made as he ate.

Danny had stayed and chatted with the two Dutch women for about twenty minutes. As it turned out, they knew little about the lawyer, Sebastian Gomez. They had met him in person only once and most of their other contact with him had taken place through their own lawyer.

What the women had told him about Hector Castillo had been worth the wait.

According to Anja and Sabrina, Castillo had first begun volunteering at the sanctuary in 1999, by which time he had already been working at MWGP four years and had just begun his consultancy work with the developers. Danny re-listened to the parts of their conversation that had interested him most.

'Tell me about Hector,' Danny's voice said on the Dictaphone recording. 'What was he like?'

Anja's voice replied: 'He was a quiet, shy man. Not the way you imagine Spaniards to be at all. And he loved animals. But he was always blue. Very blue. I am sensitive to these things in other people. I always felt he was trying to . . . I don't know, atone, I suppose is the word.'

Sabrina made noises of agreement.

'What do you think he was trying to atone for?'

Sabrina answered this time: 'We really couldn't say. Hector was a very private person. But he couldn't hide his feelings. You knew when he was unhappy.'

'Could it have been a girlfriend maybe?'

'I don't think so. Hector was shy around women. I don't think he ever had a relationship the whole time we knew him.'

'What about just before he disappeared? You mentioned that he'd been especially unhappy.'

Anja said, 'I think upset is more the word. We were used to seeing him glum, but this time he was really distressed.'

'But he didn't mention the cause?'

'No.'

'Did you mention this to the police?'

'They never asked. A woman officer came and spoke to us a week after Hector disappeared but that was –'

Danny fast-forwarded to the next section that interested him. When he began to replay it, his voice was asking, 'What about Hector's work? Did he ever mention what he did at MWGP?'

Sabrina's voice said, 'He didn't talk about work much. I don't think he was allowed to because of the nature of the work that he did. With radioactivity, I mean.'

'Radioactivity?'

Anja had put a cautionary hand on Sabrina's arm at that point, but Sabrina had shrugged it away. 'Hector was the head of a team that was analysing soil samples at that place up north, the place where the American H-bombs got dropped.'

Danny's ears had pricked at that. 'Do you mean the nuclear accident at Palomares?'

'Yes, that's the one. Hector's team was measuring the plutonium contamination in the soil up there. You know the Americans never got it all cleaned up, don't you?'

Danny did.

Journalists had been writing about The Palomares Incident ever since January of 1966, when an American B-52 bomber exploded during a mid-air refuelling and dropped its payload of hydrogen bombs onto Almería. One of the four bombs fell into the sea, but the other three fell inland, close to the tiny fishing village of Palomares. The conventional explosives within two of those bombs had detonated, causing the plutonium inside to vaporise and be spread by the wind across miles of agricultural land.

Despite the extent of the contamination, the American military prioritised locating and retrieving the intact Mk 28 bomb that had fallen into the sea, in an effort to keep its top secret design out of the hands of the Russians. As a result, the clean-up operation on land was not as thorough as it could have been. Although the Americans spent 80,000,000 dollars removing 1,750 tonnes of irradiated earth, pockets of plutonium-contaminated land were still being found around Palomares. In 2002, Spanish scientists had found several pockets of earth that were so highly radioactive the Spanish science agency, CIEMAT, had been forced to expropriate twenty-three acres of arable land and fence it off to prevent people from accessing it. The Spanish and American governments were still bickering over who should pay for the new clean-up operation. The incident was well-known locally, although it warranted little more than a footnote in most history books.

Danny sat back in his chair. So, Hector Castillo had worked on Palomares, had he? That was an interesting twist to the story. Perhaps that explained why Antonio Saez had been so cagey.

Danny tried combining a Google search for Castillo's name with Palomares. That came back blank, so Danny tried Googling MWGP and Palomares. The search result showed an April 2000 report entitled 'Palomares and Soil Contamination: Establishing the Direction and Extent of Plutonium Drift Patterns'. According to the Introduction, the report had been commissioned by the University of Almería and prepared by the university in conjunction with MWGP. Antonio Saez was identified as the chief researcher; Hector Castillo's name wasn't mentioned anywhere. Danny tried to access the report, but it was locked behind a twenty-five-euro pay wall.

Danny thought about Antonio Saez. It must have been he who had told the lawyer that Danny had been asking about Hector Castillo and that he was likely to speak to the women at the donkey sanctuary. If not, how would this Gomez have known to phone them? Danny decided he'd like to speak to Saez again. This time he'd make sure the interview was official.

MWGP's parent company was based in Regensburg, Germany. The media relations officer who answered spoke excellent English. She listened to Danny's explanation of who he was and what he wanted.

'So, you wish to interview someone from the Spanish facility about this 2000 report?' she said.

'That's right, a man named Antonio Saez. Could you arrange that for me?'

She said she didn't think that would be a problem.

Not for you it won't be, Danny thought as he hung up.

He was mopping ensadilla with a hunk of bread when his phone rang.

Tom Gibbs was editor of the newspaper chain's largest publication, Este News, which covered the Valencia and Alicante regions. Since William Fouldes had left Sureste News, Tom was unofficially Danny's boss, and Danny had to run all his stories past Tom before publication. That was fine by Danny:

Tom was an old-school type of reporter, far happier pounding the streets than sitting behind a desk, although Danny had noticed that promotion to the editorial staff had caused him to become far more cautious.

'Daniel-san,' Tom said. 'How the devil are you?'

'Not too bad. Just off to cover that short film thing we spoke about.'

'Hold your horses. I need to speak to you.'

'About?'

Tom's tone remained jocular. 'Have you been pulling the tail of someone you shouldn't have, Danny?'

'Not that I know of.'

'Does the name Sebastian Gomez ring any bells?'

For a moment, Danny was genuinely speechless. Gomez again? Who the hell was this bloke?

'Do you know who he is?' Danny said.

'Nope. But I *do* know he's been on the phone to our legal people, and that said conversation has caused them to start shitting bricks. So I'd like to know what it is you've done to upset Señor Gomez.'

'Tom, I've not even spoken to the bloke. All I've done is try to get some background on a guy whose body turned up at one of those western theme parks down here.'

Danny explained what had happened at Little Arizona and the information he had subsequently discovered.

Tom sighed. 'Well, Señor Gomez seems very het up about the issue. He's demanding to see anything we write on the subject before we go to print.'

'Tell him to go screw himself.'

'Don't worry, I will. But I'm more preoccupied with

whether he's going to have the opportunity to come back and screw us, Danny. Apparently, he represents high-power corporate clients and is monstrously litigious. He's fought numerous libel cases in the last decade and won substantial cash payments every time. And he doesn't fight fair, either. Apparently, Gomez went after some poor bastard from a local paper down your way and ruined him. The journo lost his house, his job, everything.'

'What could Gomez possibly do at this point? I've not even written anything.'

'He mentioned a possible lawsuit for emotional distress.'

'Distress to whom?'

'This Hector Castillo has cousins and an aunt in Barcelona, apparently. Did you mention to anyone that Castillo was dead?'

Danny rolled his eyes.

'Yes.'

'And do you know for a fact that he is dead?'

'I saw Castillo's DNI card in a wallet taken from the body. Anyway, I didn't contact the family. I spoke to an ex-colleague.'

'Who, according to Gomez, got straight on the phone to Castillo's family.'

'Only after he'd gone running to Gomez.'

'Danny, you know you didn't have enough information to start phoning people and telling them Castillo was definitely dead. You've left yourself wide open there.'

Danny said nothing. Gibbs was right.

'Listen, I'm on to something here, Tom,' he said eventually. 'This Hector Castillo tried to leave 30,000 euros to a donkey sanctuary. You know how Spanish inheritance law works.

It's two thirds to the next of kin, no buts, no ifs, no maybes. That means the money Castillo left the donkey sanctuary was only a third of what he had in total. He was worth nearly 90,000 euros when he died. That's a lot of saving for a single guy earning 25k a year. Plus, what is this hot-shot corporate lawyer doing messing around with a research scientist's inheritance and browbeating the owners of a donkey sanctuary? Something doesn't add up there, Tom.'

Gibbs sighed. 'Listen, if you want to sound off about the Junta or take a shot at the Guardia Civil, that's fine: everyone hates those bastards. But for Christ's sake, don't climb into the ring with someone like Gomez. Not while the coffers are so empty.'

'Let's not mince words here, Tom. Are you telling me to drop this story?'

'I'd consider it a personal favour if you did.'

'And since when do the paper's lawyers determine what news we print?'

'Danny, I'm on your side. But this isn't a good time for hard-hitting investigative journalism. Advertising revenue is way down and any legal action could sink us.'

'Spare me the sob story. I work my arse off for the newspaper.'

'Danny, that goes without saying.'

'No, Tom, it goes without *ever* being said.'

Danny hung up but felt bad about doing so almost immediately. Tom was a good guy, struggling to get by the same as everyone else. Danny decided he would phone Tom tomorrow and apologise. But if Sureste News didn't want the story, he'd find someone else who did.

Danny ordered another beer and a pork loin sandwich and ate it as the streetlights came on along the Paseo. He lit a cigarette and assessed his options.

Hell, it was Friday night. Someone else would have to write about the short film festival. Or Danny could do what ninety per cent of people in journalism seemed to do nowadays and cull the information from the internet tomorrow.

He finished his meal with a brandy coffee then strolled towards the lighted esplanade of the *Avenida de Federico Garcia Lorca,* trying to decide what to do with himself. Children played on slides and swings, while parents chatted. The air was balmy, the sea breeze carrying with it a salt tang as it stirred the fan palms at the edges of the esplanade. The road ended in a tulip-covered roundabout with a fountain at its centre. The backlit jets of water rose up blue, red and green against the night sky; the flower petals sparkled in the spray.

As Danny stood watching the fountain, a group of young women all heels and handbags clattered past, heading for the Cuatro Calles, the centre of Almería's nightlife. Danny inhaled the slipstream of their perfume and realised he knew where he wanted to go – had known since he left the bar.

First, he crossed the street to the roundabout and plucked a couple of tulips from the display. Then he walked east through the city, towards the beachfront and the El Zapillo district. When he got to number 12, Calle San Francisco, he took the lift to the fourth floor and knocked at the door of flat 4C.

Marsha's voice sounded behind the closed door. 'Who is it?'

'Open the door and you'll find out, won't you?'

The door opened inwards.

Marsha stood there in her pyjamas, smiling. 'I thought you were working tonight?'

'There's been a change of plan.'

'What are you hiding behind your back?'

Danny turned, put the stems of the freshly plucked tulips between his teeth, and spun round towards her. Marsha gave the little-girl grin she always did when she was genuinely happy.

'I learnt a good word to describe you the other day,' she said, plucking the tulips from his mouth. 'Quixotic.'

'You mean that I'm extravagantly chivalrous?'

'No, Danny: rashly unpredictable.'

She leant forward to kiss him but stopped an inch from his face and sniffed the air. 'Are you drunk?'

'Not yet I'm not,' Danny said, pulling her into his arms, 'but if you come into town with me, I promise you we damn well soon will be.

5

GABRIEL VARELA WALKED to the back of the property, where the wall that surrounded the garden was not overlooked by any of the other houses. Varela had delivered the envelope to the architect's office three hours ago, the envelope that contained the evidence of the man's crime. This was where the architect would run to, the secret house the architect's wife did not know about, the place where Phillips came to drink and fuck prostitutes.

Varela had on now the clothes he always wore when working: American M65 jacket, black leather gloves, jeans and combat boots. His hair was cropped short, but he still wore his beard long, the longest it had been since he'd served in *La Legión*.

He lifted himself up onto the wall and dropped down into the garden.

The night sky was cloudless and, by the pale light of the waxing moon, Varela realised that everything in the garden was dry and dead, even the cacti and the weeds. He crossed the remains of the lawn and saw that the swimming pool, too, was empty. It took him a moment to realise the significance of what he was seeing; his big hands balled into fists.

Earlier in the night, Varela had sat in his car with his head in his hands, smelling the canisters of petrol that lay in the boot and wondering if he could go through with what he planned to do. Now that he saw the garden he knew he would not hesitate. The architect deserved to suffer.

The back door of the architect's house had a pin tumbler lock. Varela knelt beside it, took out a torsion wrench and a snake rake pick and fiddled inside the lock until he had opened the door. Then he went to the back of the garden again and crouched in the darkness.

He had listened to the news on the radio that evening. Hector Castillo's body had been found at Little Arizona, in the place that Varela had left it the night before. Would Escobar have yet realised it had been Varela who put it there? Probably. Behind those piggy eyes, Escobar was sharp as a fox.

That meant that Escobar had most likely run straight to Gomez and Morales, the way he always had done back in the day. That was good: Varela wanted the pricks to know fear, to know that he was coming for them. Would they try to contact him now? Time would tell.

A little after 1 a.m. the gates swung open. Headlight beams swept across the garden, silhouetting the withered remains of plant life. The garage door swung upwards and the car went inside, then the garage door closed again. Varela saw a light come on in the living room and then another upstairs.

He turned his big battered face up towards the stars, wondering if somewhere little Esme was watching him.

He hoped not. Not tonight.

Varela pushed the back door open and walked through the kitchen into the living room. The architect was upstairs: Varela could hear the sound of cupboard doors banging and hurried footsteps. Then came the rasp of a match being drawn and the smell of burning paper.

Varela checked that the cable ties in his pocket were easily accessible. Then he went upstairs, flexing his gloved hands as he went.

6

AT 05:47 DANNY'S mobile began to ring. There was only one person it could be at that hour.

'Morning, Paco,' he said, rolling himself out of Marsha's bed.

'Some English bloke has been burnt alive in the north of the province. Interested?'

Danny rubbed sleep from his eyes as he listened to the photographer explaining what had happened. As they spoke, Marsha stirred behind Danny and went to the kitchen to make coffee. When she returned to the bedroom, Danny was fully dressed and lacing his desert boots.

'I'm sorry,' he said. 'Got to go.'

'Poor you,' she said, handing him a cup of coffee. 'What is it this time?'

She winced when Danny told her, then sat on the bed beside him and smiled. 'Well, before you go, I've got a little surprise that might cheer you up.'

She rummaged in the drawer of the bedside table and withdrew an envelope, which she handed to Danny. The envelope contained two tickets. It took Danny a moment to realise what they were for.

'Tonight's flamenco performance at the Alcazaba,' he said, trying hard to sound enthusiastic.

'Yep,' Marsha said. 'They cost me an arm and a leg, but it'll be wonderful. They set the chairs up on the castle's forecourt – you know, that bit by the fish pond, between the Moorish and Christian parts – and they light it with big torches. It doesn't start until half-past ten, so I thought we could go into town and have a bite to eat first, then wander on up to the castle. Sound like a plan?'

'Sure.'

She gave a momentary frown. 'You do want to go, don't you?'

'Of course,' he said, giving her a kiss. 'It's just way too early for me to react to anything properly.'

Marsha lay back on the bed and yawned. 'I think I'll have a lazy morning at the beach. Will you be home for lunch?'

'I hope so.'

'Good,' she said, snuggling her head into the pillow. 'You can make me something to eat, then. I fancy fresh fish.'

Danny headed for the lift, pulling his denim jacket on and lighting a cigarette as he went. When he got to his car, he rummaged in the glove box and found his CD of *The 109s*. He needed music that was fast and hard to rock him awake, so he turned the stereo all the way up as he took the slip road onto the motorway and drove north, tapping his hands on the steering wheel in time to the music. The band's guitar-work was superb.

Danny enjoyed driving in the dark in Spain. It gave you

an idea of just how big and empty the country was once you got away from the crowded coastal strip. The streetlights of the few towns Danny passed showed as strings of orange pinpricks amid a vast swathe of uneven darkness, the peaks and slopes of mountains just visible in the silvery moonlight.

Danny and Marsha had been together a little over two years now. As a girlfriend, Marsha ticked all the right boxes: she was clever without feeling the need to show it, cultured without being pretentious and possessed a sense of humour that made her appreciate Danny's jokes. For her part, she could also make him laugh. Hell, she even liked Black Sabbath, and that was a first for one of his girlfriends.

As teenagers they'd attended the same comprehensive school. Marsha described them sometimes as having been 'school friends', but Danny knew that wasn't really true, for the simple reason that Danny hadn't had *any* friends at school.

He and Marsha had become reacquainted while Danny was on a trip back to England covering a serial killer story and for the first year-and-a-half they had maintained a long-distance relationship, during which time Marsha had obtained a TESOL teaching certificate and secured a job teaching English in an academy in Almería. After quitting her job and renting out her English house, Marsha had moved to Almería in May.

Danny considered that as he drove. Had she really only been in Spain four months? It felt longer to Danny.

Much longer.

Marsha was another of the reasons Danny was so damned tired all the time. Since she had moved to Spain, every spare second of Danny's free time seemed to have been spent doing things with Marsha: picnics, bicycle rides, museum trips, weekends away in Madrid and Toledo and Barcelona. Now that he'd really gotten to know her, Danny had realised that life for Marsha seemed to consist of a ceaseless quest to outrun the clutches of a boredom that was constantly snapping at her heels. Quiet days spent at home on the sofa were not an option, something which had come as a major shock to Danny's system, accustomed as it was to leisure activities centred on cold beer and computer games.

Danny stifled a yawn as he thought about that night's flamenco performance. If it said 22:30 on the tickets, it probably wouldn't start until 23:00, which meant it wouldn't finish until 01:00. He'd had about four hours sleep so far. He could really do with an early night. And he'd told Marsha that the only place to see decent flamenco was at a *peña*, one of the small, specialised flamenco clubs. But what could he do? Marsha was still in that wide-eyed state of excitement that affected foreigners when they first moved to Spain. She wanted to see and experience everything. Hell, she'd even been pushing for them to head up to the north of Spain and walk part of the Camino de Santiago, the pilgrim's route that lead across northern Spain from the French border to the city of Santiago de Compostela.

'Only for a week or so,' she'd said when she suggested it. 'Then we could do a bit more every year, until we actually get to the cathedral.' Only a week? How the hell did she think Danny had time for that? Or the money, for that matter?

Still, Danny had had a good time with Marsha the previous night. First they had drunk white wine and eaten tapas at three different bars; then, they had walked arm-in-arm the whole length of the seafront promenade, talking and listening to the gentle hiss of the waves, with Marsha's head resting on

Danny's shoulder and Danny inhaling the sweet scent of her long brown hair. And Marsha was going back to England next week to visit family. The break would probably do them some good, Danny decided. At the very worst, he'd get the chance to catch up on some rest. . .

Danny drove north for fifty minutes, then took the motorway exit and followed Paco's directions until he found the scene of the incident.

It had taken place at the edge of a small rural town, where a curving terrace of newly-built houses faced a dry river bed edged with trees and scrub. The air was thick with the stench of burnt petrol and charred plants. Smoke still poured from the undergrowth, forming a channel of deeper dark that rose against the backdrop of the night sky and obscured the stars.

Danny counted three Guardia patrol cars, a fire engine and an ambulance, their flashing lights adding a macabre carnival air to the scene. Beyond them, Scenes of Crime Officers in white boiler suits knelt beside something Danny was sure he didn't want to see.

Paco Pino was already there, treading down the brush, one of his Canon 5D Mk3 cameras hanging from his neck, the other held to his eye as he photographed the scene. Danny knew he should leave the photographer to it, so he got on with the business of trying to determine what the hell had happened.

A small group of Spaniards in dressing-gowns and pyjamas stood on the pavement outside the houses, chatting in the earnest way people do when tragedy occurs on their doorstep. They all told the same story. The fire had begun around 03:30. Some had been woken by the sudden whoosh as the flames caught; others were drawn from sleep by the orange glow that had suddenly filled their rooms. One man, a former garage mechanic, said he feared a car had been set alight. 'That's what it was like,' he said, 'as if someone had dropped a match into a petrol tank.'

Danny's pen kept time as the witnesses described the confusion and terror when they realised the thing writhing in the centre of the fireball was human. Some had run for water, others merely stood frozen in horror as the victim thrashed and stumbled through his death agony, setting a twenty-yard swathe of bone-dry undergrowth alight in the process. Most agreed the victim was a man – it was something about the timbre of his cries – and that death had not been quick.

Danny thanked them and walked away. He could think of three possible explanations for what had happened: accident, suicide or murder.

None seemed likely.

If it was murder, it was a messy, noisy and brutal way to end someone's life. Criminals sometimes burnt dead bodies to hide identity or evidence, but Danny couldn't remember ever having covered the death of someone who'd been deliberately burnt alive. You heard about it happening in places like Mexico and Columbia, but rarely in Europe.

Accident? It was possible. But what the hell would someone have been doing fiddling around with a jerry can full of petrol at three in the morning? And how would they have managed to cover themselves with the stuff from head to toe?

So, it was quite possibly a suicide. But what a way to do it. Christ, a cry for help it was not.

It was 07:25 now and the sun had begun to rise from behind the peaks of the nearby Sierra Almagrera away to the east, bringing with it the day's first lazy lick of heat. Paco Pino sauntered over, scratching his belly and chewing gum.

'Have you got a name for the victim yet?' Danny said.

Paco shook his head. 'All I know so far is that he's English. But I'll have the name soon. Apparently, they're looking for his car, a silver left-hand drive Mercedes with Spanish plates.'

'So the car isn't here?'

'Not as far as I know.'

'How did the victim get here with the petrol then?'

Paco shrugged as he began checking images on his camera's digital display. Danny lit a cigarette and offered one to Paco, but the photographer winced and shook his head.

'Not after what I've just seen, *amigo*.'

'Bad one, is it?'

'Not seen one like it for years. The poor bastard's burnt to a crisp.'

Danny puffed his cigarette, thinking. 'How'd they know the guy was English then?'

Paco pointed along the line of trees to the forensic officers taking photos of something on the ground. 'According to my ambulance contact, the guy left his passport on top of some stones over there. Classic suicide behaviour, don't you think?'

Danny shrugged. 'Hell of a way to top yourself.'

'You know what some people are like. They want to top themselves but they need everyone to know they've done it. Hey, you could work that into the article, couldn't you? Something about "going out in a blaze of glory".'

Danny looked at his friend. Years of photographing all sorts of horrors had given Paco a blasé attitude to tragedy. Recently, though, Paco's quips had been bordering on the downright crass. Danny thought about saying something but decided against it.

He knew what the problem was: like everyone else in Spain, Paco was feeling the pinch. The photographer was working longer hours for less pay and the area he was expected to cover expanded another fifty miles every couple of months. News agencies were pushing in from elsewhere, nipping away at the patch Danny and Paco had carved for themselves, undercutting them on price, getting the photos through to newspapers first.

Danny was lucky: he'd kept his life simple. But Paco had kids, two of them – kids that needed uniforms, school books, ballet lessons. It was tough to show compassion when you were worrying about your own woes.

Paco insisted they eat breakfast at a nearby British bar. Since Danny had introduced him to the concept of a Full English earlier in the year, the photographer had gained at least half-a-stone.

'Look at this,' Paco said, as he examined the day's edition of *El País*. 'More austerity, more cutbacks.' He slapped a photo of a politician. 'Why don't these *hijoputas* take a pay-cut, eh? Lead from the front for once.'

'Did I tell you what happened at Little Arizona yesterday?' Danny said, hoping to change the subject: he knew from bitter past experience that once Paco started on either money or politicians, he was capable of moaning for hours.

'I saw something about it on the news last night.'

'You don't think the story is worth chasing?'

'Have you seen the papers today? Everyone's got a piece on it. And the next break in the story – if there is one – will come from the Guardia. Exclusives, Danny, that's where the money is.'

'Still, it would be nice to peg something on Sixto Escobar, don't you think?'

'Why bother when we've got a solid story here?' Paco said, then put his knife and fork down. 'Is this about that stupid translation job he screwed you on?'

'Give me some credit. But I've got an angle on this whole Hector Castillo thing that no one else has covered yet.'

'Which is?'

'Castillo was working at Palomares. He did some work investigating the soil contamination there.'

Paco's face fell. 'Palomares, Danny? Seriously?'

'What's the problem?'

'Every journalist that ever came to Almería has tried to make something out of that story. And there is nothing more to be written about it. Do you know how many readings they've taken up there since they discovered the new pockets of contaminated soil? Thousands. If not tens of thousands. Plus, I know people from Palomares and they are sick of this crap being raked up every couple of years. Do you know what it's like to have had nearly five decades of stupid jokes about glowing in the dark and house sales falling through because people don't want to get "poisoned"? There is no story at Palomares. The end.'

Danny said nothing. He knew Paco was partly right. Journalists had been watching Palomares for decades, hoping – from a journalistic standpoint – to find some evidence that the plutonium contamination had harmed the inhabitants and to write the sort of story that won you Pulitzers; but the truth was that, despite the dramatic nature of the incident, it was a non-story from a health perspective. The American military had closely monitored the inhabitants of the village for forty years and found nothing: no rash of cancer, no mysterious diseases, no deformed children. If anything, the inhabitants of Palomares were exceptionally healthy and long-lived.

Paco was mopping baked bean sauce with a slice of fried bread when his mobile rang. Paco took a pencil and began writing on a napkin.

'My contact in the Guardia,' he said. 'I've got a name and address. The car belongs to a man named Martyn Phillips,' Paco said, pronouncing it mar-TEEN FEE-leeps. The address was in Vera, a seaside town further up the coast.

'Do we know anything else?' Danny said.

'He was British, 63-years-old and married. Why don't we go see the widow now?'

'She'll probably be with the Guardia all day,' Danny said.

'There's no harm in trying, though, is there? Get in there while she's still punch drunk?' Paco said, then sighed when he saw the way Danny was looking at him. 'Hey, I'm sorry to sound callous, but this is something the nationals here will want to cover. In fact, I've already got *El País* interested as long as we can get an interview. And I need a sale, Danny.

'How about this? I'll get my Guardia contact to let us know when the widow is free. And as soon as she is, we drop what we're doing and get in there. You know that if we don't, someone else will.'

'OK,' Danny said after a pause. 'But I'll go alone, Paco. The last thing she'll need is having a camera thrust in her face.'

'That's my boy,' Paco said. When he got up to leave, he put

his hand on Danny's shoulder. 'I don't like it, but that's the way of the world. Money talks.'

That was true enough, Danny thought; it was the things money said that were the problem, though.

W HEN PACO LEFT, Danny stayed at the bar and made some phone calls, seeking information on the dead man.

Martyn Phillips was one of the province's old-school expats, and had lived in Almería more than twenty years. He had run a very successful architect's office in the nineties and early noughties and been an established doyen of the very highest stratum of expat society, the type that hung around country clubs and marinas. His wife, Sian, ran a foundation that raised money for local children with cancer.

The few photos Danny could find on the internet showed Phillips shaking hands with people at various charity and business association events. One look at Phillips and you knew he'd been one of life's successes: he had that air about him – confidence tinged with condescension, his skin tanned that perfect bronze colour only the really rich seem able to achieve.

Danny was still at the bar, checking his emails, when he noticed the Guardia had released the results of the autopsy on Hector Castillo's body:

"An autopsy performed at the *Instituto de Medicina Legal* has determined that the body found yesterday at a location in the Tabernas Desert is that of Hector Castillo Mendez, a man who disappeared in March of 2005. The autopsy found that Señor Castillo has been dead approximately seven years, and that his remains were buried in desert soil. Thanks to this, his internal organs were still well-preserved, which allowed examiners to determine the cause of death as a single stab wound to the heart, probably with some form of punch dagger, as three of the ribs in the area of the wound were also broken. There was no other evidence of injury. The assailant most likely came at him from the front and killed him with a single blow."

Danny got on the phone to the Guardia's press office.

'A single frontal blow with a punch-dagger,' Danny said. 'It sounds like the assailant wanted him dead and knew precisely how to do it. Do you think this was a professional killing?'

'I can't answer questions based on supposition. But that is certainly an angle we will be investigating.'

It was ten o'clock when Danny finished up at the bar. The heat today was almost tangible, a sweltering cloud that pressed down upon his face as soon as he walked outside.

Heading back towards the *autovia*, he drove past the scene of Martyn Phillips's death. The ambulance and Guardia vehicles had gone, now, leaving only the blackened undergrowth and the incident tape to show where he had died.

Danny drove back to Almería city, where he went to the central market and bought four mackerel fillets and a half kilo of mussels. Then he drove to Marsha's flat. Marsha wasn't home, so Danny let himself in.

Marsha had announced her decision to move to Spain during one of Danny's visits to England. The next few days had been awkward, as Danny had assumed she would want to move in with him, and he hadn't been sure if he was ready for that.

As usual, though, Marsha had been way ahead of him.

'If you're expecting me to lay the whole commitment / co-habitation thing on you just because I'm moving to Spain, think again. I've rushed into that sort of thing before, and I've learned to be wary, so I'll be getting my own place. Of course,' she'd then said, dropping her voice, 'I will be expecting you to stay over most nights.'

Danny had mimicked her tone, and asked her why on earth she would want him to do that. Marsha had pulled him towards the sofa and said it would be simpler if she just showed him . . .

Marsha was one of those girls that like to decorate with throws and drapes and scarves. A poster of the Velazquez painting, *Las Meninas*, was tacked to the wall beside the front door, and Dali's *Autumn Cannibalism* hung above the bed.

Danny put the food in the fridge, then went into the bathroom, stripped down to his boxer shorts and covered his bare skin with cold water. Then he went into the living room, turned the air con to 18°C and sat his chair directly below the wall mounted unit. Danny breathed a sigh of relief as the unit sprang into life, causing the paisley scarf on the floor lamp to flutter. Danny lit a cigarette and stared up at the face of the dwarf in *Las Meninas* staring back at him.

Marsha laughed when she came through the front door and found Danny still sitting there.

'What percentage of each Spanish summer do you spend stripped down to your grundies, my love?' she said, removing the sarong she was wearing on top of her swim suit.

'No idea,' Danny said. 'Not enough, though.'

Danny steamed the mussels with a dash of white wine and cooked the mackerel with garlic and parsley. They sat in Marsha's living room and ate at the table. Afterwards, Marsha did what she always did after eating: she put the television on and sat on the sofa with her iPad to catch up on the day's social media gossip. Danny took his laptop and went through into the bedroom.

Given the fact Marsha had lived only four months in Spain, her grasp of the language was astounding. She had begun joining in conversations during her first month and, by month three, could happily watch and understand television programmes.

Of course, the downside of that was that Marsha had developed an insatiable appetite for *tertulias*, the trashy Spanish chat shows that seemed to comprise half of all Spain's television output. Marsha's excuse was that she was improving her Spanish vocabulary, but Danny knew it wasn't that. Marsha might devour writers like Thomas Pynchon and study Open University courses 'for fun', but she seemed at her happiest and most relaxed watching C-list Spanish "celebrities" witter and argue about the latest sex scandals.

She was also a fully signed-up member of the selfie-taking, Facebook-posting social media club. Hardly an event occurred in Marsha's life that wasn't commemorated in some way on the internet and then commented on by the 579 people on her friends' list. Danny had banned Marsha from posting pictures that included him after he had spotted a comment from a girl who'd been in their school year: 'OMG!!!! He still wears desert boots, LOL. Tell him to get a life, Marsha.'

Danny sat on the bed with his laptop and began checking the expat forums. Martyn Phillips's death had been reported on the morning news and there were already a number of threads discussing the death.

That was no surprise: the internet had replaced street corners and shop queues as the central sorting house for gossip. What was surprising was the tone of some of the posts. Few had anything pleasant to say about Martyn Phillips and some were actively jubilant at his demise.

One user, identified as *Sheffield Lass,* claimed Phillips had cheated a friend of hers who had done plumbing work on Phillips's house. And it didn't seem to be just the plumber. According to one of the responses to the post, Phillips was involved in court cases with at least half-a-dozen different tradesmen over unpaid bills. Another post described Phillips as a man with a reputation for arrogance and ruthlessness in business. Others claimed that he had had numerous affairs, and that he drank too much.

Danny took the negative comments with a pinch of salt. Ugly rumours follow a rich man's death the way that seagulls follow a trawler and the anonymity of the internet meant people could – and would – vent as much half-baked spleen as they wanted. Still, it was an interesting angle to the story.

Danny was still reading the forums when Marsha came through and sat on the bed beside him.

'Come on,' she said, massaging Danny's shoulders. 'You've done enough work. You're mine for the rest of the day now.'

She must have felt Danny tense, because she lifted her head immediately and said, 'I have got you for the rest of the day, haven't I?'

Danny's shoulders slumped.

'I might have to do something later on. I promised Paco.'

Marsha looked away. Then she sighed.

'Oh well, it's what I get for falling in love with a reporter, I suppose. Where are you going?'

When Danny told her, she frowned. Danny asked her what the matter was.

'Do you know what you said when we started going out together? You said that good journalism should do two things: comfort the afflicted and afflict the comfortable. Which one are you doing by going to bother a widow twelve hours after her husband was burnt alive, Danny?'

'I can't help it. Sooner or later someone is going to talk to her and that someone might as well be me. I'm a reporter. It's my job.'

Marsha went to say something, but paused, so Danny said, 'What?'

She sighed again. 'You always do that.'

'Do what?'

'Talk about journalism as your "job".'

'What should I call it then?'

'It's your career, Danny.'

'Is there a difference?'

'Yes. A job is something static. A career is fluid. It changes. It goes places. I'm not going to tell you how to live your life, Danny, but sometimes I can't help wonder whether this ambulance chaser type of work is really the best use of your talents. You're a damned good reporter. You should be looking to get a permanent position at a national newspaper.'

Danny said nothing. They'd had this conversation a number of times before. Marsha had made it clear she didn't like the tabloid work Danny did for The Daily Mail and The

Sun – she loathed both newspapers – and she had been a sworn enemy of Sureste News ever since they'd buggered about with Danny's working conditions.

'Don't worry,' Danny said. 'I'll be back in good time for the concert.'

'You'd better be,' she said with mock severity.

Later that afternoon, they both fell asleep on the bed listening to an episode of Hancock's Half Hour, the one about the poison pen letters.

A couple of hours later, Danny's phone woke him.

He peered through bleary eyes at Paco Pino's name on the screen then looked at Marsha's face as she dozed peacefully beside him on the bed. Part of him wanted to carry on sleeping, so he let the phone ring until Marsha murmured, 'Either you answer the phone, Danny, or it's going out the window.'

Danny answered the phone.

'Time to go to work, *amigo*,' Paco Pino said. 'The widow's back home.'

8

An hour later, Danny was in Vera, sitting in his car outside Martyn Phillips's house. It was late afternoon now and the day's heat had reached its sweaty, energy-sapping apex, but Danny's skin felt cold, and his throat was dry.

In twenty years of journalism, Danny had been insulted, chased and threatened more times than he cared to remember, and it was nearly always the result of doing a death knock: you never knew how bereaved relatives would react when a reporter turned up asking for quotes.

To make matters worse, Paco Pino had already phoned twice to ask him how he was getting on. Danny had finally turned his mobile off.

Danny took a deodorant can from the glove compartment and sprayed himself all over, then checked his hair and got out of the car.

The Phillips' house was on the beach front in Vera. The walkway that led to the garden gate was shaded by trellised jacarandas that formed a canopy of green and pink. Danny could hear splashing from a nearby swimming pool and the dull thwack of tennis balls. The asphalt was sticky-hot beneath his desert boots as he crossed the pavement and pressed the button on the intercom.

A woman's voice answered almost instantly, asking who he

was. Nearly a minute of silence followed Danny's explanation, then a buzzer sounded and the garden gate clicked open.

The sixty-something woman who greeted Danny at the door explained that she was Barbara, one of Mrs Phillips's friends. She pulled the front door half-closed and dropped her voice to a whisper.

'I just want you to know, you've a bloody cheek turning up like this. A damned cheek. I would have told you to bugger off, but Sian is adamant she wants to talk to you. I'll be listening to every word, though. I know what you bloody people are like.'

Sian Phillips was a similar age to Barbara and was putting a brave face on the situation, the way British people of her generation tended to deal with bereavement, but anyone with experience of grief could see she was clinging to her prim composure like a life preserver. She greeted Danny and offered him coffee. Danny told her not to worry, but she insisted. Both women disappeared into the kitchen to make it, leaving Danny alone in the living room.

The patio doors at the far end of the room opened onto a balcony that overlooked immaculately pruned palm trees and a stretch of lawn. Beyond that were sand and the silver-blue waters of the Mediterranean. That view alone was probably worth more than Danny's entire house.

The furniture in the living room was what you'd expect from people of the Phillips' social standing: tastefully expensive and upholstered in autumnal tones. Glass cabinets contained antiques and objets d'art. Only the drinks bar seemed out of place. The decor would have suited decanters and crystal tumblers, yet it was loaded with half-empty bottles of cheap supermarket spirits, as if whoever used it preferred quantity to quality.

The photos on the walls attested to Mrs Phillips's beauty in former years. She'd been an absolute bombshell at thirty, Danny thought, just the type a successful architect would marry.

Most of the photos of Martyn Phillips showed him at various social events: in top hat and tails at a race meeting, standing in front of an F1 car with his arm around the shoulder of a helmeted man in a race suit.

One photo drew Danny's attention, though. It showed Martyn Phillips and his wife standing either side of a young boy in a wheelchair. The boy wore a bobble hat, but lacked eyebrows and his skin had an unhealthy, greyish pallor. A drip hung on one side of the wheelchair.

But what really drew Danny's attention was Martyn Phillips's expression. Gone was the confident captain of industry of the other photos. Now Phillips's eyes were bloodshot, his skin puffy and flushed and he carried about three stones of unhealthy weight.

Danny's eye went to the corner of the room and the drinks bar. So, the rumours about his drinking seemed true. But it was unusual for someone to go off the rails so late in life. What could have prompted it?

Sian Phillips brought a coffee pot and cups and laid them on the table. Now that Danny was closer to her he could see she was sedated: her eye sockets were blue-grey beneath the make-up, her expression vague and distracted and a slight pause preceded each of her movements, as if she needed to remind herself of how to perform it. The friend, Barbara, sat next to her, dividing her time between making soft, consoling coos and shooting daggers at Danny.

Danny began with neutral questions about the Phillips' life in Spain and the architectural business. Once he'd got her relaxed and talking, he turned the conversation round to her husband.

'Have they made a positive ID yet?'

Sian Phillips nodded, dabbing her eyes. 'Martyn had had surgery. They used that to identify him. That, and his teeth.'

Danny raised a hand to indicate he understood. Unless extremely hot, flames normally only damaged the exterior of corpses, leaving the viscera relatively unscathed. Evidence of surgery on specific organs was a useful way of identifying victims of burning.

'I expect you're wondering why I agreed to talk to you,' she said.

Danny had angled his chair diagonally towards her. Experience had taught him that was best: to sit opposite was too confrontational; beside, too familiar. He replaced his coffee cup in its saucer. 'Not really, Mrs Phillips. As I mentioned earlier, I'm primarily here to offer my condolences on behalf of the newspaper and to see if there's anything we can do to help. But if there's something you feel you need to get off your chest, I'd be happy to listen.'

That wasn't a lie: *pretending* to care didn't work on death knocks; it was only by rolling up your sleeves and offering to shoulder part of the grief – however infinitesimal that part may be – that you got anywhere. Danny was ready and willing to help the woman with whatever she needed: explanations of the laws pertaining to Spanish funerals or the pitfalls of transporting coffins back to the UK. God knows, he'd done it enough times in the past ten years.

Sian Phillips mustered the faintest of smiles, a gesture of gratitude that dissipated when she said, 'I want to talk to you because people have been writing all sorts of nonsense about Martyn on the internet. They're such cowards, these people, hiding behind their stupid aliases. It's just an open invitation for gossip. And people were always jealous of Martyn because he was such a success.'

Danny eased pen and notepad from his shoulder bag as he let her explain the rumours to him. Then he said, 'How do they make you feel?'

'Bloody furious.' For the first time, focus returned to her fogged expression. 'What right do people have to make up these lies? It makes me sick to my stomach. That is why I want you to state, categorically . . .' – it took her two attempts to say the word – '. . . that there is no foundation to these rumours. Martyn was a hard-working man and a good husband. I don't care what people say. And as regards what they say about Martyn and other women . . . well, that was between me and him.'

She sniffed. Barbara put a hand on her forearm.

Danny thought carefully about his next question.

'Have the police told you what they think happened?' Danny said.

She shook her head. 'But then I don't need a stranger to tell me what happened. I already know.' Her right eye twitched. She played with her coffee cup. 'Martyn had a nervous breakdown a number of years ago,' she said slowly. 'That's no secret. And no shame, either. These things can happen to anyone, especially someone as hardworking as Martyn. I thought he'd gotten better. Clearly he hadn't. I don't think people ever really recover from something like that. It caused him to become very . . . unstable.'

'Unstable enough that he might have taken his own life?'

Her eyes became moist. 'What other explanation is there?'

Danny didn't answer that one. She seemed to draw solace from the thought her husband had committed suicide.

'What did the doctors say caused this breakdown?'

'Martyn refused to see his doctor.'

'So who was it that said he'd had a nervous breakdown?'

'*I* said it. Do you think a wife can't tell when her husband has a breakdown?'

'How did the symptoms manifest themselves?'

'I really don't think it appropriate to go into specifics, Mr Sanchez. Suffice to say, Martyn became very . . . *hypochondriac* would be the word, I suppose. He suddenly had a number of health tests.'

'Tests for what?'

'Pretty much everything that was going. And he insisted on moving house. We had previously been living elsewhere in the province. Of course, I wasn't really that upset about that, as I'd always preferred this property.'

'Were there any problems with work?' Danny said after a pause. 'Perhaps related to a difficult contract? Or any other sources of stress in his life?'

She shook her head. 'Martyn had been semi-retired for three years. He had a few projects on the go – he didn't want to go to seed – but nothing remotely stressful. But, now that you mention it, one of Martyn's friends killed himself earlier this year. I think it must have affected him even more than I imagined.'

'Could I ask who it was?'

'A man named Florentino Yagüe.'

'And how did your husband know him?'

'They were involved in a business project many years ago. And they were both tireless fundraisers for the charity I run.'

'Is that a photo of one of the children to whom you donate money?' Danny said, indicating the photo that had drawn his attention.

'Yes,' Mrs Phillips said. 'We try to help three or four children each year. Although, in some cases, we can do little more than ease their suffering. I think poor Florentino became far too involved with the children. When one of them died at the end of last year, he went into a very rapid and obvious mental decline.'

'Do you feel up to telling me about what Martyn did yesterday?'

She nodded, chewing her lip. 'He'd been out playing golf in the morning. He lunched at the club. In the afternoon, he went to the office. I was preparing his dinner when he phoned and said he wouldn't be home and that I wasn't to wait up for him.'

'Did you ask him where he was going?'

The question flustered her. Tears came into her eyes. 'Martyn didn't react very well to me "meddling", as he used to call it.'

'Did he often go out at night?'

'Sometimes, especially in summer. I think he liked to drive at night. He enjoyed the mountain air, the coolness.'

Barbara's expression warned Danny not to press her further, so he dropped the conversation to a lower gear. They talked about the funeral arrangements – unlike in the UK, it was not uncommon for someone in Spain to be buried within thirty-six hours of dying and, now that the coroner had signed off on Phillips's death, his widow would be expected to lay him to rest in Spain or ship him back to the UK. Then the conversation drifted towards the Spanish life insurance policy that Phillips had bought. When Danny mentioned some of the pitfalls of making a claim, Sian Phillips looked worried and said she needed to check the paperwork in her husband's office.

She left the living room and went into a room opposite, leaving Danny alone with Barbara. When sounds of rummaging came from the office, Barbara leant towards Danny and hissed, 'Five more minutes and then you're gone, buster, even if I have to hoik you out myself. Sian's got enough to put up with without you reminding –'

She was going to say more when Sian Phillips reappeared, holding a pile of papers in her hands.

'Is everything OK?' Danny said as he noticed the perplexed look on the woman's face.

'Look,' she said raising the paperwork, 'there are bills here going back years for our old house on the Bellavista urbanisation. There are gas and electricity bills in Martyn's name. And grocery bills. And for the satellite television.' She paused. Some thought seemed to be trying to pierce her Valium fog. 'Why would Martyn do that? He told me he had rented this property out.'

Danny kept his expression neutral, although one possible

reason leapt instantly to his mind. The internet forums had mentioned Phillips's philandering: he wouldn't have been the first rich man to have set up a mistress in rented accommodation and taken charge of the bills himself. Danny made split-second eye contact with Barbara and realised she had drawn precisely the same conclusion.

Sian Phillips saw them exchange glances. Still standing in the doorway, she frowned and one of the papers fell from her grip and drifted to the floor. Danny tried to change the subject, but it was too late: the penny had dropped.

'Take me there,' Sian Phillips said. 'I want to see her.'

'I really don't think that's a good idea,' Danny said, but Sian Phillips began speaking over him, her voice rising.

'I can't believe he's done it to me again. Tell her to go and identify his body. Tell her to clean up after him when he wets the ruddy bed.'

Barbara put an arm around her shoulders. Sian Phillips shrugged it away. Then she took car keys from the wall and headed for the front door.

Danny got there first, blocking her path, saying, 'I don't think driving at the moment is a very good idea, Mrs Phillips. Why don't I go round there and see what's what? All this might just be in your imagination. It's on my way home.'

Sian Phillips turned eyes ringed with smeared mascara towards him. 'You find the bitch's name and you print it, Mr Sanchez. I want her named and shamed.'

Outside, Danny sat in his car. When he lit a cigarette, he noticed his hand was trembling.

Death knocks: Lord, how he hated them. And now he had to call on this other address, unsure of what he would find there. Maybe he would have to go through another version of this whole bloody scene.

As Danny leant forward and turned on the ignition, he was sure of one thing: Paco Pino owed him, big style.

9

Towards the middle part of the afternoon, Gabriel
Varela awoke. He stretched and rose from the mattress at the
back of the lock-up where he'd slept. The ceiling here was
cracked and allowed a light breeze to enter, but the heat inside was stifling. Varela poured water into his hands and
rubbed it over his shaven head, then looked at his big, heavy
face in the cracked sliver of mirror glass that remained on the
wall.

He'd lost weight in prison. His scarred skin was now
stretched taut over the blunt and crooked angles of his face.
It made him look older. He flexed the slabs of muscle in his
shoulders, feeling the ache of a hundred different fist-fights.
How old was he now? Fifty-five? Or was he still only fifty-
four? It surprised him that he didn't know immediately, that
he had to work it out on his fingers. But then he had thought
of nothing but Esme and revenge for the last eighteen months.

The lock-up was in a poorer part of the city of Almería,
where residential areas merged with industrial parks and factories. Half the buildings here seemed abandoned. Varela walked
to the nearest shop and bought a copy of *La Razón* newspaper.

Outside, he turned to the back pages and looked at the
personal ads. He sat on a wall and scanned through them one
by one, keeping his place with his cracked fingernail. When

he had done this twice he folded the newspaper and tossed it away.

Nothing for him yet, but the news of Phillips's death was only just breaking. He would check again tomorrow. Sooner or later one of the pricks would try to contact him.

He walked back to the lock-up and opened a tin of peaches. He began pricking the slices out with the tip of his punch dagger, but after only a few mouthfuls nausea overwhelmed him and he rushed outside and was sick on the floor.

He couldn't eat. Not now, not so soon afterwards: the smell of Phillips's burning flesh was still in his nose.

Despite what others thought of him, Varela had little experience of killing. Gabi had always been smart enough to know that others only had to believe you *capable* of killing in order for them to fear and respect you.

The first man he had killed had been Hector Castillo. Martyn Phillips was the second.

Varela leant against the wall of the lock up and thought about Phillips, the way the man's eyes had bugged and stared as Varela doused him with petrol. Right at the end, Varela had removed the gag. He'd wanted to hear Phillips repent, but instead he had merely blubbered in Spanish and called on God's mercy.

God's mercy? After what he and the other pricks had done?

After that, Varela had laid a trail of petrol away from where Phillips was trapped on the floor, struggling and kicking against his restraints. Then Gabi had lit the match.

The memory of the deed sickened him. He felt no sensation of triumph, no elation, no sense of justice having been served. There was only the memory of those terrible high-pitched screams, the waves of heat and the terrible stench of burning flesh as the restraints burnt through and Phillips began to stumble and thrash around.

Varela had planned to burn all four of the men, but he knew now he could not go through with it again. He would have to find some other, cleaner way to kill the three that remained: Escobar next; then Morales; and, finally, Gomez.

Varela took his coat and withdrew the two photos of Esme that he kept in the breast pocket. The first showed her at ten years old, looking into the camera and smiling, her face fresh and framed by long auburn hair. The second was of Esme two years later, lying in a hospital bad, her scalp piebald, faint wisps all that remained of her hair, the fleshless skin wrapped tightly to the bones of her face.

He kept the first photo to remember her by; the second, to remind him of what it was he had to do.

Varela propped the photos of Esme against the wall and swallowed hard. Then he picked up the tin of peaches and began to eat, his eyes fixed on the photos.

10

Twenty minutes after leaving Sian Phillips, Danny rounded a curve in the steep road that wound down out of the mountains. Below him, the Bellavista urbanisation stretched out across the plain, more than a thousand houses organised in neat terraces and cul-de-sacs, the red roof tiles following the undulating curves of the landscape.

An archway of mud-coloured bricks and terracotta tiles ran over the entrance to the urbanisation and was obviously meant to give the place a Texan, hacienda type feel: split-rail fences curved away on either side of the arch and the main roundabout had a bronze sculpture of a wagon wheel and a coiled lasso in its centre.

When he saw them, Danny wondered what the Bellavista's cowboy connection was – Tabernas and the Spaghetti Western film sets were thirty miles away inland.

Then he saw the faded advertisement on the billboard.

Doug Sampson was one of those B-list actors whose face you might vaguely recognise, but recalling whose name re-quired a bit of effort. At the height of his fame in the late seventies he had clawed himself a niche as a type of ersatz Eastwood, playing tough-but-honourable soldiers and police-men, but it was when making his early Spaghetti Westerns he had come to Almería. The faded billboard depicted Sampson's leathery face smiling beside the slogan, 'I'm hitching my horse here – how 'bout you?'

Danny drove through the streets, thinking back on conversations he'd had with other journalists. Sampson had had something to do with the building of the urbanisation back in the nineties. Something had gone wrong and Sampson had been kicked out early on, although the development company had somehow ended up with the rights to use Sampson's image. Danny made a note to look into it.

On the eastern side of the urbanisation, the side that nestled amid the foothills of the Sierra Almagrera, the houses were bigger and detached. Martyn Phillips's property was at the end of a cul-de-sac, a chalet surrounded by a half-hectare of land.

Danny peered through the bars of the garden gate, shielding his eyes against the glare of the sun on the tiled pathway. If Phillips did have a mistress living there she clearly wasn't the house proud type: the place was a tip. The windows were covered with years of dust and one of the shutters hung from a single hinge. Four date palms rose up from the corner of the garden, but they seemed to be dead: the long feather-like leaves were brown and withered and hung in scruffy clumps from the trees' tops.

When Danny pressed the buzzer at the intercom he saw the panel was broken. He looked up and down the road. A Spanish woman was sweeping the pavement outside her house. Danny crossed the road to speak to her.

'Do you know if anyone lives there?' he said.

She shook her head. 'Señor Phillips goes there sometimes,' she said, 'but, no, he doesn't live there. Not anymore. He moved out a number of years ago.'

'Has anyone lived there since?'

'There have been some tenants in the past, but no-one has lived there for about three or four years. It's hard to rent out because of the state of the garden.'

'When was the last time you saw Señor Phillips at the house?'

'Last night. I saw his car. And I saw lights on inside.'

'Did you see anyone else there?'

'Not last night.'

'What about on other nights?'

She frowned. 'I saw other people. Women. Women who were not Señora Phillips, if you catch my drift.'

'Did you see him leave last night?'

'No. But then I do not pay much attention to him. Not since he went funny.'

'Funny?'

She whirled a finger next to her temple. 'In the head. Mad. *Loco*. Go and take a look at his garden if you don't believe me. He had one of the best gardens on the estate and then, suddenly, about seven years ago, he moved out and let the whole thing dry up. Go take a look at it if you don't believe me. I think it's the sun we have here,' she said with an air of finality. 'It is too much for foreigners.'

Danny opened the garden gate and went inside. He saw immediately what the woman meant about the garden.

There had been a lawn at one point, a big, expensive swathe of it running all the way around the house, but little now remained except tufts of brown straw. The hedgerows that edged the lawn were brown ruins of skeletal twigs. Hell, even the cacti looked on their last legs. The ochre earth either side of the pathway was parched and cracked: Danny's shoes stirred white dust as he walked.

Beyond the desiccated remains of the hedgerow there was a swimming pool, the biggest Danny had ever seen at a private house, perhaps 15 x 10 metres, but there was no water in it. The tiles at the bottom were cracked and obscured by dust and dry leaves.

The sun was low in the sky now, a huge red welt that shimmered on the horizon. The heat sucked at Danny's energy. He fanned his face with his notebook and knocked at the front door. He looked around him again. Jesus, to own a property like this and to let it go to pot in this way. Some people had more money than sense.

There was no answer. The front door was locked. Danny walked across the dusty earth to the back door, which he found half open. Danny pushed the door and it swung inwards.

'Hello?' he said. He said it twice more then walked into the kitchen.

The air inside smelt stuffy and old. Crumpled beer cans and empty whiskey bottles covered the kitchen work surface. Next to the sink there was a five-litre carafe of mineral water. Danny looked inside the pantry. The shelves were stacked with cans of baked beans. On the floor there were more of the carafes of water, dozens of them.

Danny turned the tap. It gave a dry choke. Something banged somewhere upstairs, a muffled interior thud, but nothing emerged from the tap. That was strange. Why continue to pay the electricity, gas and satellite bills but neglect the water? Especially when your entire garden was turning into desert?

The kitchen gave onto the living room. The furnishings here were extremely basic. A sofa and armchair were drawn up in front of a huge plasma television screen. Cigarette butts lay in an ashtray, and a half empty bottle of DYC whiskey stood on the coffee table. An interior door gave access to the garage. Danny pushed it open.

Martyn Phillips's silver Mercedes was parked inside.

Danny took his camera and began photographing everything on the lower floor. He would need to phone the Guardia and alert them to the discovery of Phillips's car, but he would take a good look round the house first.

The upstairs rooms had the same air of abandonment as the ground floor rooms. Some were empty, others contained the barest rudiments of furniture. Only the master bedroom was fully furnished.

Two hard shell suitcases lay open on the bed in this room, big black ones with extendable handles and wheeled bottoms. The first contained a jumble of clothes. The clothing smelt fresh and clean, but was scrunched up, as if Phillips had packed in a hurry. The second suitcase contained more scrumpled clothes, toiletries and Phillips's wallet. There was a boarding card beside it, the type travellers could print out in advance. The flight was for a 09:30 Gatwick flight out of Malaga airport that same morning, Saturday, August 25th, 2012.

There'd been a fight in the room, Danny realised as he explored: on the far side of the bedroom the carpet was stained with blood and there was a broken tooth on the floor. Droplets of dried blood led away from the blood stain and into the en-suite bathroom.

Danny took out his mobile phone, rang the Guardia Civil

and told them what he'd found. The call-taker told him to wait at the house and not to touch anything. Danny said, 'Sure'. Then he hung up and picked his way past the blood stains into the bathroom.

The bathtub was filled with ash and burnt scraps of paper. Matches were scattered on the floor and across the ashes.

Danny leant over the bath and looked at one of the larger scraps of paper. Most of the page was burnt, but part of it could still be read. Danny rubbed his thumb across the ash and held it up to the light. There was a letterhead at the top of the page: *Laboratorios Florentino Yagüe S.L.*

Florentino Yagüe? That was the friend Sian Phillips had mentioned, the one that had committed suicide.

A brown A4 jiffy bag envelope rested on the sink. There was no address on the envelope, but the words MARTIN FILIPS were written on it in marker pen. It looked to Danny like someone had been trying to burn the contents of the envelope inside the bath. He opened the envelope and peered inside. It contained a single sheet of foolscap paper. Someone had written on the paper in Spanish. Judging by the handwriting, it was the same person who had written Phillips's name on the outside.

It said: *Ahora te toca pagar.*

It's time for you to pay.

11

It took the Guardia Civil twenty minutes to show up after Danny's phone call. He sat outside while he waited for them and thought about what he'd found inside the house: the tickets, the packed luggage, the signs of a struggle. Phillips had been set to flee the country, but someone had caught him. But from whom had he been running? And why?

Danny thought of the message left in the envelope: it's time for you to pay. But pay for what? Because whoever had sent that note had most likely captured Phillips before he could leave for the airport and then burnt him alive. That same person had also taken his passport and left it at the scene of Phillips's death.

What could the architect have been mixed up in that could have warranted such a cruel punishment? It probably had something to do with the papers he'd been destroying in the bathtub. Danny had looked them over, but only a letterhead and some meaningless numbers had been legible.

The first Guardia officers to arrive came on motorbikes. They were of the type that always irritated Danny: deadpan, suspicious and authoritarian, speaking with thumbs tucked into their belts. They asked Danny to repeat his story twice, then made him wait outside while they checked with Sian Phillips his explanation of why he was there – a process which took an hour, because a translator had to be located. By that time, detectives from the *Policia Judicial* team that was investigating Phillips's death had turned up and for Danny the real fun and games started.

The plain clothes officers made him tell his story at least another three times, then started firing questions at him. Did he have an alibi for the previous night? Had he ever met Martyn Phillips? How well did he know Sian Phillips?

After that, Danny was sucked into the time-warp of a crime scene. He was specifically told not to leave, but no-one seemed particularly anxious to do anything with him. More officers from the homicide department arrived; then came the forensics with their white overalls and plastic boots. Photos were taken, evidence collected. Danny occupied himself for some time by looking through his notes, before remembering that his phone was still turned off.

There were 14 missed calls: ten from Paco Pino, four from Marsha. For a moment, Danny wondered why Marsha would have been calling him at 19:47, 20:01, 20:22 and 20:38. And then he remembered.

The concert.

He looked at his watch. It was nearly nine now and he was still an hour's drive from home. There was no way he'd make the concert. He would be stuck here for hours yet.

'Danny. Where are you?' Marsha said when he phoned.

When Danny explained, Marsha said, 'The Guardia haven't arrested you, have they?'

'No. At least I don't think so.'

'But you've stumbled across a crime scene?'

'Yep.'

'So, basically, you're saying the concert is off.'

'No,' Danny said, rising now to the cold tone of irritation in Marsha's voice. 'What I'm saying is that I'm going to be stuck inside a Guardia barracks answering questions over and over until the early hours of the morning. Christ, don't you think I'd much rather be at – '

The phone went dead.

Two minutes later, Paco Pino phoned.

'Danny, what the hell is going on? It's nearly nine o'clock. I've spent the whole afternoon sucking up to the news editor at *El Pais* and now we've missed their evening deadline. Where's the text?'

It took all of Danny's restraint not to tell Paco to go to hell. Here he was standing around in the heat, while Paco was likely sipping beer on his balcony. Danny counted to three, then said, 'I've seen where Phillips was abducted. It's definitely a murder. Phone the news desk and tell them we've got an exclusive. I bet they'll give us some leeway.'

Danny was right. Paco came straight back to him and said they had twenty minutes. Danny spent ten of these arranging his notes and sketching out 300 words in shorthand. Then he phoned Paco's number and dictated the whole article down the phone, while Lourdes typed it up.

Danny kept to the facts and reported it as a straightforward news story, omitting mention of anything he wasn't sure about. He described the plane tickets he had seen and the burnt pages in the bathtub, but did not mention *Laboratorios Florentino Yagüe S.L.* by name. He didn't want other reporters sniffing around until he'd had a chance to investigate further.

This frenetic activity provided Danny with a welcome distraction, but once the article was done boredom set in again. The minutes dragged by like hours. He'd upset Marsha. It wasn't his fault he'd found a crime scene. But, if it wasn't his fault, why did he feel so damned guilty?

Part of the reason was that Marsha tended to react badly to disappointments. She had been hurt badly in the past by her ex-husband and, when she and Danny first got together, had made a point of describing herself as 'damaged goods'. Danny didn't really know the whole story – he had quickly learned that Marsha's divorce was not a subject you approached without either angering or upsetting her – but he knew the basics: in her late twenties, she'd done the whole fifty-grand fairy-princess type of wedding at Guildford Cathedral, with horse-drawn carriages and hundreds of guests, only to discover eight years later, that her husband had cheated on her half-a-dozen times.

Added to that, Danny was struggling to make the transition from bachelorhood to full-time boyfriend. Sometimes, having Marsha in Spain seemed the most wonderful thing in the world; at other times, he felt constrained, and the two emotions usually came so close on each other's heels that Danny struggled to work out exactly how it was he felt about the whole thing. Anyway, he would just have to apologise about the concert and find some way to make it up to her.

At 23:00, the lead detective decided he wanted Danny to make an official statement. They took him in a squad car to the Guardia barracks at Vera, where he had to wait again, sitting on a plastic chair in a windowless office.

After midnight Danny heard a commotion outside. He stood up, opened the door and peered out. The Guardia had brought Sian Phillips in. He saw her walk past, crying as she went.

At one-thirty a.m. one of the plain-clothed *policia judicial* officers came into the room and introduced himself as *Teniente* Fernandez. He gave Danny a bottle of mineral water and took his statement.

They finally finished with him at about 02:30. Fernandez said Danny could go. Danny asked if Sian Phillips was still there. Fernandez nodded.

Danny looked at his watch and said, 'You do know she lost her husband yesterday, don't you?'

The tone of reproach made Fernandez look up from his paperwork.

'She'd have been out of here an hour ago if she hadn't gone all legal on us,' he said, 'but she insisted on bringing in her lawyer. That's the only reason she's still in there.'

Danny's eyelids were drooping, but he decided he would wait outside the barracks and try to get a quote from Sian Phillips when she came out. He wanted to ask her what the hell was going on.

The air outside was deliciously cool after hours spent in the stifling room. Danny sat on a bench and listened to the arrythmic chirrup of cicadas, before picking up a stone and hefting it into the darkness. The noise stopped instantaneously, leaving only a deep, uneasy quiet.

Only four more weeks, he told himself, fighting sleep. Four more weeks, then the temperature would begin to drop and the hell of summer would be done with for another year. . .

The arrival of a car woke him. Headlight beams swung across Danny's line of vision as a 4x4 sped across the car park and pulled up sharply before the steps of the Guardia barracks. Danny rubbed sleep from his eyes and stretched as he saw a lithe, muscular man in a tight white T-shirt – the type worn by guys that work out and want people to know it – jump out of the driving seat, jog up the stairs and disappear inside.

Danny yawned and looked at his watch. It was 05:50. He walked to the bottom of the steps.

Ten minutes later, the doors opened and white T-shirt appeared, walking beside Sian Phillips, guiding her down the steps. Behind them came a podgy, moustachioed man in an expensive suit. He was carrying a briefcase. The exterior light reflected on the lacquer in his hair.

Danny stepped forward and began to say, 'Mrs Phillips, would you care to comment on –', but white T-shirt spun round at the sound of his voice.

It happened faster than Danny could see. The guy did some combination of a split second elbow and foot sweep and Danny went down on his arse, hard. He landed on his coccyx and it drove all the breath from him.

'How's that for a comment, asshole?' the man said in American-accented English. Then he smiled, revealing sharp white teeth.

Danny was still on the ground when the car doors slammed and the vehicle sped away, spraying him with gravel.

He climbed painfully to his feet, rubbing his rump. His nose wrinkled: there was a slipstream of sickly-sweet eau de cologne wafting in the air.

A Guardia Civil officer appeared at the top of the stairs.

'What the hell was that?' Danny said, pointing towards the faint dust trail the car had left. 'Who were those guys?'

'The fat one with the curly hair was the Phillips woman's lawyer. He's a real hard ass. I've not heard anyone talk to my captain like that before. The other one was some private security guy that belonged to the lawyer.'

'Got a name for them?'

The Guardia officer checked inside.

'The security guy is called Tomás Shrike.'

Danny wondered why the surname sounded so familiar and quickly realised: the shrike was a type of bird, known also by its nickname, The Butcher Bird.

Right. A private security guy called Shrike. That couldn't be his real surname. What a wanker.

Danny shared a laugh with the Guardia officer then said, 'You got a name for the chubby lawyer?'

The Guardia nodded.

'His name is Gomez,' he said. 'Sebastian Gomez.'

12

AFTER MARSHA HUNG up on Danny, she sat with her hands resting on the clasp of her macramé bag, feeling her face flush beneath the carefully applied make-up. She had suffered badly from depression when all the business with her ex-husband had unravelled, and she felt the flutter of its black wings now, so she took out paper and pen and started doing one of the coping strategies her therapist had taught her.

She wrote on the piece of paper:

Danny has let me down. I feel hurt and rejected.

I really wanted to go to the concert. I feel disappointed.

I feel resentful towards the amount of time Danny dedicates to his job.

She got as far as number five, then stopped and screwed the piece of paper up. She wasn't depressed or resentful. She was bloody furious. And with good reason, too.

That same afternoon, when Danny had got up to go out and interview the widow, she had nearly reminded him, had nearly said, 'Don't forget that we're going out tonight. You will be back in time, won't you?'

Something had stopped her from doing it. She sat quietly and tried to work out what it was that had prevented her from saying it. Had she been testing him? Yes, she realised, she had wanted Danny to remember without reminder, because that way she would have known that the concert meant as much to him as it did to her.

Bloody Danny.

He hadn't wanted to go to the concert. She had noticed his reticence as soon as she mentioned the tickets. That was one thing about Danny Sanchez, she could read him like a book. It was the thing that made him so much of a known quantity and, at the same time, so infuriating.

She entered the kitchen and poured herself a nice big glass of wine. Then she took out her secret packet of Marlboro Lights. Marsha had ostensibly given up smoking the year before and was trying to encourage Danny to quit – or, at least, to cut down – so she avoided smoking in front of him, but every once in a while she felt the need for a quick ciggie.

She looked at herself in the mirror, at the new outfit she'd been looking forward to wearing tonight. She stood sideways on, trying to decide whether the skirt made her tummy and bottom stick out. A little, perhaps. But then she'd put on nearly half a stone since she'd moved to Spain. It was difficult not to, what with all the beer and wine and tapas.

She leant closer to the mirror, examining her face now. She'd used a new technique for her eye shadow, something she'd seen on the internet, where you applied it to the outer corners of the eyes then drew a line back along the creases to the inner corners and blended it. It was supposed to make the eyes looked wider and the lids longer. It hadn't really worked, she decided. 'I look like a ruddy panda,' she thought.

She walked into the bathroom and sponged the make up from her face. Then she carefully unrolled the thigh-high stockings from her freshly-shaven legs and changed out of her Victoria's Secret underwear.

'You'll never know what you missed, Sanchez,' she thought as she put the stockings back in the drawer. It made her feel a little better, as if the situation had been moved back in her favour. She poured herself another glass of wine.

The problem with Danny was he was always trying to help people. In the four months since she'd moved to Spain she'd seen it on half-a-dozen occasions already: Danny sitting around with complete strangers, trying to unravel their problems, translating, explaining for hours on end. It was admirable in some respects, but it was a question of priorities. Just once, she would like to see him apply himself with equal vigour to making *her* feel special and needed. Didn't he realise how lonely she felt sometimes, so far from home, trying to participate in the noisy, lightning-fast free-for-all that constituted conversation at social gatherings between Spaniards?

But that was the problem, wasn't it? Danny didn't realise. He was bilingual and had grown up speaking both languages, so he didn't know what it was like to be lost in waves of half-understood words. But then, Danny was such a loner, he didn't really seem to need anyone or anything.

That thought did little to improve her mood. She felt her anger return. Back in the dark days, when the truth had come out about her ex, she had sworn never to allow her happiness to become dependent on a man again and yet here she was, sitting around moping because she'd been stood up.

She lit another cigarette.

It wasn't true what she'd just been thinking about Danny, she realised. There *was* something Danny needed. He needed his work, needed it the way that a fish needs water or a bird the wind. When he got the bit between his teeth, he ceased to care about anything else.

When she'd first met him, she'd found that intensity intriguing. Now she wondered whether it was something she really wanted to have to accommodate for the rest of her life. Because, if there was one thing of which Marsha was certain, it was that Danny wouldn't change. Jesus, he still wore the exact same shoes he'd worn at school, beige desert boots, size 9. He bought the things in bulk now. She'd seen them stacked in his bedroom cupboard. Danny wore one pair until the soles wore out. Then he threw them away and unboxed a new pair.

Still, it wasn't surprising that Danny was a bit odd, given the childhood he'd had. He had been raised by his Spanish grandmother, the *abuela*. Marsha remembered her from a parents' evening at school, a grim-faced Mediterranean matriarch dressed head to toe in black, listening carefully to the teachers' reports, even though she was unable to speak a word of English. Marsha wondered if Danny had translated everything the teachers had been saying to the woman. She remembered Danny was quite badly behaved at school in a stubborn, sullen kind of way. He didn't like being told what to do.

And then there was Danny's mother, off gallivanting around the world with one man after another while her son stayed at home with the grandmother.

At thought of Adriana Sanchez, Marsha frowned. She was remembering something the woman had said to her the last time they'd met. They'd been at a restaurant and Adriana had begun one of her monologues about why all men were bastards and couldn't be trusted.

'Of course, I don't mean our Danny, though,' she had said suddenly, while Danny was at the restaurant bar. 'He's a different kettle of fish entirely. One of your non-commitment types, isn't he? I don't think any woman's ever managed to nail him down for more than a couple of months before he bolted for the hills. But then you know all this already, don't you, Marsha? I mean, you would hardly have come trailing halfway across Europe otherwise, would you?'

Then she had leant across the table, her voice conspiratorial.

'And that was a smart move not moving in with him straight away. Softly, softly, catchee monkey, eh?'

Marsha hadn't paid much mind to it at the time – Adriana Sanchez was one of those women who had a knack for saying hurtful things while smiling with an expression of heartfelt commiseration – but now the words churned around in her mind.

She had come to Spain because she, Marsha Constance, had wanted to. The move to Almería was supposed to be about personal development – a new career, life challenges, a second language – and yet everyone seemed to assume it was all about Danny.

Well, balls to that, she thought, draining her glass. She wasn't going to let Danny mess her around. She needed more and she was going to tell him so. And if he couldn't give her that, well . . . she would cross that bridge when she came to it. That was one of the things her therapist had encouraged: not to feel guilt over pursuing the things that made her happy.

But she was going to sort things out, one way or another.

And if he couldn't be bothered to find time to go to the flamenco concert, Marsha was damned if she would waste the tickets.

She didn't have time to redo her make-up, but that didn't matter. She pulled on a pair of leggings and a faded old Morrissey T-shirt, looking at her watch. She still had time if she took a taxi.

She looked at herself in the mirror. Then she smiled and blew herself a kiss. She'd worry about Danny Sanchez tomorrow.

13

Sunday, August 26th, 2012

T HERE WAS NO point in going home, so Danny took a
taxi back to his car then stopped at a café and drank coffee
and smoked cigarettes. The pharmacy opposite the café had a
digital display that showed the time and the temperature. Danny shook his head when he saw the numbers displayed there:
06:55 and it was already 25°C. Today was going to be torture.

He had too many thoughts in his head to worry about the
heat, though.

Sebastian Gomez, again. Who was this bloke? Danny
Googled the name but found nothing. That in itself was interesting, as it probably meant that Gomez was well-known
enough not to need to advertise his services.

Still, Danny could learn more about Gomez later on. The
important thing now was that Gomez's presence meant the two
stories – Hector Castillo's body at Little Arizona and Martyn
Phillips's death – were linked. They had to be. It couldn't be
a coincidence that the same hot-shot corporate lawyer was
throwing his weight around in both cases.

So Danny started searching for further links between the
two stories. The obvious starting point was the construction
industry. Phillips was an architect, Castillo had worked as a

consultant for a development company and Sixto Escobar had run a construction company.

He began by searching for their names. It yielded results immediately.

The photo he found online showed Martyn Phillips shaking hands with a Spanish man in front of a group of suited onlookers who were smiling and clapping. Danny wondered why the dumpy Spaniard clasping Phillips's hand seemed so familiar. It took him a moment to realise why: it was Sixto Escobar's father.

And there was Sixto, now that Danny looked, standing amid the crowd of suited men applauding the handshake. Sixto looked younger and perhaps four stone lighter, but it was definitely him. And there was another face there that Danny recognised: the actor, Doug Sampson, looking out of place in a suit, his hair dyed that awkward jet black colour that vain old men think makes them look younger.

The photo was dated 1997. The caption read, 'Councillor Pedro Escobar celebrates the signing of an agreement with The Sampson Consortium to build a 1,214 house urbanisation in the Las Redes zone of Las Jarapas', but the link to the article kept delivering an error message.

1997. That must be the Bellavista Urbanisation, the place where Phillips's other house was. Danny cursed. If he'd learned that yesterday, he would have asked Sian Phillips a whole different set of questions. What was the betting that Phillips's architectural company had had something to do with the development?

He looked for information on the Sampson Consortium, but there wasn't really anything of interest: 1997 was before most newspapers had developed digital editions.

At 07:30 Danny drove to Paco Pino's house in Retamar.

Paco's wife, Lourdes, was getting their two daughters ready for a day out at the beach. Normally, Lourdes was one of those Andaluz women who plonk food in front of you as soon as you enter their houses – Danny had learned long ago never to eat before visiting Paco's house close to a meal time – but today she merely greeted him with a terse nod of the head and went on brushing her daughters' hair.

Paco was sitting on the balcony in his underpants, eating a breakfast of toast and cold meats.

'You look rough,' Paco said around a mouthful, gesturing for Danny to join him.

'Thanks. I've been awake most of the night. Have I done something wrong?' Danny said, nodding towards Lourdes.

The photographer shrugged.

'Marsha and Lourdes were chatting on Skype early this morning.'

'Right, so Lourdes is giving me the cold shoulder because I missed the concert last night?'

Paco dabbed the corners of his mouth with a napkin. 'I think it's more the fact that after missing the concert last night, you came straight here to see me, rather than going to square things with Marsha.'

'Your house is on the way home. And I need to speak with you.'

'Just make sure you go home after this and apologise. Marsha's a great girl, Danny. You don't want to lose her.'

'I don't plan on losing her. Unless you've heard different, that is?'

Paco lit a cigarette and looked away.

'Have you heard different, Paco?'

'No, of course not. But I think the general consensus of opinion is that, on occasions, you take her for granted. She's given up a lot to be with you.'

Danny rolled his eyes to indicate he was tired of the subject. A few seconds later, though, he said, 'Anyway, why is it always the man that has to go crawling back apologising whenever there's a problem?'

Paco's hands flapped upward in exasperation. 'How should I know why? Why is it always the man that sleeps on the sofa? Or has to make a big fuss about anniversaries? Some things in life just *are* and it's simpler if you go with the flow.'

'I'm not a go-with-the-flow type of guy.'

'Anyway, I've got some news that will cheer you up,' Paco said. He reached below the table and withdrew a copy of *El Pais*. 'There we go,' he said, spreading the newspaper in front of Danny. 'We got half of page 4. Not bad, eh?'

Danny nodded, munching toast as he read the article entitled 'Almería killer burns victim alive'.

'What's the matter?' Paco asked when he saw the look on Danny's face.

'Nothing. It's a good article, given the time we had. But I just wish I'd known then what I know now.'

'Which is?'

'It's all linked.'

'What's all linked?'

Danny said, 'First of all this Hector Castillo – a placid, teetotal boffin-type guy who spends his spare time rescuing donkeys – disappears in what looks to have been a professional hit. Then, seven years later, his body turns up strapped to a wagon wheel at Sixto Escobar's place. Then it turns out he had roughly ninety grand in the bank when he died – money that he supposedly got working for a development company.

'Then, the very same afternoon I begin doing background research on Castillo, a lawyer named Sebastian Gomez starts phoning round, berating people, telling them not to speak to the press. Then he gets on the phone to my newspaper. Now, this same Gomez guy has turned up and hustled Sian Phillips out of the Guardia headquarters like his very life depended on it. Not only that, Gomez has some hired goon called Shrike with him. The bastard put me on my arse so fast I didn't actually see him do it. He's a cocky sod, too: he did it right in front of the main entrance to the Guardia barracks. I reckon he's –'

Danny paused as Paco began making frantic shushing gestures.

'Did I say something wrong?' Danny said.

Paco checked to see Lourdes was out of earshot. 'It's just that after the whole Scarecrow business, Lourdes isn't keen on me taking risks at work. Or rather, taking risks that might put the family at risk again. And neither is Marsha, now we're on the subject.'

'How do you know that?'

'What the hell do you think they talk about when they get together here, Danny? It ain't haircuts and lipstick, *amigo*, I can tell you that.'

Danny lit a cigarette.

'What about this lawyer, Paco? Have you heard of him?' Danny said, watching the photographer closely: he was sure that Paco had recognised Sebastian Gomez's name when he'd mentioned it before.

Paco seemed about to say "no", but then nodded slowly.

'Be careful if you go up against him, Danny.'

'Why?'

'Because he's got the morals of a sewer rat and teeth twice as sharp. Trust me, he's vindictive and he doesn't play by the rules. A few years ago he went after a reporter from *La Voz* and he destroyed him.'

'You're the second person to mention that. Who was this journalist? What happened?'

Paco sighed, as if he regretted mentioning it.

'His name was Eduardo Bolaño.'

'Did you know him?'

'We never worked together, but we started out in journalism at the same time. We'd see each other in the pubs sometimes in the evenings, or have a coffee together when we were covering the same story.'

'What happened?'

'It was around the turn of the century. Apparently, Bolaño had some story that the newspapers wouldn't print for fear of the repercussions. So Bolaño published it on a webpage.'

'What was the story?'

Paco shrugged. 'I never saw it. The thing was only up for a day or two before this Gomez bastard got an injunction to bring the webpage down. Then he hit Bolaño with a libel suit. Bolaño lost everything: his job, his house, his savings. The poor sod ended up throwing himself under a train.'

'As long as we print solid facts, libel is nothing to worry about.'

'Take it from me, Danny, you won't sell anything involving Gomez's name locally. Everyone's shit scared.'

'If we get our facts straight, someone will print it.'

'I wouldn't be so sure. Gomez's cousin is Emilio Morales, and he manages a local investment fund, the sort where you need a million euros minimum to invest. That's who Gomez works for now. Between them, they've got some powerful friends.'

'Big deal. I'm still going to try to speak to this Gomez guy.'

'Danny, if he's hired himself a bodyguard, that really isn't a good idea. Remember, I've had some experience of these private security bastards, doing paparazzi work. There's nothing they like better than an excuse to give someone a good kicking.'

'So, what are you saying then? That we should drop the story?'

Paco shook his head. '*El País* are really keen on this whole murder angle in the Phillips's story, so that's what we should delve into. Let's work on finding the link between Phillips and Escobar. If we can establish why Castillo's dead body was dumped on Escobar and then link it to Phillips's death, we'll have a really solid story. Nobody's going to shed a tear if we pin something on a crummy bastard like Escobar. By the way, what does the Sheriff of Little Arizona have to say about all this?'

'He's gone off the radar. And I mean totally disappeared. He's not been home for two days, nor has he been to work. No-one knows where he is. That's why I'm going to speak to Jorge Salamanca later on today.'

'What the hell do you expect to learn from Jorge? He's been out to pasture for years.'

'He's still the best court reporter in the province. I bet he will have covered Escobar's divorce. And I want to speak to someone at the analytical laboratory, too.'

Paco ran a hand over his big bald head.

'What does an analytical laboratory have to do with Phillips's murder?'

Danny pointed at the copy of *El País* which contained their article.

'Have you actually read this article? An article with your name on the byline, might I add.'

Paco laughed. 'If I wanted to worry about sorting all this crap out I'd be a reporter. But I'm not. I'm a photographer. I point my camera at things and press a button. The end.'

'A man named Florentino Yagüe was Phillips's friend. He committed suicide recently. And the papers that Phillips was trying to burn were from Yagüe's laboratory.'

Paco nodded, only half listening as he looked at Danny's notes. 'It's time for you to pay. That sounds like blackmail, don't you think?'

'As a rule, blackmailers don't tend to burn their victims alive.'

'Who do you think is doing it?'

'No idea. But the spelling of the name on the envelope I saw is significant.'

'Why?'

'Martin Filips. That's not how his surname's spelt.'

'Isn't it?'

Spanish is a phonetic language: there are five vowels which produce five fixed sounds. The seemingly random way the English language throws letters together proves a constant source of wonder – and bafflement – for Spaniards. Danny explained the correct spelling. Paco shook his head. 'It starts *ph*? And why two *l*'s? Why do you English have to make everything so complicated? Anyway, what does it tell us about the person who sent the package?'

Danny smiled. 'Either they were extremely bad at spelling, or they were Spanish.'

'Or they were like me,' Paco said, stifling a burp. 'Both.'

14

DANNY HAD A busy day ahead of him, but he knew he wouldn't be able to concentrate until he squared things with Marsha. On the way to her flat, he stopped at a petrol station and bought a box of chocolates, feeling a dull ache in his back and buttocks as he crossed the forecourt. He decided he'd better not mention Shrike to Marsha. She would only worry.

Close to Marsha's flat, some idiot on a moped pulled out without looking, forcing Danny to slam on his brakes, which sent the chocolate box flying. Danny swore when he saw the box edge had crumpled and split apart.

When he got to Marsha's flat, he rang the doorbell. Almost instantly, he heard the approaching slap of Marsha's flip flops on the tiled floor.

'Hello,' she said after opening the door.

Danny handed her the chocolates, which she accepted with a slight frown as she noticed the crumpled box lid.

'You may notice some superficial damage to the packaging,' he said, quoting one of their favourite comedies, 'but the chocolate inside is still perfectly edible.'

Marsha smiled at that. They went through to the living room.

Marsha's displeasure normally manifested itself in cold, quiet indifference, parrying all enquiries as to what the matter was with a terse, 'Nothing, I'm fine'. But today she seemed completely normal – affable even.

'So you're OK, then?' Danny said. 'I mean, I thought you'd be upset about missing the concert.'

'I was upset last night. But then I thought, "Why waste all that money?" So I went on my own. I even managed to sell the other ticket outside.'

'Well, that's great,' Danny said, relieved.

'But that doesn't mean we're going to avoid discussing what happened,' she said, patting the sofa to indicate Danny should sit beside her.

Danny's shoulders slumped.

The conversation began with Marsha asking him to tell her what had happened the night before, which he did – everything bar the part where Shrike had thrown him over.

'I suppose what I really want to ask,' Marsha said when he'd finished, 'is whether last night is what the rest of our life together is going to be like. Me sitting here like a lemon waiting for you, while you're off chasing around after stories long into the middle of the night? Because I really don't think I could stand that, Danny.

'This might sound terribly middle-aged, but at the moment I just want a quiet, comfortable life with the man I love. I want to sit next to you in bed and read books and watch television with you and do all the things that happy, middle-aged couples do. And I don't want you running any more stupid risks for the sake of a story. Move on, Danny. You're not a young man anymore. Let someone else run around after all this crap.'

Danny scoffed at that. Marsha turned towards him.

'You don't think your work is dangerous? Tell me this,

when I asked you before to tell me everything that happened last night, did you?'

Danny was going to say, 'Of course', but the lie died on his lips when he saw the way Marsha was looking at him.

Shit. She knew about Shrike.

Danny held her eyes for a moment, then looked away. 'I take it Lourdes overheard me talking to Paco and told you about it?'

'Yes, she did. She phoned me while she was on the way to the beach. She didn't want to make a scene with Paco while you were there, but rest assured she will be having the exact same conversation with Paco later on. Do you seriously think either us of want our men getting physically hurt just because of a job?'

'Well, she's exaggerated.'

'Has she? Like she exaggerated what happened with that wretched Scarecrow business? Because when you told me your version of events, you didn't mention anything about being locked in a burning building. Or about Paco being stabbed. Or Alejandra being kidnapped.'

Danny said nothing. Marsha gave an ironic smile.

'God, listen to me: I sound like my bloody mother.' She stood. 'Listen, I don't mean to be a nag, Danny. But you run far too many risks for *far* too little pay.'

'So, you wouldn't mind me running risks if the money was better?'

She frowned. 'Have you not listened to a word I've said? I don't want you running risks, full stop. The fact you do it for rubbish pay is just the icing on the ruddy cake.'

The conversation was drifting towards an argument now,

so Danny got up and went to the toilet. He splashed cold water on his face and stared into the mirror, his hands gripping either side of the wash-basin. Then he tried to examine the damage his fall had caused by standing in front of the bathroom mirror and craning his neck around. All he could see were two red-purple blemishes that started somewhere on his arse and carried on up about six inches of his spine.

Feeling calmer, Danny went back to the living room and rejoined Marsha on the sofa.

She sighed and looked at the floor.

'Look, I can tell you're onto something with this latest story,' she said. 'You've got that look you always get when something has caught your interest. But you upset me last night. That concert was something *I* wanted to do with *you*. Now, I know it wasn't your fault. Not entirely. But when you get the bit between your teeth, you're only ever half there. So, I guess what I'm saying is, don't shut me out.'

'Fair enough,' Danny said.

They kissed.

'So what is it?' Marsha asked. 'This story.'

Danny told her everything. About Martyn Phillips and Hector Castillo, about Sixto Escobar and the Palomares Incident.

'That sounds fascinating,' she said when he'd finished. 'But just please tell me it's not anything dangerous.'

'Of course it isn't.'

She looked deeply into his eyes.

'You promise, don't you?'

'I promise.'

'Because when I go back to England next week, I don't

want to be worrying about you.'

'Scout's honour.'

Marsha looked at him, smiling sadly, the way she did when she was trying hard to believe him.

15

'LOOK AT THIS,' Jorge Valenzuela said, gesturing towards his plate of tapas. 'Two prawns. *Two*,' he said, holding up thumb and forefinger for emphasis. 'Time was you'd get six or seven in this place.'

Danny gestured towards the empty tables all around them in the bar. 'Time was they would have had more than two customers at lunchtime. But don't get sidetracked. Tell me more about Sixto Escobar's divorce, Jorge. How messy was it?'

Jorge Valenzuela had been court reporter for *El Mundo* for as long as anyone could remember. Court reporting was boring but comfortable work, two adjectives that described the rotund fifty-five-year-old's life perfectly. Any investigative zeal he might once have possessed had died out long ago, which made him a good sounding board: you could ask Jorge about stuff without any danger of him going off snooping around on his own. Besides that, he was a veritable gold mine of gossipy scuttlebutt. It wasn't the sort of stuff you could print – not without serious risk of libel – but it was perfect to get an idea of what was really going on behind the scenes of life in Almería.

'All in good time,' Jorge said, wiping prawn juice from his fingers with a napkin. 'Do you know, when I saw it was your number, I nearly didn't answer.'

'Why's that?'

'Because whenever you phone it's always to ask me for something.'

Danny smiled at the truth of that. 'So why did you answer?'

'I've got an ulterior motive.'

'Which is?'

'You've met my daughter, Manuela, haven't you?'

'Yes.'

'Do you know how I scrimped and saved so I could send her to that English school in Granada? Ten years at four grand a term, Danny. Do you know what that meant on my wage? But it was all worth it just to get her to speak fluent English.' He shook his head sadly. 'I envisaged her being a university lecturer or an interpreter. But do you know what? She can't even get a cleaning job. She's twenty-seven with a first-class degree in English Philology and yet she's never had a job. You should see the way she mopes around the house.'

'And you want me to help her?'

'Yes. I want you to get her a job in England.'

Danny's smile faded when he saw Jorge was serious.

'Why Britain?'

'Why not?' Jorge said, and for a moment his voice rose. 'I'm sick of Spain. I'm sick of all the corruption and the bullshit. All that EU investment money we got, where did it end up? In the pockets of the usual cheap pimp bastards. ¡*Joder*! my toes curl when I imagine what the French and Germans must think of us.

'And that's the worst part, isn't it? Because it's not the ordinary Spanish people that fucked things up, is it? No, they're always too busy getting shafted. It's the politicians and the bankers. All of them. They're rotten right to the core.' He laughed bitterly. 'It took us thirty years to create an educated, affluent middle class and just three years to piss it all away. Where are all our best and brightest now? They've all gone abroad. Why Britain, you ask? If I was younger, I'd go with her.'

Danny motioned for the waiter to bring another round of beers and said he would see what he could do. Jorge relaxed.

'Come on, then,' Danny said when the fresh drinks arrived. 'Tell me about Sixto Escobar's divorce.'

'OK. First, I'd better give you some background.' Jorge cleared his throat. Danny got his notepad and pen out. 'Right, in 1993, Sixto Escobar married a woman named Lucia Borja. It was a marriage made in hell. Both of them were just as greedy and corrupt as each other. Back then, Sixto was still on his way up, courtesy of the juicy building contracts Papa Escobar was putting his way, so Lucia set up an estate agency to sell the properties Sixto was building.

'As of 1996, Sixto and his father decided to make a bid for the serious money and the Bellavista urbanisation project was born. They were one of the first in the province to wake up to just how much money they could make by building houses and selling them to retired foreigners. And the Escobars made sure they had their snouts in every trough going. Then again, the whole rotten council up at Las Jarapas was in on it.'

'Why did people keep voting for them, then?'

'Firstly, it was a socialist stronghold. And secondly, you could have got a monkey elected to that council back then as long as it knew how to rubber stamp planning proposals and keep its mouth shut. The whole place was awash with crooked money. Do you know what they used to call the town hall in Las Jarapas? *Los Correos*, the Post Office, because it used to take delivery of so many brown envelopes stuffed with cash.'

'And all this money came from the Bellavista urbanisation?'

'That's right. Anyway, by the start of this century, Sixto Escobar and Lucia Borja were absolutely loaded. That was when Sixto bought himself that wretched theme park in Tabernas and started dressing up as a cowboy. They were both so rich, in fact, that they begin to indulge themselves in every way possible. Rumour has it that Sixto had a taste for poker, cocaine and strippers, while Lucia basically went after anything in trousers.' Jorge sipped his beer. 'God, can you imagine those two going at it in bed together?'

'Hey,' Danny said, 'I've enough horror shows in my head already without you adding a naked Sixto Escobar.'

Jorge smiled. 'Anyway, the infidelities began to mount. Eventually, in May 2008 they decided to divorce. Sixto was the petitioner, Lucia the respondent. It was a messy split. Sixto cited irreconcilable differences as the reason, but after fifteen years together they were so financially entwined it was always going to end up in court.

'Lucia insisted on a public hearing, thinking that the dirt she could make public would scare Sixto into settling out of court. Escobar, like the hothead he is, fought her tooth and nail and agreed.

'The first day of the trial covered all the usual crap. Both sides called in character witnesses to testify as to what fantastic human beings they were. But you could tell Lucia had something up her sleeve. After working the courts, you get to know the look. She just sat there, taking everything Escobar's lawyer threw at her with a little half-smile on her face, as if she was thinking "just you wait".'

'What was it?'

'The trial started on a Thursday. On the Friday, about twenty minutes before the trial was due to end for the day, Lucia's lawyer suddenly mentioned a property that had belonged to them both on the Bellavista estate, one that Sixto had supposedly sold to a business associate. Lucia claimed Sixto had sold it for a vastly reduced price – sold it practically for cost, in fact – and Lucia wanted him to cover what she would have got had they sold it on the open market.

'"Who is this business associate?" the judge asked. Lucia was smiling. Beaming. "He was a gentleman that handled corporate security for Señor Escobar's development company," her lawyer says.

'You should have seen the look on Sixto's face. I've never seen someone so pale and yet so angry at the same time.'

'Corporate security meaning dirty work?'

Jorge shrugged. 'Well, the inference was very definitely that this chap had received the property in lieu of services rendered, if you catch my drift. It was well-timed, as well. Lucia's lawyers brought it in right at the end of the Friday session. It gave Sixto the whole weekend to sweat.

'Anyway, Monday morning, Sixto Escobar came in with a new set of lawyers, real sharks. A guy named Sebastian Gomez had taken over handling Sixto's case. The first thing he did was ask to show the judge and Lucia's legal team something in closed chamber.'

'Any idea what it was?'

'Rumour had it Gomez had a videotape that showed exactly what sort of things Lucia Borja liked to do in the bedroom and with whom she liked to do them. Apparently, they had evidence of Lucia going at it with about six different guys – and not always on separate occasions, if you catch my drift.'

'She can't have been happy about that.'

'Nor was Sixto, to judge by his face when he came back into court. You know what Spanish society is like about female infidelity, it reflects badly on both parties: the woman is a *puta,* but the guy gets to be called *cabrón* for the rest of his life.'

'So, you think Sixto had the tapes, but Gomez forced him to use them?'

'Yes.'

'How come none of this got reported?'

'Someone got to my editor and threatened to pull a lot of advertising. Plus this Gomez threatened all sorts of legal nightmares if we did print.'

'What about the house? Have you got an address?'

Jorge shook his head. 'This was four years ago. If it was read out in court, I didn't make a note of it.'

'Is Lucia Borja still around?'

'She lives locally, yes. But there's no point in talking to her. A friend of mine on *ABC* tried to get her to talk just after the trial, but this Gomez had forced her to sign some form of non-disclosure agreement – one that promised to rain hellfire and brimstone down upon her were she to break it. I can tell you one thing, though. Borja wasn't best pleased about the settlement. Let me show you a photo of her.'

The woman in the photo was around Danny's age. She

wasn't ugly, but she was far from attractive. It took a special talent to make all those designer labels and haute couture look so. . .tacky. The photo showed Borja on the steps of a big glass building, her eyes like freshly-opened furnaces.

'She looks pretty pissed off,' Danny said.

'Hell hath no fury, eh?'

'Tell me more about the other guy,' Danny said. 'I take it this corporate security guy was really a hatchet man?'

'You'd have thought it to see the guy. He had a heavy-weight's physique, but a face that was pure bare-knuckle, if you know what I mean. He was ex-Foreign Legion, too, and you know how they can be.'

Danny nodded to show that he did. The Spanish Foreign Legion – *La Legión* as it was known – was a strange military organisation, obsessed with honour and death. The unit's motto was *Viva la Muerte* – Long Live Death – and it prided itself on taking only the toughest of the tough.

'Apparently, this chap had been eking out a living as one of the stunt riders at Escobar's godawful Western park, but found a sideline doing strong-arm work: industrial espionage, sabotage, burglary, that sort of thing. And, of course, going around collecting the brown envelopes for Escobar and all his cronies.'

'Have you got a photo of the hatchet man?'

Jorge laughed. 'I wasn't about to go up and shove a camera in his face. You should have seen the guy. He must have weighed eighteen or nineteen stone and none of it was fat. Plus he had a police guard with him.'

'Really?'

'That was the interesting bit. As it turned out, a year earlier, there had been a big police corruption trial here in Almería.

Some *policia local* admin officer had been selling favours, creating alibis, losing witness statements, that sort of thing. The hatchet man got caught up in it.'

'Interesting. Have you got a name for the hatchet man?'

Jorge thumbed through his notes.

'His name is Varela,' he said. 'Gabriel Varela.'

PART II

EL ANÁLISIS

1

Maria Esmerelda Varela Schmidt was born at
02:17 on April 10th, 1998. She measured 52 centimetres and
weighed 4.4 kilos.

That first night of her life, Gabriel Varela sat awake in a
chair beside the exhausted mother's bed; and when little Esme
stirred within her glass cot and made soft sounds of distress, he
lifted her out and laid her upon his broad chest. She quietened
immediately, and he watched in fascination as her tiny fingers
curled inwards and clung to the fabric of his T-shirt. Later that
night, to his surprise, he found himself stroking his little finger
through the soft down on her skull and whispering soft words
to her: '*Te quiero, mi angelito*' – I love you, my little angel.
He had repeated the words over and over, wondering at the
strangeness of the sounds they made – his mouth had never
before expressed such genuine tenderness.

Father, mother and child had lived together for only a few
months after the birth. Then had come the night when Varela
had been out into the small hours, collecting money for one of
the *Flecha Rota* pricks – Gomez, probably, or Escobar – and,
on the last call of the night, Varela had had to bust someone's
nose in order to get him to pay. When he arrived home, as was
his wont, he walked upstairs, went into Esme's room and lifted
the child from her cot. She made soft noises and snuggled into

the crook of his arm. He held her that way for a number of minutes, feeling her heartbeat beneath his fingers.

Next morning, the mother called Varela into the room and showed him the smears of dried blood his knuckles had left on Esme's skin and clothes. She said, 'If you've been out beating on people at night, Gabi, wash your fucking hands before you touch our daughter.'

Varela had moved out that same day. He had tired of the mother's griping, anyway, but that was only part of the reason: he had realised that he could not allow the sump that had become his own life to stain little Esme's. He would be a father to the child and would do his best to make her feel comforted and loved, but he would have to keep his distance.

Of course, the mother would have preferred that he'd disappeared from their lives altogether, but a few days after he moved out he contacted her with an offer of financial support. After all, Varela could afford to be generous: the amount of work the *Flecha Rota* pricks had been putting his way back then, he had had more money than he knew what to do with . . .

But that was then. Now, Varela had a different type of work to do. There were still three of them left.

He sat on the mattress at the back of the lock up and spread his copy of *La Razón* open to the personal ads, scanning down the columns. He paused halfway down the third column.

There it was.

GENEROUS OPPORTUNITY FOR FORMER LEGIONNAIRE.

Willing to discuss full compensation of outstanding

amount, plus a bonus of twice the initial premium. Call 626 365 779

Varela snorted as he re-read the message. So, they were offering him money, were they? That was no surprise. It had always been their solution to everything.

He cast the copy of *La Razón* to one side and began looking through the other newspapers he had purchased. He had bought copies of all the major national and local newspapers today. He wanted to see how Martyn Phillips's death had been reported.

Most of the articles covered the same ground, merely stating that a British man had burnt to death, without saying whether it was suicide, accident or murder.

El País was different. The article in that newspaper described Phillips's death as murder. Varela's eyes narrowed as he read the article. The reporter also described the scene inside Phillips's house and mentioned the papers Phillips had been trying to burn.

How the hell had the reporter learned that?

He looked at the names at the top of the article: Danny Sanchez and Paco Pino.

He re-read it.

The journalists weren't really that close to the truth. Still, it was early days. If these two began sniffing around, it could be a problem. Varela decided he would keep an eye on their work. If they got too close, Varela would have to warn them off.

But as he considered further he realised it could also work to his advantage.

Varela looked across the lock-up to the folder Lucia Borja

had brought him while he was in prison, the proof he had of what the men had done.

Yes, once he had killed the three remaining men, he could send the proof he had of their crime to the journalists. There would be something satisfying in that. Not only would he kill them, he would destroy their names, too. Yes, he decided, that was how he would do it. Varela made a note to find out the journalist's mobile number.

He folded the newspaper and stood up.

Sixto Escobar was next.

2

Eᴀʀʟʏ ᴏɴ Mᴏɴᴅᴀʏ morning, Danny drove to an industrial park on the outskirts of Almería city, heading for the premises of *Laboratorios Florentino Yagüe S.L.*

Analytical laboratories were big business in Almería, where fruit and vegetable production was a mainstay of the local economy. Labs analysed produce for quality and checked skins for traces of pesticides prior to export. They also took care of water analyses for the semi-private companies that supplied the province's tap water.

According to Danny's research, *Laboratorios Florentino Yagüe S.L.* was one of the most prosperous labs in the province. Despite that, at the beginning of 2012, the 66-year-old owner and founder of the company, Florentino Yagüe, had driven out to a remote mountain road, run a plastic tube from the exhaust to the driver's side window and turned the key in the ignition.

Newspaper reports at the time had linked the suicide to the economic crisis – hell, between failing businesses, redundancies and house repossessions, the suicide rate in Spain had rocketed in recent years – but Danny had discovered that Yagüe's business had been doing all right at the time, all things considered.

Yagüe's son, Nacho – short for Ignacio – had taken over the running of the business since his father's death, but rumour had it he wasn't really up to the task.

Danny had also done some checking on the links between Yagüe and Martyn Phillips. Not only had the two men engaged in lots of charity work for Sian Phillips's foundation, Danny had also discovered that Yagüe had been an investor in The Sampson Consortium, the development company that had built the Bellavista urbanisation. The previous evening Danny had phoned Anja at the donkey sanctuary and asked whether The Sampson Consortium was the developer for whom Hector Castillo had acted as consultant.

'Yes,' she had said almost immediately. 'The American cowboy. That's the one, I remember now.'

That was one mystery solved. It still didn't explain why the hell a research scientist was working for a property developer.

Once Danny had found the Yagüe lab, he parked and walked to where he could watch the entrance to the car park from a patch of shade. The car park was already full: most companies in Spain worked a modified timetable in summer that started and finished early to avoid the worst of the day's heat. Danny kept his eye on the parking bay closest to the entrance, the one that had the word *reservado* painted on the floor.

At 09:45 a black Porsche swept into the car park and a bearded Spaniard of around Danny's age emerged.

Nacho Yagüe had dark curly hair slicked back from his forehead and wore an electric blue sports shirt with a pale yellow jumper resting on his shoulders, the arms tied loosely below his neck. He closed his car door, paused and burst into raucous laughter as he talked into a smartphone.

'She was twenty-six, you bastard! Anyway, I'm seeing her again next week so I'll check her DNI when she's in the pisser. And you still owe me for those bottles of Dom Perignon. Anyway, I'll be –'

'Hello, Señor Yagüe,' Danny said.

Nacho Yagüe spun round.

'Who are you?'

'Danny Sanchez, we spoke last night.'

Yagüe's face darkened. 'And I told you I had nothing to say to you.' He turned and headed for the building.

'Do you know this man?' Danny said, keeping pace with him and angling himself so that Yagüe junior got a good look at the photo of Martyn Phillips Danny was carrying.

Yagüe's eyes flickered towards the photo. He stopped. 'What the hell is all this about?'

'So you do recognise him?'

'No, I don't. But I want to know why you're pestering me.'

'This man was an architect named Martyn Phillips. In the early hours of Saturday morning he was abducted from a house on the Bellavista estate. Someone then poured petrol on him and burnt him alive.' Yagüe's eyes widened at that, so Danny said, 'There were papers from this laboratory at Phillips's house – papers he had been trying to destroy before he was killed. Perhaps you saw the article I wrote in *El País*?'

Yagüe shook his head.

No, Danny thought, he didn't look the type to read a left-leaning, liberal newspaper.

Danny said, 'There was also a handwritten message left

there: *It's time for you to pay.* It could be someone was trying to blackmail Mr Phillips, perhaps by using information from this laboratory. Do you remember your father ever mentioning Mr Phillips?'

Nacho Yagüe scratched the stubble on his chin and rolled the name around, making great show of trying to remember. Up close, Danny realised Yagüe junior wasn't quite as well groomed as he first appeared: he'd missed a patch shaving and his bloodshot eyes had a greyish tint to them. He looked like a man who had drunk too much and slept too little the night before.

Yagüe shook his head. 'I don't recognise the name. Perhaps if you tell me more about him I might remember.'

'Mr Phillips's widow seemed to think your father and Mr Phillips were friends.'

'Then she was wrong.'

'So, you don't know about your father's involvement with Mrs Phillips's charity?'

'No,' Yagüe said, and for the first time Danny felt the man was telling the truth.

'What about a man named Hector Castillo? Does that name ring any bells?'

Nacho Yagüe frowned. 'Are you just going to reel off a list of random names at me?'

'Castillo was a research scientist. Your father ran an analytical laboratory. It doesn't seem too far-fetched that they might have known each other. What about Sixto Escobar? Do you know him?'

'Only by reputation. And my father was the scientist. I deal in real estate.'

Danny didn't press the point, but he knew the bastard was lying. You learned to spot that momentary hesitation when someone wanted to answer a question to their own advantage.

'There's just one more thing,' Danny said. 'Did you get on well with your father?'

'What business is that of yours?'

'Rumour has it you hadn't spoken for years. And that makes me wonder whether all those answers you've just given me might not be wrong. I mean, if you weren't speaking to your father, how would you know? And it's interesting that you mention working in real estate. Because, as it turns out, your father and Martyn Phillips were both major investors in the Bellavista urbanisation – and yet you don't seem to know about it. Doesn't say much for your professional acumen, does it?'

Yagüe's cheeks flushed red beneath his beard. His voice trembled when he spoke. 'You people. God, I despise you.' His voice rose. 'I want you to go. Now. Go on, before I throw you out.'

Danny flipped his notebook shut and walked back to the patch of shade across the road. Journalism was fun sometimes, when it provided the chance to ruffle existences unused to being ruffled. He leant against the wall and began searching through his address book.

A few years back Danny had written an article on three Britons in Almería's El Acebuche prison – two drug smugglers and a hit-and-run drunk driver – and Esteban had been the guard who had shown him round. Danny got on well with the man, and had ended up giving Esteban's daughter English lessons. Esteban worked in prison admin now.

'Hello Esteban,' Danny said into the phone. 'I need to ask a favour.'

'You always do.'

'Can you find me some info on a prisoner named Gabriel Varela?'

'What sort of info?'

'Well, for starters, whether he's still in prison.'

Danny heard fingers clacking on a keyboard.

'Yes, here he is. Gabriel Varela Bahamonde, age fifty-five. He's an ugly bugger. Got seven years in 2007 for perverting the course of justice, but was released after five.'

'So he's out?'

'Yep. He got out June 29th according to this. He served three years in El Acebuche, then was transferred up to a prison in Cantabria.'

'That's the other side of the country. Why'd he get taken all the way up there?'

'It doesn't say why, although Varela applied for the transfer himself.'

'Can you try to find out for me? Also, I need to know some background on the guy. Did he receive any visits? Did he get any mail?'

Esteban's voice dropped to a whisper. 'Before I risk my job by doing this, tell me it's *really* important.

'Esteban, it's REALLY important.'

Esteban agreed.

Danny hung up and looked back across the road, towards the laboratory. Nacho Yagüe was standing in an upstairs window, looking down at him. Danny gave him a cheery wave. Yagüe jerked out of sight.

Danny crossed the road and walked up the stairs to the lab's main entrance, where the secretary buzzed him in. Danny handed her one of his business cards and asked her to give it to Nacho Yagüe.

'Why shall I say you've left this?' she said.

Danny thought about this for a moment and then smiled. 'Tell him to give me a call if he decides to start telling the truth.'

3

Nacho Yagüe watched through the blinds as the reporter crossed the road, climbed into a battered maroon Escort and drove away. Seeing the car made Nacho feel better: the reporter couldn't be much good if he drove a piece of shit like that. But it irritated Nacho that the reporter had been able to see through him so easily. If there was one thing Nacho Yagüe was normally good at, it was lying.

He crossed the office and sat in his father's chair, a huge swivel thing decked out in black leather. Nacho swung back and forth in the chair, massaging his temples with his fingertips. He had a real bastard behind the eyes this morning.

He reached into the desk drawer, withdrew the bottle of Smirnoff he kept there and poured himself a two finger measure, which he used to wash down a couple of paracetamol tablets. The vodka made him feel a little more human, so he took a pad of paper and wrote down the three names the reporter had mentioned: Martyn Phillips, Hector Castillo, Sixto Escobar.

He underlined Castillo's name. That was the only one he didn't recognise. He would need to find out more about him. Nacho sat back in the chair, thinking about the Bellavista.

¡Joder! he hadn't heard that name for years. Of course he

remembered: it had been the source of the rift between Nacho and his father.

He let his mind wander. That had been a good time for Nacho, back when the development project had been getting off the ground: lots of parties, lots of corporate events, lots of easy money. And lots and *lots* of women. There hadn't been a single corporate event where Nacho didn't end up banging at least one of the hostesses The Sampson Consortium had hired.

When had that been? Was it 1997? No, it was '96, the year the English put Spain out of the European Cup on penalties. He could remember that bastard Phillips ragging them about it over dinner one night, the remains of 170,000 pesetas' worth of shellfish, suckling pig and Chateau Lafitte on the table between them.

Naturally, Sixto Escobar had been there, too: when had he ever missed out on a good feed? Nacho could picture him now, his sweaty pimp's leer emerging from the fug of cigar smoke that surrounded him, swilling whiskey and coke and telling everyone they were going to make so much money 'we'll be able to wallpaper our fucking houses with it'.

There had been a lawyer there, too – had his name been Gomez? – and some creepy banker, a relation of the lawyer, someone that everyone else had seemed to want to suck up to.

And, of course, Escobar's wife had been there.

Nacho couldn't forget her.

As always when he thought of Lucia Borja, Nacho felt a sudden flush of warmth in his crotch at the same time as his face reddened with shame.

He turned the computer on and went to the *El País* website and searched for the article the reporter had mentioned. After

he'd read it, he poured himself another vodka and began massaging his temples.

This was all he needed.

The article didn't mention the lab by name, but it did
mention the possibility of blackmail and the fact that Phillips
had been trying to burn papers when he'd been abducted. But
that was only the article in today's paper. It was obvious the
reporter was following up on the story. Who knew what the
bastard might write in the coming days?

Nacho needed to find out more about the links between
his father and this Phillips guy, so he drank the rest of his
vodka, crunched a handful of breath mints in his mouth and
headed downstairs to the basement of the building to look for
Kiko.

The laboratory's basement was originally an underground
car park, but after more than thirty years of business, the lab's
records had become so extensive that the whole of this space
was needed to house them. As Nacho descended the steps the
smell of old, dry paper rose to greet him.

It was typical of his father to have insisted on keeping
paper records of everything. The bloody results were all dou-
ble-backed on floppy disk and microfiche but, no, his father
had kept hard copies, too. Who would ever want to look at
any of this ruddy stuff anyway? There were analysis results
here going back three decades.

Nacho paused at the bottom of the stairs and peered into
the gloom.

'Kiko?'

As always, Nacho stifled a smile as the little crook-backed
figure shuffled out from behind a stack of shelving, bringing

with him the mingled stench of sweat and black tobacco that always accompanied the cripple.

Kiko had been the right hand man of Nacho's father for as long as Nacho could remember. God knows what his father had seen in him: Kiko was such a smelly little troll, always dry washing his hands and addressing people with the formal *usted* pronoun, his red eyes bulging.

'Can I help you, sir?'

'Martyn Phillips, Kiko. Do you remember that name?' Nacho said, making a point of referring to Kiko with the informal *tú*.

Kiko nodded and ran a hand through his wispy hair.

'He was an Englishman.'

'What connection did my father have with him?'

'I believe he was a shareholder in the investment group to which your father belonged. For the Bellavista development.'

'Do you mean The Sampson Consortium?'

'No, sir,' Kiko said, shuffling awkwardly, as if contradicting Nacho caused him physical pain. 'I mean *Grupo La Flecha Rota*.'

Nacho laughed at the sound of the name. 'The Broken Arrow Group? Who the hell were they?'

'The Sampson Consortium was only the developer. It was *Grupo La Flecha Rota* that actually dealt with financing the whole operation.'

Nacho thought about that. So, Nacho's father had kept him out of the loop. That was typical of his father.

'Are there any paper links to this Phillips man?'

'It's quite possible, sir.'

'Someone burnt him alive the other day. I want to know if

there's any possible comeback on us, so drop whatever you're doing and find the records. I want to see everything relating to any business my father might have had with Martyn Phillips.'

After that, Nacho climbed into his Porsche Cayman and drove into the city centre.

One thing was certain, he'd be upgrading his car before long. It had always galled him that he had to drive one of the more modest Porsche models – it was as if he could afford the name but nothing else. Once he managed to find a buyer for the lab he would be rolling in it. Of course, selling the lab would probably mean that all the current employees would lose their jobs, but that wasn't Nacho's fault, was it? He needed the liquidity. His estate agency was dying on its arse.

He did the rounds of some of the city centre bars, talking and gossiping, and drank three more beers, enough to put his hangover firmly to bed. Then he drove over to his father's house in Roquetas de Mar.

This was another of the problems his father's suicide had lumbered him with, a big five-bedroom property on the outskirts of Roquetas, the type known as *chalets* in Spanish, with 1,000 square metres of land around it.

The trouble was, not only was the property market dead in the water, the house was a fucking eyesore. His father had decked the place out with so many expensive and gaudy features – marble tiles on the exterior walls, stone architraves around the windows and doors – that it looked like one of those places rich Romanian gypsies built. Sure, everything was ornate and of the very best quality, but the cumulative effect was depressing. There was no flow to the architectural style. The house crowded down upon the eye like hawkers at a middle-eastern bazaar.

Nacho had only been to the place once since his father's death, and that was to make sure it was all properly locked up. Nacho's notary had handled most of the paperwork relating to the building. But it occurred to him now that there might be documents relating to his father's business affairs inside the house.

He pushed the key into the lock and opened the front door.

The interior of the house mirrored the exterior, in that there was an abundance of expensive features that seemed to have all been chosen independently of one another. And there was religious stuff all over the place: an ornate crucifix hung on the wall opposite the front door and the living room had huge photographic portraits of the last Pope and the *Virgen del Mar,* the patron saint of Almería.

Nacho climbed the stairs and went into his father's upstairs office, where he began rummaging in the drawers of the desk, looking for paperwork that might explain his business relationship with Martyn Phillips. The desk drawers were stuffed with papers, so he pulled the whole lot out and sat on the floor with them, sorting them into piles.

After thirty minutes of this, Nacho lit a cigarette and leant back against the desk.

There were more crucifixes and religious pictures in this room, too, and on the top of the desk Nacho found a well-thumbed Bible and rosary. A red leather bookmark protruded from the Bible's gilt-edged pages. Nacho puffed idly on his cigarette as he took the Bible and opened it at the bookmark.

A part of the left-hand page had been highlighted with fluorescent marker.

2 Corinthians 7:10: *For the sorrow that is according to the will of God produces a repentance without regret, leading to salvation, but the sorrow of the world produces death.*

Nacho frowned as he flicked through the Bible and saw that other pages had also been marked. All the quotations related to repentance and contrition.

What had happened to the old man? Nacho had heard that his father had found God late in life. He'd assumed the old bastard had been working some angle, but now Nacho wasn't so sure. But then his father had always been a weak man, the sort that would disappear for a whole weekend, only to come home blubbering and begging forgiveness of Nacho's mother. That was one of the reasons Nacho had despised him – that, and the fact that his mother had always forgiven the bastard.

There was another drawer in the desk, but this one was locked. Nacho had no idea where the key might be, so he went down into the garage, found a hammer and chisel and broke the thing open.

The drawer contained a pile of framed pictures, placed face down. Nacho picked the top one up and turned it over.

Someone had written something on the glass in black marker pen, but the letters had been smeared and rendered illegible. Nacho took a tissue and wiped dust away from the glass.

The picture showed a photo of Nacho's father crouching beside a child in a wheelchair. The girl was about eight years old, but her head was nearly bald, her eyebrows non-existent. An IV drip dangled above her, attached to her arm. Nacho looked more closely at the photo. Everyone else in the photo was smiling, but Florentino Yagüe's face was a pale rictus as he posed beside the sick girl.

There was an inscription cut into the picture's mount, written in English: *Dear Florentino, thank you for all your help with the fundraising for little Gillian. Sian Phillips.*

Nacho put the picture down.

Shit, this was the thing the reporter had mentioned, the wretched charity.

He picked up the next picture, which again depicted his father with a different sick child and held a dedication from Sian Phillips. Someone had written on the glass of this picture, too, but this time the words were still legible: *Arderé en el infierno.*

Nacho checked the other pictures in the drawer. The subject matter was always the same and the same message was written across the glass of each.

Nacho blew air as he realised the handwriting was his father's. All this religious bullshit was getting him down. What had happened to his father to cause him to write those words on each of the pictures?

Arderé en el infierno.

I will burn in hell.

4

W HEN DANNY GOT home, he did what he'd been doing every couple of hours for the last few days. First, he phoned Sixto Escobar. Then he phoned Sian Phillips. Sixto Escobar was not answering his phone; Sian Phillips simply hung up on him. It was curious that since Sebastian Gomez had come on the scene, Mrs Phillips was refusing to speak to Danny. Danny thought about the lawyer, about his sudden involvement with so many disparate cases: Escobar's divorce, Martyn Phillips's death, Hector Castillo's corpse. He wondered whether the lawyer's efforts were really dedicated towards protecting his clients' interests or his own.

He went into his office and started looking for background information on the Bellavista urbanisation. That was the logical point where all these men's interests coincided: Phillips, Escobar, Castillo, Yagüe, Gomez.

According to the information he'd found, Martyn Phillips's architectural company had designed the houses on the Bellavista; Sixto Escobar's construction company had done all the earth-moving and pipe-laying; Lucia Borja's estate agency had helped to sell the properties; and the Almería-based investment fund for which Sebastian Gomez worked, Inversiones Emilio Morales S.L., had provided a lot of the backing.

Although the developer of the Bellavista was officially The

Sampson Consortium, Danny had it on good authority that Doug Sampson had only ever been a straw man – the investors had wanted a (relatively) well-known face to sell their product. Rumour had it that Sampson had also been a minor investor in the project, but had been ousted when he began playing fast and loose with property buyers' deposits.

Danny smiled when he saw one of the early publicity photos: it showed Doug Sampson in full cowboy regalia, waving pistols and beaming at the camera, looking not a day over sixty despite the best efforts of the make-up artist and the photographer.

Danny found the investment fund's webpage, but it was light on solid fact: there was just enough to give an impression of its classy credentials and to ensure that casual browsers knew that plebs were not welcome. There was a great deal of information about the fund's directional and arbitrage strategies, and graphs showing the risk and returns. There was also a link that allowed potential investors to apply for a memorandum which detailed the fund's investment strategy. It stated that applicants would be vetted for suitability before any details would be supplied. Its corporate message was written in English: *Making the world a better place.*

Danny had to laugh at that one. From what Danny knew of the fund, the chances of it improving the world for anyone but its investors were slim. As an investment group, it had a reputation among competitors as being rapacious and utterly ruthless – no small feat in a market packed with predators. Since the economic crisis, the investment fund had specialised in stripping companies of their assets.

Danny managed to find one photo of Sebastian Gomez on

the website. He printed it out and tacked it to the wall. Gomez was snappily dressed. He had thick, luxuriant hair, lacquered back from his forehead and an extravagantly coiffured moustache, the tips waxed and curled upwards. Gomez liked his food, too, that much was clear: he wore his puppy-fat right up to his cheekbones. He looked like a podgy little cherub shoved into an Armani suit.

The webpage also had a photo of Emilio Morales, Gomez's cousin. Morales was stick thin, tall and creepy-looking and wore his hair in a widow's peak. There was a glint deep within the cold pools of his eyes – something both sharp and ruthless – that made you know he was not a man to be trifled with. Danny thought of what someone had said of the man: 'He looks a bit like Sherlock Holmes, but his scruples are all Moriarty's.'

Danny tried the investment fund's telephone number and got through to a snooty secretary. As soon as he mentioned he was a journalist, she told him that no-one was available for comment and that he should not bother phoning again.

After that, Danny continued to look for information on the Bellavista. He was idly clicking through links when Marsha phoned.

'Danny, I know you always sneer at me using Facebook, but I've just had a bit of a result. I've been chatting with one of my contacts, and it turns out a Welsh lass I met at one of my Spanish classes over here lives near the Bellavista. Anyway, I gave her a bell, and she told me about this website, www.bellavistatruthnow.es. I think you should take a look.'

The web address opened with a short animation: a radioactive trefoil symbol pulsated in the centre of the screen, then disappeared as the words Truth Now slammed down from above and crushed the symbol.

Danny clicked the pulsing ENTER button and was then directed to the home page of something called Bellavista Residents for Truth.

The home page opened with a lengthy open letter from the anonymous creator of the webpage, explaining that threat of legal action had prevented him from publishing most of the information he had gathered on the subject of the "cover-up" at the Bellavista urbanisation. Instead, he would state "the facts" and let the public decide.

There was an enormous amount of information about the Palomares Incident: a detailed breakdown of how H-bombs worked, explanations of the difference between a fission and a fusion bomb, photos of the damaged casing of the bombs involved in the accident. Another section gave a detailed map explaining exactly where the Palomares bombs had fallen and to where the vaporised plutonium had spread. Another map marked the places scientists had discovered patches of irradiated land missed by the American clean-up operation.

A photo gallery showed black and white shots of American Air Force personnel in boiler suits and face masks shovelling irradiated earth into oil drums. There were other links leading to separate sections on 'How Radiation Causes Cancer' and an explanation of how ionizing radiation causes cell molecules to change into ions. There was a mass of links to other webpages and Wikipedia pages.

The bottom of each page of the website bore a stark warning: 'Do you know how much plutonium-239 the human body can safely contain? Six tenths of one *millionth* of a gram. That's o.6 × 10 ⁻6 grams. There is still more than a whole *kilogram* of plutonium unaccounted for in and around Palomares.'

Although the website never quite came out and said it, the inference was clear: if you lived on the Bellavista urbanisation, you were at risk from plutonium-contaminated soil.

Danny leant back in his chair, tapping his fingers on the table top. He wasn't inclined to give too much credence to the website – like most journalists, he had a deep-seated mistrust of online conspiracy theorists – but sometimes these things were worth following up. Danny would look for another opinion on the matter. He went online to look for the number of the Bellavista residents' association.

His call was answered by a man named Alan Neave, who identified himself as the organisation's co-ordinator. When Danny mentioned the webpage, Neave sighed.

'I wondered when the press would get hold of this.'

Danny clicked his pen. 'What can you tell me about these Bellavista Residents for Truth people?'

'Let me start by saying that the name is a complete misnomer, as the organisation consists of only one man.'

'Kind of like the Popular Front of Judea?' Danny said.

'I beg your pardon?'

OK, Danny thought, Neave wasn't a *Life of Brian* fan, then.

'So who is he,' Danny said, 'this one-man protest movement?'

'His name is Louis Margaux. He was once a valued member of the residents' association, but a few years back the poor chap lost his wife to cancer and . . . well, he lost his head.

He became obsessed with all sorts of wild ideas and conspiracy theories.'

'Such as?'

'Before I tell you, I want it made perfectly clear that his theories have been categorically disproved. In fact, I am telling you this off the record. I don't want his nonsense being reprinted.'

'OK. You have my word.'

Neave sighed again. 'Margaux claims some of the houses on the Bellavista were built on contaminated soil.'

'By contaminated, you mean soil that contained plutonium? From the Palomares Incident?'

'As you'll probably know, the southern edge of the Bellavista borders the municipality of Palomares. We had a terrible problem with Margaux a few years back. He was climbing into people's gardens in the middle of the night with a homemade Geiger counter, digging up soil. The bloody idiot got himself bitten by a dog one evening. Obviously, we had to expel him from the residents' association. Some of the things he was saying were highly libellous. Since then he has confined his activities to the webpage you have seen.'

'I'm going to play Devil's Advocate here, Mr Neave. You sound very sure that Margaux's claims are false.'

'I *am* sure, Mr Sanchez,' Neave said with a note of irritation. 'As head of the neighbourhood association, I made it my job to be *damned* bloody sure. Christ, man, you don't think I'd let people's children play in the gardens if there was any chance of the soil being contaminated, do you?

'As soon as Margaux started spouting his nonsense, we contacted the science team that had prepared the original report. By then, Margaux had got people so lathered up that we had to commission an independent survey of the supposedly affected areas and it found absolutely nothing. Not one single trace of anything that shouldn't have been there. We even had a few people buy their own Geiger counters and go round measuring the earth. Guess what they found.'

'Nothing?'

'Exactly. The soil here is not contaminated in any way, shape or form. I'd appreciate your mentioning that in any articles you might write on this subject. It's bad enough trying to sell these properties with the bloody mess the Spanish economy is in without this ridiculous story about the contaminated soil being dug up again – if you'll pardon the pun. Anyway, we have a far larger problem here on the Bellavista.'

'Really? What's that?'

'The water supply. It's an absolute bloody disgrace. For the last three years some parts of the urbanisation have only had an intermittent domestic service. They're lucky if the tap water is accessible for eight hours a day, so people have had to shell out fortunes having water deposits installed. And you can forget about filling swimming pools.'

Danny turned his eyes heavenwards. He didn't want to get sidetracked with this, but Neave was on a roll.

'And do you know what the worst thing is? The really galling thing? There's a bloody great aquifer right below the urbanisation. That was one of the reasons the developers chose this spot to build on. In fact, when the development was still in the planning stage, the developer *promised* us there wouldn't be any water shortages, and yet we've had nothing but problems.'

'What's happened to the service, then?'

'The private water company that got the municipal charter to supply the urbanisation went bust a few years back, and since then we've been mired in litigation. And the water company's lawyers have used every crummy trick in the book to string the process out. Did you ever hear that expression: If you want justice, go to a whorehouse; if you want to get screwed, go to court. Well, that's what's happening here.'

Danny nodded, only half-listening. Stories like these were ten a penny in Almería, where thousands of houses had been built – and sold – without any consideration for whether their residents would have access to the most basic of amenities. To make matters worse, Spain's courts we're Kafkaesque at the best of times. People could lose years in the pursuit of justice. Even before the economic crisis, the entire system had been groaning beneath a backlog of cases, but strike action by Justice Department bureaucrats had worsened the situation. It was currently estimated that the courts had three times more work than they were able to deal with.

'In fact, we are holding a protest meeting this Saturday outside the government buildings in Almería city,' Neave said. 'I take it we can count on your support, Mr Sanchez? I've long been an admirer of your journalism in Sureste News.'

What could Danny say? He said, sure, he would pop along.

He put the phone down, thinking, *More work, and on a weekend, too. Just what I need.*

5

DANNY LIVED IN a rural property outside the city of Almería. He had four thousand square metres of land filled with rows of olive trees, seventy-seven of them in total – Marsha had counted them for him. Watering the trees was a ritual he had to go through every six weeks and each October, his trees would yield roughly one-and-a-half tonnes of olives, all of which had to be collected, put in crates and driven to the nearest *almazara*, where they were pressed into oil.

Laziness had caused him to leave them to ripen and fall one year: that had been a big mistake. By November, his property had been ankle deep in rotting olives, which seemed to have infused the very earth with the smell of semi-rancid olive oil. The smell still lingered when the wind blew in a certain direction.

It was seven o'clock now and Danny had been at it for about three hours, moving the stiff plastic pipe that carried water onto his land. Not for the first time he wondered why the hell he'd ever thought buying land with so many olive trees was a good idea.

It took about five minutes to fill the three-metre hollow around the trunk of each tree. Marsha had helped him at the beginning, wearing a swimming costume beneath a tie dye sarong; but when it had transpired that Marsha was far more interested in soaking Danny with the hose than actually getting any work done, Danny had suggested she go inside and plan the barbecue they were holding for friends on Wednesday.

About eight, Danny heard the Star Wars ring tone on his mobile sound inside the house. When Marsha brought the phone out to him, she was frowning.

'It's Her,' she said, handing Danny the phone.

It was Danny's turn to frown. There was only one woman in the world to whom Marsha habitually referred using the third person pronoun.

'Hello, mother,' Danny said.

'God, I hate it when you call me that,' Adriana Sanchez said. 'You make me feel like I'm a hundred years old.'

'Listen Mum, I'm busy with the olives at the moment. How can I help you?'

'I've just been flicking through *El País* and I've seen the article you wrote about Martyn Phillips the other day. I just wanted to say that there are certain – what's the word? – lacunae, and I wanted to help you fill them.'

'Go on,' Danny said.

'What would you say if I told you that Sian Phillips's precious foundation is racist?'

'I would say you'd started drinking earlier than normal.'

'This is no joking matter, Danny,' she said, talking now in the solicitous purr she employed when going all out to convince another person of her point of view. 'I've been told by a very credible source that Sian Phillips herself ensures that the financial aid her foundation provides *only* goes to British children.'

'Come off it.'

'There have been a number of children from other nation-
alities that have applied in recent years and they've all been
turned down. Phone the foundation up and ask them about it.
I bet you'll hear them start to wriggle.'

'How do you know this?'

'A friend of mine has a source close to one of the foundation's board members.'

'And how well does this friend know her source?'

'Better than said source's wife would like.'

Danny lit a cigarette. 'What's your beef with the foundation, then?'

'My *beef*?'

'Come on. I know that tone of voice. This is personal
between you and her.'

Adriana Sanchez was quiet for a moment. Then she said,
'Well, if you must know, we did have a slight falling out last
year.'

'About?'

'I offered to donate some of my paintings to the foundation. Mrs Phillips couldn't have been more condescending in
the way she refused.'

'Trying to get some free advertising, were you?'

'I don't need advertising of any kind. I'll have you know
my oeuvre is gaining recognition in the very best circles.'

Danny smiled at that. Adriana Sanchez was sixty-two now
and was officially retired – although quite how you retired
after an entire life doing nothing still mystified Danny – and
had decided to dedicate her time to becoming an artist: the sort
of artist whose *oeuvre* consists of abstract swirls and blobs
with portentous titles like "Incandescence" and "Covenant".

Then again, Adriana Sanchez was just the type to get ahead in the art world. If there was one thing she was perfectly geared for, it was talking pretentious crap to people with more money than taste.

He was about to ask more when he heard the muffled sound of a car horn at his mother's end.

'Anyway, I have to run, now, darling,' his mother said. 'Phone me tomorrow if you need any more info. Ciao.'

Danny tucked the phone into the elastic strap of his boxers and went inside.

'So, what did she want?' Marsha said, as Danny took a beer from the fridge.

'Nothing,' said Danny, then laughed when he saw the look on Marsha's face.

Marsha and Adriana Sanchez had met perhaps six or seven times altogether. At first they'd got along famously, mainly because Danny's mother had gone into pyjama-party, all-girls-together mode, walking arm-in-arm with Marsha, whispering and giggling with her, pouring her wine. But recently Marsha's attitude towards her seemed to have cooled, probably because Marsha was coming to realise that Adriana Sanchez's inter-personal relationships only took on two guises: men were ex-pected to fall at her feet, and women to follow in her wake.

Danny put in another hour on the olive trees, then went inside to eat the dinner Marsha had prepared. They chatted as they ate, but Danny found his mind wandering. He was think-ing about what his mother had said about the foundation.

Experience had taught him to take anything his mother said with an entire fistful of salt, but, then again, she knew better than to bother Danny with rumours that were totally unfounded. And perhaps chasing up this story would give him an insight into what was happening with Sian Phillips and why she was refusing to speak to Danny.

After dinner, he found the foundation's telephone number on the internet. When he rang, a familiar voice answered: it was the friend, Barbara.

'I don't believe you people,' she said when Danny said who he was. 'Sian won't speak to you, so you come slithering round the back. I've got absolutely nothing to – '

'I've received some rather worrying allegations about the foundation,' Danny said, enjoying being able to cut the woman off. 'I just want you to comment on them.'

Barbara said nothing for a moment. 'Go on then.'

She scoffed when Danny explained.

'Right, this rumour has gone on long enough,' she said. 'Yes, there was an effort to prioritise sick children from the Bellavista urbanisation, something that, given the Phillips' connections with the building of the houses there, is hardly surprising. And for the record, I can assure you that Sian Phillips was against the move. It was her husband that insisted sick children from the Bellavista be moved to the front of the queue. But I can assure you this foundation *has* helped and will continue *to* help children of any race, colour or creed.'

'Are there a lot of sick kids on the Bellavista, then?'

'Mr Sanchez, there is nothing in this world more tragic and traumatic than a seriously ill child. I hope you're not going to start trawling through people's problems in an effort to spice up your story.'

'How do you think the rumours started?'

'How they started I don't know. But how the rumours were

propagated is another matter. There is a group of women that has taken against Sian, Mr Sanchez and . . .' Barbara's voice trailed off into silence. Then she said, 'Actually, Mr Sanchez, might I ask your mother's name?'

Danny's heart sank. When he said nothing, Barbara said, 'If I'd known you were related to *her*, I would never have let you anywhere near Sian. You tell that toxic harpy if she spreads any more slander about the foundation, we'll see her in court.'

The phone went dead.

6

THAT MORNING GABRIEL Varela drove up into the heart of the Sierra de los Filabres. Buildings here were rare and isolated, and the roads that crossed the mountain range snaked on for miles without sign of human habitation.

Varela parked a mile from his destination and walked the rest of the way, hiking across mountain slopes dotted with slate outcrops.

Killing Phillips had been easy: he'd had the element of surprise. Things would be more difficult with Sixto Escobar, he was sure.

Varela sat among the trees on the slope overlooking Escobar's remote house and took out his binoculars.

Escobar was planning to run somewhere, that much was clear. Varela saw a lot of coming and going during the day, and luggage being loaded into the 4x4. By the afternoon he was certain that there was only Sixto Escobar and some big muscled goon inside the property.

That was good. Escobar thought that no-one else knew about his mountain hideaway.

In the late afternoon Varela watched as Sixto Escobar emerged from the rear of the house and crossed the patio beside the swimming pool, his hairy gut bulging through the front of his towelling bathrobe. He looked nervous as he talked into a mobile phone, gesticulating with his hand. The goon sat on a sun lounger beside the pool.

As dusk set in, Varela picked his way down the mountain slope. He came at the house from the front, picked the lock on the main door and walked through the house.

Both men looked up as Varela slid the patio doors open and stepped out, his hand wrapped around the grip of his punch dagger.

For a moment they both simply watched. Then Escobar ran for the poolside shed, while the goon stood up, smiled and came towards Varela, cracking his knuckles.

Varela let the man approach. He knew his opponent would do something stupid: the young man's eyes had lit up when he saw Varela, and he'd adopted a flashy, loose-limbed fighting stance.

He does not respect me, Varela thought. He is too eager to fight me.

Still two yards from Varela, the man kicked out at his head. Varela caught the foot, twisted it inward then out, breaking the leg at the knee. The man fell heavily onto his back with a scream. Varela released his hold on the man's foot and dropped to a crouch beside him, using the momentum to drive his punch-dagger through the other's heart.

The blow landed with a dull thud. The man exhaled and shuddered, then lay still.

Varela rose and wiped blood from his knuckles. He was striding towards the poolside shed calling Escobar's name when Escobar emerged, holding a 12 gauge shotgun.

Varela dived to the right as Escobar levelled the weapon at his hip and fired.

The poolside table shattered, glass flew into the air and both sun loungers were shredded. Varela winced as he felt sudden pain in his arm and calf, like a dozen simultaneous hornet stings. The report of the weapon echoed off the stony hillsides that surrounded the house.

Varela rose quickly and examined the damage.

The sleeve of his M65 jacket was torn and the skin beneath it was covered in blood. He could see the dark dots of shotgun pellets embedded in his flesh. He had a similar injury in his leg.

He'd been lucky, though: only the outer edge of the shotgun blast had caught him. As the spread pattern had been so wide, the gun's barrel must have been fitted with a cylinder choke.

He advanced towards Sixto Escobar, wincing as he had to put his weight on his wounded leg.

The blast had blown Sixto Escobar backwards and he lay on the earth between two cacti, his bathrobe snarled on the plants' spines. He struggled as Varela limped towards him, a huge bruise already forming on his hip from the shotgun recoil.

For a moment, there was only fear in Escobar's eyes. Then his gaze fell on the blood dripping from the punch dagger on Varela's fingers.

'You sonofabitch, Gabi. You're mad. Do you hear? You're out of your tiny fucking mind, you dumb bastard. I'm going to –'

Varela kicked him hard between the legs with the tip of his combat boot.

Escobar screamed and put his hands to his groin. Varela stood over him, silent, as Escobar writhed. Eventually, Escobar began to breathe normally. He dried the tears from his eyes.

'Gabi, I know Lucia came to see you when you were in prison. I don't know what the hell she told you, but it's all lies. She hates me because of the divorce. She'd do anything to hurt me. But I've settled accounts with that bitch, believe you me. And I'll get you the money I owe you, the money I said I'd pay you when you went inside. I've already spoken to Gomez and we'll pay you triple the original price. It was Phillips's fault you didn't get paid. But you've settled accounts with him. Let me do the same. I'll –'

'You think this is about the money you owe me, you prick?'

Varela's words stopped Escobar dead. He spluttered and blinked for a few moments, trying to assimilate what Varela had just said. Then he shook his head.

'What else could it be?'

Varela reached inside his jacket and withdrew the cardboard folder. He threw it at Escobar.

Escobar opened it and looked at the pages inside.

'What is this, Gabi? Is this from Yagüe's laboratory?'

'That's a copy of the documents Lucia brought me when she came to see me in prison.'

Escobar said nothing, but he began to tremble all over as he flicked through the pages.

'You knew, didn't you?' Varela said. 'You all knew. And yet you did nothing. For years.'

'It was Morales, Gabi, I swear. And Gomez. It wasn't my fault. It was –'

Varela drove his left-hand fist hard into the flab of Escobar's stomach. Escobar wailed. Varela began walking up and down before him. Pain from the wound had made him mad.

He could feel the hatred bubbling in him, even more so than with Phillips.

'You're wondering what this has to do with me, aren't you?' Varela said. 'I can see it in your face. You're thinking "why does he even care?" Shall I tell you?'

Varela took the photos of Esme from his pocket. He showed the first to Escobar.

'Do you see this girl? Do you see how beautiful she is?' He withdrew the second photo. 'This is what she looked like a week before she died of stomach cancer. That was the first thing they diagnosed, anyway. By the time this photo was taken, it had spread to her intestine and then on to her liver. She was a fucking skeleton. No hair. No fingernails. The doctors said there was nothing they could do because it hadn't been diagnosed in time.

'Do you remember the fucking house you sold me, Sixto? This girl lived in that house from 2003 onwards. She lived on the Bellavista, Sixto.'

The colour had drained from Escobar's face. His lower lip trembled.

'Oh God. Don't burn me, Gabi. God's mercy, Gabi, please, not that.'

'God?' Varela said. 'Did you just say God? What is it with you pricks? Do you think God will help you after what you've done? Do you?'

He dragged Escobar across the patio and turned him so he was looking up towards the darkening sky.

'Do you think God is up there?' Varela said. 'Do you think he can hear you? Let's find out, shall we?' Varela looked at his watch. 'I'll give you ten minutes to get God on your side, Sixto.

Tell him to come down here and save you. Pray all you want. Because, as soon as your ten minutes are finished, I'm going to string you up and gut you like a fucking pig.'

7

Danny rose early and drove out to Little Arizona. He wanted to know more about this Gabriel Varela character and, if Varela had once worked at the park as a stunt rider, there was a chance someone there would remember him. Besides that, Danny also wanted to ask about Sixto Escobar, because the impresario had completely dropped off the radar. His phone no longer even went to voicemail, it returned a number-not-recognised tone.

The twenty-minute drive took Danny through the heart of the Tabernas Desert, a lunar landscape of bleached ochre, coloured by occasional pastel shades of mauve and grey where the wind had stripped hillsides down to their seams of mineral deposits. Slot canyons and cacti were the only indications water had ever visited this arid world, and yet it was only thirty minutes' drive from the Bay of Almería and its tourist beaches; drive an hour north towards Granada, and you could ski most of the year round.

Little Arizona was open for business. Danny parked outside and headed towards the main gate, where he spoke to a bored-looking Spanish girl who told him to wait while she called the manager. Danny lounged in the shade and watched the groups of sun-pinked German and British tourists that wandered the dusty streets of the wooden town, taking photographs with the costumed staff-members and examining the tourist tat on sale in the gift shop.

Ten minutes later, a man appeared wearing a flat-brimmed hat, duster, leather chaps and spurs. The guy was obviously a *gitano*, a Spanish gypsy. There was no mistaking his combination of swarthy skin and sparkling green eyes. He introduced himself as Sergio, but hesitated before shaking the hand Danny proffered.

'What is it you want?' he said.

'Are you the manager?'

Sergio looked around him as if considering this for the first time, then shrugged. 'I'm in charge for the time being, I suppose.'

'Still no sign of Escobar?'

'Nope.'

'You don't sound too upset about it.'

'Things run smoother without that fat idiot around. Plus, I get to keep an eye on the admissions coming through the gate each day.'

'The park doing good business, is it?'

He nodded slowly. 'Why that bastard can't afford to pay us is beyond me. But he won't get away with it anymore.'

'Does he still owe you for the unpaid wages?'

'Three months of them.'

'Any idea where Escobar might be?'

Sergio shook his head. 'Nobody here has seen him since that business with the dead body. He left the park the same afternoon and he's not been back since.'

Danny offered him a cigarette. Sergio took it, but his dark-lashed eyes watched Danny from beneath the brim of his hat.

'How long have you worked here?' Danny said, lighting the man's cigarette.

'Twenty-nine years.'

'Do you remember a man named Gabriel Varela?'

The cigarette paused. Green eyes watched Danny from behind a veil of smoke.

'Why do you want to know about him?'

'So you do know him?'

'I *knew* him, sure. I've not seen him for ten years or so. Maybe more.'

'Can you tell me about him?'

Sergio took two long draws on his cigarette. 'Gabriel Varela isn't a man whose name you mention lightly. What's in it for me if I tell you about him?'

'If you give me what I need, I'll do a big exposé piece on Sixto and the unpaid wages. Name and shame him. And I still owe Sixto a half-page feature on the park. I could come down here, interview some of the stunt riders and do a piece on you all.'

Sergio scratched his stubble as he considered this. Then he motioned for Danny to follow him. They kept to the shade as they walked past the blacksmith and went into the Last Chance Saloon. Danny ordered a mineral water, Sergio a coffee. They sat at a corner table. Sergio toyed with his coffee spoon.

'So, what do you want to know about Varela?'

'What was he like?'

'Quiet. Secretive.'

'So, the strong, silent type then?'

'Strong, silent and dangerous type. He was ex-Foreign Legion. He made it to the rank of sergeant. Or so I heard, anyway.'

'How did he end up at Little Arizona?'

'He'd served in the cavalry, so he was good around horses. He was taken on as a stunt rider.'

'I've heard he did other stuff for Escobar. Strong-arm stuff.'

Sergio nodded his head. 'Yeah, I heard that, too. Varela had connections in the police and the Guardia. But that all started way before Sixto Escobar came on the scene, back when this place belonged to Sampson.'

It took Danny a moment to realise what he was saying: with Sergio's thick Andaluz accent, he pronounced the surname *tham-THON*.

'Little Arizona used to belong to Doug Sampson? The actor, Doug Sampson?'

Sergio nodded. 'But it wasn't called Little Arizona back then. It was called Broken Arrow. Escobar changed the name when he bought it.'

'Why did Sampson sell it?'

'Sampson didn't want to sell the place, but he was flat broke. That's why he sold it.'

'So you remember Doug Sampson, too?'

'Yep.'

'What was he like?'

'He wasn't much better than Escobar. He liked his poker, liked to party. And he threw money around. That's why he ended up in such a mess, financially speaking.'

'Tell me more about Varela.'

'Like I say, he started out as a stunt rider, around '85 or

'86. But pretty soon after, Sampson took him on at the park as a kind of security guy. They used to have these big high-stakes poker games here, and Varela would go with Sampson to withdraw his money.'

'So, he was a bodyguard then?'

'It was more than that. While they were actually playing, Varela was always on hand. You know how these things can be, you get a guy that loses big and he starts accusing everyone else of cheating. Basically, that was when Varela would step in.'

'And do what?'

Sergio laughed. 'He never had to *do* anything. He'd just walk up behind Sampson and stand there. Believe me, that was enough.'

'What else did Varela do for Sampson?'

Sergio scratched his stubble. 'There was a big film festival they held here at the beginning of the nineties. The mayor wanted to give it to one of the other theme parks, but Sampson went to see him one night with Varela, and the mayor "changed" his mind. Then when Sampson started with the development company, that was when Gabi started getting into a lot more of the other stuff.'

'Like?'

'Well, I only heard rumours. But when they began with the Bellavista, there was a lot of bickering over who was going to get what contract. And there were a lot of bungs going on, a lot of envelopes with cash changing hands. Varela was the guy Sampson and the others used to keep everyone in line. For example, I heard that a big building contractor wouldn't play ball. A few weeks later, his business premises burned down.

And there was some kind of labour dispute during the construction of the Bellavista. They used Varela as a bodyguard.

'Anyway, this is all just rumour. By that time, Varela had become super secretive. No-one even knew where he lived. He didn't even have a telephone number. He'd just turn up one day, sort things out, and then he'd be gone again for a few weeks.'

'If no-one knew where he lived and he didn't have a telephone, how'd they get hold of him?'

'They had some type of system. They left him a message in the newspaper when they needed him.'

'That's a bit old-fashioned, isn't it?'

'Hey, I'm just telling you what I heard. I don't know if it's true or not. And this was the late eighties, early nineties. There weren't any mobiles or internet. At least, there weren't many here.'

'And this was work that Varela did for the development company, The Sampson Consortium? The one that built the Bellavista urbanisation?'

Sergio smiled. 'No, The Sampson Consortium was just the front company. Gabi worked for the people who really ran things.'

'Who was that?'

'*Grupo La Flecha Rota.*'

'The Broken Arrow Group?' Danny said. 'What was that?'

'That was the inner circle. They used to meet here, in the saloon after hours. That was where the whole Bellavista thing was hammered out. And the poker games gave them access to lots of investors. That was how Sixto Escobar first turned up here.'

'So they named this *La Flecha Rota* company after Samp-son's theme park? Broken Arrow?'

Sergio nodded.

Danny rummaged in his shoulder bag and withdrew the photos he had of Martyn Phillips and Florentino Yagüe.

'Did you ever see either of these guys at the parties?'

'Yep, I remember that one,' Sergio said, pointing to the photo of Martyn Phillips. 'He always used to speak to Sampson in English.' He looked at Yagüe's photo. 'This one was there, too, but not as often.'

'What about these two?' Danny said, showing him the printouts of Sebastian Gomez and Emilio Morales.

'They were here, but they didn't play poker. Then again, when they were around, things tended to be more business-like.'

Sergio sat in silence while Danny scribbled his notes down in shorthand. When he'd finished, he realised that Sergio was lost in thought.

'Is there something else?' Danny said.

Sergio considered this, then nodded and got up. When he came back, he brought with him an envelope filled with old Polaroids that showed riders in western clothes. The photos were blurry and ill-defined, the way photos taken back in the eighties tend to be.

Danny looked more closely at the photos. It wasn't clearly visible in the first of the shots, but in the second he could discern through all the horses' legs and dust, a figure with its back tied to a wagon wheel. The other shots showed the wagon wheel being dragged away by a horse, the rope tied to the back of the saddle of one of the riders.

'Who's this? The guy strapped to the wheel?'

Sergio looked at him, as if debating whether to tell him. Then he said, 'That's Gabriel Varela.'

Danny looked back at the first shot, the one that showed the whole scene. The wagon wheel was propped between two teepees.

'How do you know it's Varela? You can't see his face.'

Sergio scoffed.

'Because Varela was the only one crazy enough to do that stunt. He's got upwards of a dozen horses there, with fake guns going off, and he's tied flat to a wagon wheel being dragged through the middle of it all? You know how heavy horses are? You have one step on your gut and you're a goner.'

Danny looked at the photo. It was the exact same place, the exact same position in which Hector Castillo's body had been left, sat upright, tied to a wagon wheel at the entrance to the Indian Settlement.

It had been a message.

Danny looked at Sergio.

'There's just one last thing,' he said. 'Do you know where Doug Sampson lives now?'

∾

An hour later, Danny pulled his car over and checked his directions. He was in the open country beyond the town of Níjar looking for Doug Sampson's address. The sky was bright blue and cloudless, the heat unbearable.

Marsha had suggested he buy one of those fancy phones with GPS, but Danny wasn't a fan of technology. Part of the adventure of journalism was in trying to find out-of-the-way places, taking wrong turns, knocking on strangers' doors for directions. Having a computerised voice guide you straight there felt like cheating, somehow.

After leaving Sergio, he had tried to learn something about the company the cowboy had mentioned, *Grupo La Flecha Rota*.

There was nothing on the company anywhere. The only thing that Danny had been able to discover was that the company had ceased trading in 2008. Apart from that, he had managed to determine only that it seemed to have been a paper corporation, as there were no records of the company ever having owned business premises. That was why he wanted to speak to Doug Sampson. If anyone knew anything – and would be willing to spill the beans – it would be Sampson.

As he drove, Danny considered what he knew about the man.

Doug Sampson was the sort of minor celeb that often washed up on Spain's shores, the sort that Spanish mayors and businessmen liked to parade around. Newspapers still described Sampson as a "film star" although that was stretching the term. Sampson's career had withered in the eighties, reduced to straight-to-video releases, television shows and adverts for cheap whiskey.

But it wasn't his films or his adverts that people remembered now.

After nearly a decade out of the show business limelight, Sampson had hit the headlines again in the late nineties when a Spanish gossip magazine had published a 4-page special revealing that big, butch, man's man Douglas Sampson had a taste for young Latino men. Although the allegations were never proven – there had only been some grainy photos and an interview with a rent boy who claimed to be a former lover – it was the sort of story on which the gutter press thrived, and Sampson did everything he could to worsen his own predicament.

Not only did Sampson prove to possess a volcanic temper, he had a tendency to get drunk in public and had failed to find anything humorous in being outed. That had made him precisely the sort of guy the tabloids enjoyed ripping to pieces, and for a period of about three months they had engaged in baiting him. Then, after a string of very public meltdowns in hotel foyers and restaurants, Sampson had officially "retired" from public life and sworn never to have dealings with the Press again.

That had been more than twelve years ago. Danny was banking on the fact that Sampson's feelings towards the Fourth Estate had mellowed in the interim.

Danny was following a pitted country road that wound between low, rounded hills. Doug Sampson's house was at the end of the road, a white property surrounded by ill-tended almond trees. A rusty iron gate gave access to the property. A battered orange pick-up was parked next to the house. Danny rang the intercom beside the gate and a man with a soft, South American accent said, '¿Quién es?'

'My name is Sanchez. I'd like to speak to Mr Sampson.'

The same voice said the word 'Dougie' and Sampson came to the intercom.

You would have known Sampson was an actor purely from his voice: it was like a radio presenter's, deep and honeyed.

'Who is this?' he said.

'Danny Sanchez.'

'What do you want?'

'I'd like to speak to you.'

'About?'

Danny hesitated, weighing whether to tell the truth now or get inside first.

'I'm a journalist,' he said.

There was a momentary silence. Then something buzzed, and the door within the gates sprang open.

A gravel pathway lined with cacti and sandstone led across the garden and up to the house, some fifty yards distant. As Danny walked towards it he saw a tall man in white shorts step out onto the decking that covered the porch. Danny was going to wave when the man knelt and pointed something towards him.

The branch to the right of Danny's head cracked and split apart.

He turned and stared at it, still trying to assimilate the fact that Doug Sampson had shot at him, when a second bullet hit the earth to the side of his feet with a dull thwock.

A third bullet had snicked the trunk of an almond tree before Danny turned and began to run. Two more shots followed, followed by Sampson's voice, bellowing something of which only two words were clear: *sonofabitch* and *kill*.

Given the context, Danny could guess the rest.

Danny got to his car and jumped inside, heart thundering.

The old bastard had shot his rifle at him.

He was considering what to do when he saw Sampson in the rear view mirror, coming out of the gates and standing in the middle of the road, still holding the rifle.

Danny didn't wait around. He hit the accelerator. The front wheels were spinning, a cloud of dust surrounded him, the tyres bit and the car shot away.

Danny drove straight to the nearest bar and ordered a glass of *anis* to steady his nerves.

He knew he should report Sampson to the police, but he had no proof of the incident. It would be his word against Sampson's. Danny smoked a cigarette and finished his drink, feeling calmer.

No, he wouldn't report it, he decided. He could lose the rest of the day with the police. If Sampson wouldn't give him the information about *Grupo La Flecha Rota* he needed, he'd have to look elsewhere.

8

Danny PARKED ON the outskirts of the town of Las Jarapas, trying to remember when he had last visited the place: five or six years ago, probably, when he'd interviewed someone from an agricultural union.

The town had seemed vibrant and filled with bustle then. It was different now. Many shops had closed down and their glass windows were whitewashed from within. Fluorescent posters with the words *Se Vende* and *Se Alquila* – For Sale and To Let – were everywhere.

Despite the Bellavista development and the influx of around 4,000 foreigners it had brought, Las Jarapas was still a small Spanish town at heart. You could see it in the way old men in berets gathered around benches to gossip and housewives walked the streets in their dressing gowns clutching loaves of bread. For all its ersatz grandeur, it would take another generation to wash the whiff of peasant from the town.

The town square was typical of southern Spain, a rectangular space twenty yards wide by fifty long, flanked on all four sides by white buildings that shone in the sharp sunlight. The *ayuntamiento* was located at the far end of the square, a huge glittering building of glass, brick and marble, a monument to the town's construction wealth. The plaza before it was decorated with pale tiles and ornate iron bollards; fountains trickled in its centre, shaded by tastefully arranged clumps of fan palms.

'Is that to stop councillors talking paperclips home?' Danny said as he stepped through the metal detector on the door of the *ayuntamiento* and had his bag searched by a grey-haired policeman. The policeman didn't return Danny's smile.

The *ayuntamiento's* open plan lower floor mirrored the modernistic architectural style of the building's exterior. Danny followed corridors to the office of the mercantile register, which consisted of a glass window manned by a young woman. A red machine dispensed tickets below a sign which said, "Wait for your number to be called". No-one else was waiting, but Danny took a ticket anyway, number 87. The digital sign above the counter said "Now Serving: 23".

Danny stared at the empty plastic chairs either side of him. The woman continued typing at her computer.

'*Hola*' he said when the woman made no sign of acknowledging him. Her eyes remained glued to the screen, but she held up a hand to silence him.

Danny hated dealing with anyone in public administration in Spain, the infamous *funcionarios*, the bête noire of most of the country's population. Unlike their British counterparts, *funcionarios* obtained their posts via *oposiciones,* public exams. The exams were supposed to ensure that only the brightest and best were employed after having competed with their fellow citizens in rigorously fair competition, but in reality the system exposed Spain's bureaucracy to the worst type of cronyism, and ensured that anyone who managed to obtain a position – with their generous pay scales, attractive hours and guarantee of a job-for-life – had nothing but contempt for the mere mortals to whom they were supposed to attend.

Danny gestured towards the 'now serving' sign. 'I appreciate you must be terribly busy dealing with the other sixty-four people ahead of me in the queue, but I am in something of a hurry.'

The woman looked at him over the top of her glasses.

'What do you want?'

'I'm looking for details on a company that operated in this municipality, *Grupo La Flecha Rota*.'

The name seemed significant to the woman. For a moment, she looked panicked. 'Hold on,' she said, and disappeared into another room, where Danny heard her murmuring on the telephone. Five minutes later, she returned shaking her head. 'We don't have any records on that particular company.'

'How the hell not? It financed the Bellavista urbanisation. And who were you on the phone to just now?'

'We had a move. The records probably got lost. Or water damaged. And who I speak to on the telephone is no business of yours.'

Next, Danny went to the office of the mayor and asked the secretary there to show him the records for the council's plenary sessions from 1996 onwards. The secretary showed Danny into a side room filled with desks and chairs, where she invited him to sit while they found the records he had requested. A few minutes later, the woman from the mercantile register came into the room, wheeling a librarian's trolley. She unloaded a number of blue boxes and piled them next to Danny's table. 'They're all yours,' she said, with a faint smile.

Danny held her eyes.

There were two ways bureaucrats could screw you. The first was by claiming the records you wanted no longer existed; the second was by swamping you with so much paperwork, it was impossible to find what you needed. Danny tipped an imaginary hat towards the woman in appreciation of the double whammy she'd managed to lay on him.

He cracked his knuckles and set to work on the laborious process of going through the minutes of each plenary session.

The first thing he noticed was that the records were not complete. They were bound together in red leather tomes, one for each month, but Danny could see where entire pages had been cut out with a razor blade. He went through the whole of 1996 and 1997 without finding a single mention of *Grupo La Flecha Rota*.

In April 1998 there was a single mention of the company, although it wasn't conspicuous – Danny very nearly missed it. According to the minutes, *Grupo La Flecha Rota* had purchased a piece of council land for eighty million pesetas on April 17th, 1998. Danny started making a note of the details of the sale, copying them into his notebook, but he quickly realised the page held too much important information.

To hell with it, he thought, pulling a ruler from his shoulder bag, he'd just rip the whole bloody page out.

Danny was halfway through carefully removing the page from the book of minutes when the door opened and the woman from the mercantile register appeared, looking flustered.

'I'm sorry,' she said, 'the office is closing. You'll have to come back tomorrow.'

Danny had slammed the book closed as soon as he heard

the door opening. He looked at his watch. It wasn't even midday yet.

'A little early for lunch, isn't it?'

'Didn't you hear me?' the woman said, looking over her shoulder nervously. 'We're closing.'

'No,' Danny said, 'at two o'clock you close. I know, I checked. These minutes are a matter of public record. You can't stop me from looking at them.'

The woman threw her hands up in exasperation and left the room.

Danny opened the book, yanked the page free, folded it up and tucked it into his pocket. He was about to open another tome from the box when the door reopened. Danny was going to say, 'Now what is it?' but the words died on his lips.

It wasn't the woman standing there. It was Tommy Shrike, Gomez's security guy, in a short-sleeved shirt and mirrored sunglasses, his arms folded.

Shrike stepped into the room and pushed the door closed behind him.

'You heard the lady,' he said in English. 'It's time for you to leave.'

Danny realised now that he heard Shrike speak that he was undoubtedly American. His voice had a distinct New Jersey twang to it.

'What are you doing here?' Danny said, hoping he sounded more confident than he felt. There was something about Shrike. The bloke radiated latent menace, as if the eyes behind the mirrored sunglasses were considering which bits of Danny's anatomy to break first. Shrike had a body that you knew was hard and lithe by design, and he moved with a gymnast's ease.

'Where's your boss today?' Danny said when Shrike did not reply, scraping the chair on the floor as he stood up. 'And how's Sian Phillips? I've not been able to contact her since she hired your boss. Strange that Gomez seems so interested in stopping me from speaking to anyone. What happened today? Did someone phone and tell him I was here?'

Shrike said nothing but took three rapid steps forward, coming at Danny from the left side of the table. Danny moved backwards, keeping the table between him and Shrike. Part of him could not believe that Shrike would attack him in such a public place, but both of Shrike's hands were balled into fists.

The two men continued to circle, Shrike now wearing a cocky smile, when the door opened again and the grey-haired policeman who had been standing at the main door came into the room.

'Is there a problem here?' he said.

'No, problem,' Danny said in rapid Spanish, hoping Shrike would not understand, 'apart from the fact this fuckwit has decided to chase me in circles around the table.'

Shrike smiled. 'I'm doing nothing of the sort,' he said in rapid and flawless Spanish. 'I was just informing this gentleman that the mayor's office is closing down for the day.'

The policeman looked at them. 'You're both a bit old for games, aren't you? And I'm sorry, sir,' he said, turning towards Danny, 'but this gentleman is correct. Something is going on and we need this room. Whatever it is you're looking at will still be here tomorrow.'

Danny seriously doubted that.

He walked downstairs, sticking close to the policeman until he got outside. Then he walked back to his car, took his map of the province from the boot of the car and found the land survey reference for the plot the council had sold to *Grupo La Flecha Rota*. Whatever it had been used for, it was up in the mountains above the Bellavista, in the Sierra Almagrera.

Danny folded the map and closed the boot.

Someone whistled loudly.

When Danny turned to look back along the road, Shrike was there, leaning against the wall of a building and looking straight towards him.

Danny yanked the door of his car open and jumped inside. Shrike was still there at the end of the road when Danny drove past. Shrike stepped to the edge of the pavement and drew his thumbnail in a horizontal line across his throat. Danny hit the horn and gave him the finger.

When he got to the outskirts of the town, it suddenly occurred to him that if Shrike was following him, perhaps today wasn't a good time to drive out into the middle of nowhere. He pulled over at a petrol station and bought a can of coke. He leant against his car, sipping the drink and watching the road. If Shrike was following, the bastard would have to pull in and stop, too.

After ten minutes Danny decided he wasn't being followed. Even so, he opened the boot, took out the tyre iron and laid it on the passenger seat.

Better safe than sorry.

From what he could see, getting to the plot of land purchased by *Grupo La Flecha Rota* was going to be a problem. Sierra Almagrera had been a major centre for mining in the 19th and early 20th centuries, and dozens of dusty disused roads remained that led to absolutely nowhere.

After half-an-hour driving around in circles along roads that were barely wide enough for two vehicles to pass, Danny pulled over outside one of the few houses he'd encountered.

The adobe house was so old and ramshackle it was difficult to tell where the human dwelling ended and animal pens began. Chickens ran free on the dusty ground outside and smoke curled from a crooked chimney stack. The ground behind the building fell away from the house in terraces buttressed by curving stone walls, but there was no sign of agricultural activity; the only things growing on the terraces were swathes of prickly pear and esparto grass.

Danny gave a few long beeps on his horn.

The man who shuffled out belonged to another, older Spain. He was as nicked and pitted as the cliff faces that surrounded his home and he wore an old blanket draped around his shoulders and a black beret on his head. He walked painfully towards Danny, a dog yapping at his heels.

'I'm looking for a plot of land that was sold by the council. Do you know where it might be?' Danny said.

The old man nodded. 'It's up there,' he said, pointing with his stick along the road. 'You mean the old gold mine. The council sold it to some developers.'

'What would developers want with a mine?'

The old man shrugged. 'How should I know? But they were doing something up there back when they bought it. The lorries came by for about a week. Always at night. The bastards kept me awake. And it's because of them all my land is dead.'

'What do you mean?'

The old man beckoned for Danny to follow. They crossed

the patch of dust in front of the house and stopped by a sandstone well-head. Despite his seeming frailty, the old man hefted
the metal cover from the top of the well-head with ease and
lowered the bucket. When he pulled it back up, he showed
Danny the water.

'Look at this crap,' he said, showing Danny the cloudy
brown water. 'It's full of grit and God knows what else.'

'What does that have to do with the developer?'

'When they bought the plot of land, they had to widen the
access road so their wretched lorries could get in. While they
were doing it, they blocked off a stream and now when it rains
the water washes down off the mountain slopes and straight
into the mine shafts. And every time the mine shaft floods, it
washes this brown crap into my well. This whole mountain
range is like a honeycomb and some of the shafts go down
nearly a kilometre. Who knows what sort of chemicals they
were using down there?'

'Do you remember when the lorries came up here?'

'Right after they sold the place.'

'So, in 1998?'

'I think so. Yes, I think it was. My wife was still alive and
the Lord took her in '99.'

Danny thanked the man, got into his car and drove up the
road, taking the turning the man had indicated, a narrow dirt
road that had been carved through the slopes of the mountain.
The road snaked back and forth before opening out onto a
long, thin valley, a half-mile in length.

There had been a major mining concern here at one point,
but all that remained were the crumbling remnants of buildings and machinery. There were perhaps forty buildings still

standing, all of them in various states of disrepair, and three huge concrete bowls, fifteen yards in diameter, were situated around the pithead beneath the rusting machinery.

Danny walked between the buildings, taking photos, toeing the detritus. The pithead itself was a vast ragged hole in the ground, ten yards in diameter. God knows how deep the ruddy thing was. The wind whistled through the steel girders of the head frame.

Danny picked up a stone and threw it into the darkness at the centre of the mine shaft. If it ever hit bottom, Danny didn't hear it.

He could see where floodwater had passed through. A channel of dried mud, ten yards wide, led directly down the nearest mountain slope and ran straight into the gaping maw of the mine. Layers of broken boulders and vegetation lined the edges of the channel, washed down from higher up in the mountains.

Danny stood and looked back along the valley.

He was no expert, but he couldn't see what possible use the plot of land would have been to a development company. The strip of land occupied by the pithead and the admin buildings was narrow and surrounded on all sides by rocky slopes that were scarred with the marks of industry – hardly the type of view to attract British pensioners.

He thought about what the old man had said about the lorries he'd seen coming up here. There was no sign of any work having been done at the mine, no digging, nothing. They hadn't even begun to clear away the ruined buildings. The old man could have been mistaken, but Danny didn't think so. He'd seemed quite sharp.

One thing was certain: Danny wasn't going to get any answers at the *ayuntamiento*.

He headed back towards his car.

9

THE WHEELS OF Nacho Yagüe's Porsche crunched gravel as he pulled off the N-340a and parked on the scrap of waste-land beside the lap-dancing club. He was feeling horny and restless. He knew why: it was thinking about Lucia Borja again. It was strange, the power she still had over him after so many years.

Nacho first met her at one of the corporate events held to promote the Bellavista development, back in '96. He remembered the blue suit-dress she'd worn, just tight enough to show she wasn't wearing any panties.

Their affair began that same day.

Nacho had been a young man then, and he'd never experienced anything like Lucia Borja. That first night, they went at it fast and hard on the backseat of Lucia's Mercedes – hell, Nacho was only nineteen at the time, what else did he know? – slipping around on the slick leather. Lucia had run him ragged for about twenty minutes. Then she had given a huge shudder-ing moan and dug her nails into his back so hard she'd drawn blood. Then her face changed.

'Get off me, I'm finished,' she said, passion replaced now with barely concealed distaste. Seconds later, they'd been back out on the road, Lucia driving in tight-lipped silence, swerving through the traffic in her haste to get rid of him. She'd ordered

him out at the first bar they'd come to and left him there on
the side of the road, his trousers still unbuckled, the fly open.

The humiliation of that still burned. And yet they'd continued like that, screwing every chance – and every place – they
had the opportunity. Sometimes she would keep him up all
night, other times it was all over in ten minutes and to hell
with whether Nacho came or not. But her unpredictability
only added to her allure. She became like an addiction.

Like all addictions, it ended in tears: Nacho's father had
discovered what was happening.

Nacho could still see his father's face now, purple with
rage, screaming at him, 'You dumb little shit,' as he bunched
the front of Nacho's shirt in his fists and shook him. 'Do you
know how much I've got invested in this project? How much
I've had to kiss Sixto Escobar's fat ass? And meanwhile, you're
sticking it to that fuck-machine he calls a wife. What were you
thinking? You could have ruined me.'

That had been the end of Nacho's relationship with The
Sampson Consortium. And the last time he'd spoken to his
father. . .

He pushed open the big metal door of the lap-dancing
club, sat in a leather booth close to the bar and ordered himself
a vodka and coke from the Russian girl that was waiting tables
in panties, boots and nipple tassels.

Nacho sipped his drink as he watched the girls on stage
go through their moves. The girls looked tired and haggard
beneath their make-up, but Nacho liked that: it made them
seem more accessible.

He'd pulled in with the idea of having a little fun with one
of the girls – nothing helped cheer him up like a lunchtime

blowjob – but as he sipped his drink and watched the women's blemished arses grinding in front of him, he realised that for all his restless horniness, he wasn't in the mood.

It was because of those pictures he'd found in his father's house the day before.

Try as he might, he couldn't get them out of his mind. Even after he'd locked his father's house up and driven home, he had awoken during the night with a dose of the horrors, sweating and nervous, the nightmare of hairless kids in wheelchairs still fresh in his mind.

Nacho finished his drink and walked outside, squinting as he emerged from the club's gloom into the glare of the summer sunlight. Then he drove to the laboratory and walked down into the basement, calling Kiko's name.

The cripple shuffled out of his office. Nacho lit a cigarette.

'What the fuck happened to my father?' he said. 'At the end, I mean.'

Kiko winced at the expletive and began scratching the dry skin on his knuckles.

'I don't really think it's my place to say.'

'Why not?'

'I don't want to speak ill of the dead.'

'Come on. I'm his son. I know my father was far from perfect. Did you notice a change in him? Towards the end of his life, I mean.'

'Of course. I always got the sense he laboured under a great weight. His suicide came as no surprise to those of us who knew him best. He had been unravelling slowly for years.'

'Why are there so many pictures of sick kids in my father's house?'

'I mentioned the connection he had with Señor Phillips and his wife's charity. Your father was a tireless fundraiser. And together with Señor Phillips, he helped prioritise children that were falling ill on the Bellavista urbanisation. I'm afraid it began to weigh upon him in the end. Some of the children did not survive their illnesses. I think your father became too emotionally attached.'

Nacho laughed. 'He never gave a shit about his own children. Why should he care what happens to someone else's?'

Kiko dry-washed his hands. 'Your father was a changed man. I believe he cared very deeply for those children. You could ask your father's priest, Padre –'

'I've had enough religious bullshit for the moment,' Nacho said, relishing the way the profanities made Kiko's face pucker.

'That priest was your father's confessor. He did your father an enormous service by securing him a decent burial. Without his intervention, you would never have been able to bury your father's remains on holy ground.'

'What about the information I asked you to find? Did you find any records of the business links between the lab and Phillips?'

'There are two pieces of business we did for Señor Phillips. The first was a series of medical tests undertaken in March of 2005.'

'What types of tests were they?'

'Oncology tests. Cancer.' Kiko leafed through the paperwork. 'In fact, he seemed to have had himself tested for just about every type of cancer that was going.'

'What's the matter?' Nacho said when he saw the little man frown.

Kiko continued to leaf through the paperwork. 'With tests of this type there are normally details as to which doctor or clinic asked the patient to undergo the tests. But it seems that Señor Phillips referred himself. That's very unusual. He's had a blood chemistry test, a cancer gene mutation test, a CBC – that's a complete blood count – a cytogenetic analysis, a urinalysis, and urine cytology.'

'And what did they show?'

Kiko flicked through the results. 'He was clean. But I don't understand why he would have had all these tests.'

'Perhaps he was hypochondriac. Let's face it, with his wife's foundation, he must have been around sick kids the whole time. What was the other business?'

'Between the years 1999 and 2009 we conducted bi-weekly water analyses for a company named *Suministros La Flecha Rota*. I believe it was part of the investment group, *Grupo La Flecha Rota*. Martyn Phillips was a cosignatory on the company. This is the file relating to the analyses we carried out,' Kiko said, holding up a cardboard file.

Nacho took the file and opened it. There was nothing inside.

'Where are the analysis results?'

Kiko looked at the ground.

'A few years ago, a woman named Lucia Borja came to the laboratory to see your father.'

'*The* Lucia Borja? Sixto Escobar's ex-wife?'

'Yes. She spoke with your father for an hour in his office and I know it had something to do with this company, *Suministros La Flecha Rota*. I don't think the conversation was entirely amicable. I remember your father had been crying.

Afterwards, they came down here, to look at the records. Ten minutes later she was gone.'

'And you think she took the results of the analyses away with her?'

'It's the only explanation I can think of for why the hard copies are not here. And now that I think of it, there was something else irregular about this company's account.'

'What?'

'We employ a laboratory information management system here, LIMS, which helps with the tracking, traceability and reporting of data. When a sample enters the lab, it is logged into the LIMS system and all the relevant information relating to the sample – its source, the date it was taken, storage conditions, what tests are required – is captured by the system. Then, a label is generated and the testing schedule is printed out.

'After March 2005, your father insisted on carrying out all the tests on these water samples himself, and the samples were no longer logged into the LIMS system. Nor did he allow the peer review of the analyses that we normally carry out to ensure no mistakes are made.'

Nacho swore. This scientific crap was making his head spin. 'I want to see the originals of these analysis files.'

'The only other copies will be on floppy disk.'

'Find them. I'm going to speak to Lucia Borja. I want to know what the hell she wanted with that paperwork.'

Nacho went upstairs to his office and made some phone calls, asking for Lucia Borja's home number. He ended up with two numbers, a landline and a mobile. He phoned them both.

There was no answer.

Ten minutes later he tried again, but both numbers just rang and rang.

He slammed the phone back into its cradle, cursing. There was nothing for it, he would have to drive round and see the woman. He wouldn't be able to rest until he spoke to her and found out what she had wanted with those analysis results.

Borja's address was in the northeast of the city, a place where the suburban developments had spilled out into the marshy scrubland beyond the city's limits. Most of the houses here were built in long terraces with white doors and barred windows, but in Lucia Borja's road the properties were larger, detached and interspersed with clumps of reeds.

Nacho parked and looked at the house. Judging by the height of the walls that surrounded the villa, Lucia Borja hadn't done too badly out of her divorce settlement. Not that she would have been happy with it. A woman like that never was.

Nacho crossed the road and pressed the intercom button.

No answer.

He peered through the barred gates. There were two cars on the drive. He pressed the button again and held it down longer this time.

Still no answer.

He pushed at the metal gate and found it was open, so he walked up the path to the front door and knocked.

Nothing.

The living room window was wide open. From somewhere towards the back of the property he could hear a screen door banging in the hot, dry wind blowing in from the scrubland behind the house.

Something about the situation was wrong. As he neared the back of the house, he heard the buzzing of flies. A window at the back of the property was open about six inches. Nacho's nose wrinkled. The air here smelt rank and rotten, as if a huge mound of rubbish had been left to fester.

The window was covered in iron bars. Nacho pulled a ceramic plant pot across to the window, upended it and lifted himself up to see in, calling Lucia's name.

10

DANNY WAS WALKING through the centre of Almería city. He'd been thinking about the labour dispute that had taken place during the construction of the Bellavista, the one that the cowboy, Sergio, had mentioned. That was why he was going to speak to a friend of Paco Pino's at the *Unión General de Trabajadores*.

The UGT trade union is one of the largest in Spain and has strong links with the socialist party. Although the two organisations share a political credo, they do not always get on: the UGT represents the more traditional, militant form of socialism that sometimes clashes with the political expediency championed by sections of the modern PSOE party.

The union's Almería branch occupied a grimly functional five-storey building in the centre of Almería city. Danny had often thought it fitting that such an old-school left-wing organisation should be housed in a building that, architecturally, looked to have been transported straight from the former communist bloc. The décor inside followed suit: walls painted in dull, matt colours, scuffed and dirty linoleum on the floor. Danny didn't fancy the rickety elevator, so he took the stairs up to the fourth floor and knocked on Iñaki Arroyo's office door.

Arroyo was in his fifties and had an enormous grey bush

of a moustache that obscured his top lip; the hairs in the centre were stained that particular tarry yellow-brown caused by smoking dark tobacco. He greeted Danny with a firm handshake and invited him to sit down.

'What's this all about, then?' he said. 'Paco mentioned that you wanted details on the Bellavista development. I have to warn you that, from a union perspective, that's a pretty big subject.'

Danny smiled. 'Did the developers cause problems?'

Arroyo nodded. 'When do the bastards ever play by the rules?'

'Talking of the developers, did you have much contact with The Sampson Consortium? Or with something called *Grupo La Flecha Rota*?'

'Who the hell do you think we were up against most of the time?'

'Can you tell me about them? How are the two related?'

'Put very simply, The Sampson Consortium was what investors paid their money into, but *Grupo La Flecha Rota* was where that money got spent. Bascially *La Flecha Rota* was the developers' own company – an inner cabal, if you like – and they had it arranged so that they were in charge of all the subcontracting that went on. About 90% of the work on the Bellavista was done by outside companies, but everything – and I mean *everything* – went through *Grupo La Flecha Rota*. Not a single droplet of sweat fell on that site without those bastards taking their cut.

'If I remember correctly, *Grupo La Flecha Rota* had about two dozen different off-shoots. They had a company for each area of profit potential on the project: the plumbing, the plastering, the electricians, the swimming pools, the accounting, human resources. Basically, every time a new opportunity to screw people presented itself, they created a new company.'

'This inner cabal you mentioned: who are we talking about?'

'Doug Sampson, although he got thrown out early on. Sixto Escobar. There was a lawyer, Gomez, and his cousin, some banker – I forget his name. And there was an English architect, Phillips. And Escobar's wife, Lucia. God, you don't forget a woman like that. There were probably one or two more, I don't really remember.'

'I've heard the whole set up around the Bellavista was pretty corrupt. Is that true?'

Arroyo scoffed. 'You had companies competing for multi-million euro contracts. Let's just say there was a lot of cash swilling around that ended up being stuffed into brown envelopes. Plus the Bellavista was one of the first big development projects in the province. I suppose in some ways you could say it was the benchmark for all the incompetence and corruption that came after it. And let me tell you, they set the bar pretty high.'

'Didn't anyone try to stop them?'

'There were protests from the usual sectors. But when something like the Bellavista happens to a small town, a gold rush mentality takes over. Besides, who the hell was going to complain when Sixto Escobar's father had the whole council feeding from the trough as well, fudging the rules, approving business licences, handing out contracts. And remember, before the Bellavista, Las Jarapas as a town was dead in the water: no jobs, young people moving away in droves. And then suddenly, there was work for everyone. And not only that, work you could get rich from very quickly.'

'Did the UGT do nothing to stop the corruption?'

Arroyo scrutinised Danny, trying to decide whether his words contained a note of reproach.

'I heard rumours about what was going on, but it wasn't my job to investigate allegations of corruption. My only concern was to ensure that all the easy money floating around didn't result in corners being cut and workers' lives put at risk. Especially given the political pressure. The Bellavista was a big deal, the first big development in the province, and it was occurring in a PSOE stronghold. The word from on high was to get the thing done with the minimum of fuss – no ifs, no buts.'

'Talking of fuss,' Danny said, 'what I really wanted to ask about was the labour dispute that occurred.'

'Again, you've come to the right person. I remember it well. Strangest damned situation I've ever seen.'

'What happened?'

'At the beginning the union really had its work cut out on the Bellavista. There were upwards of three hundred people working on site some days and, due to all the sub-contracting that took place, there were dozens of different companies that we had to monitor. Added to that, we had all the usual problems that you get on a big project: workers being forced to work extra hours for free, missed lunch hours, no social security payments, lack of on-site toilets, unsafe working practices.'

Spectacles hung from Arroyo's neck by a chain. He lifted them up now and perched them on the edge of his nose, angling his head to look over them as he examined the paperwork he had on the desk in front of him.

'The actual building work was staggered across the four phases of the development. You'd have earth-moving and pipe-laying first, then the foundation and brick-work; after that came the plumbers, sparkies and roofers. Finally, in came the plasterers and the tilers to finish things off.

'The earth-moving began in January, 1998. Everything was fine for the first three months and then one day in the middle of April, *bang –*' he clapped his hands together – 'Seven in the morning, my phone started ringing off the hook: the site gates were locked and no-one could get in.

'I got there by nine and the situation was ugly. Someone from The Sampson Consortium came and read some cock-and-bull statement about there being a temporary problem with the building permits and that everyone was to take the rest of the week off – without pay, naturally – while they assessed the situation.

'I got on to the developers and read them the riot act. Then, at the end of that first day, someone noticed there *were* people inside working. The bastards had bussed in a load of cheap immigrant labour.'

'What type of work were they doing?'

'Who knows? But they had them working all through the night with flood-lights. Anyway, the type of work wasn't really the issue. It was the fact they were doing any damned work at all, when everyone else had been laid off. After that it was chaos. Some of the lads chained tractor tires together, pulled them across the main road to Las Jarapas and set them alight. You could see the plumes of smoke for miles. The council had to bring in the local police to protect the site gates.

'This continued for eight days and nights. We were settling in for a long fight and had started to organise a protest march when, just as suddenly, everyone was back at work and everything was hunky-dory again. The Sampson Consortium just rolled over, took everyone back on and forgot all about it.'

'What happened to the immigrant labour?' Danny said.

'We never saw them again. Like I say, it was the strangest situation I've ever encountered in thirty years of union work.'

'Do you remember a guy that used to do the corporate security for the developers? A man named Gabriel Varela.'

'The name's not familiar. But, yeah, there was a big nasty-looking guy that used to follow the nabobs around. Kind of like a bodyguard.'

Danny showed Arroyo a photo of Hector Castillo.

'What about this guy?'

'I recognise him. But then again I saw his photo in the paper a few days ago. This is the guy that was found out at Little Arizona, isn't it?'

Danny nodded. 'Apparently he was a consultant for The Sampson Consortium. Have you any idea what sort of consultancy work a research scientist might have been doing there?'

Arroyo laughed. 'A "consultant", was he?'

'What's so funny?'

'Back then, "consultant" was the catch-all phrase for "bribed by the developer". Every time they hit a snag with someone that could hold the project up, that person mysteriously started working for the developers as a "consultant". I reckon they must have had about fifty people on the books drawing wages that nobody could put a face to.'

'Why didn't they just pay them a bung?'

'Some people are happy to receive an envelope stuffed with

cash, but others have a slightly higher sense of morals. Plus, you know what it's like with large sums of cash with no legal source. If you're a normal person, you can't really do anything with it apart from sit on it or fritter it away, can you? Whereas, if you're receiving a nice fat "consultancy" wage packet every month, you can spend to your heart's content.'

Danny nodded to show he understood. The biggest problem with illicitly-obtained money was that, unless it was properly laundered, it could only be spent on illicit goods.

'However,' Arroyo said, 'now that you mention this Castillo fellow, I do remember something about him.' He began flicking through paperwork. 'Yes, here it is: he was granted a permit to enter the building site right at the beginning of the project.'

'Any idea why?'

'I remember something about some research he was conducting. Apparently, he'd set out some form of equipment that was taking readings from the soil before the land was sold and needed access to gather the data. I would have had paperwork relating to it at one point, but it's so long ago now I wouldn't even know where to start looking.'

Danny would have asked more, but his mobile began to ring.

'Sorry, about this,' he said, cancelling the call. 'I forgot to switch it off before I began the interview.'

Arroyo waved his hand to say it was OK, then broke into a smile when, seconds later, his own phone began to ring.

'I'm sorry, I don't have the luxury of hanging up on calls,' he said as he lifted the receiver.

He listened for a moment and frowned.

'It's for you,' he said, handing the receiver to Danny.

'Danny?' Paco Pino said. 'Whatever you're doing, drop it and go to the address I just texted to your mobile. No, you listen, this is a big one and we both need to be there. Lucia Borja has just been found at her house with her head caved in. As God's my witness. She's been dead for days. Some bloke went round there and got a whiff of the stench. But do you want to know the best bit? It sounds like the police have already got Sixto Escobar in the frame for it.'

11

GABRIEL VARELA WOKE suddenly, gasping for air. He tried to sit upright, but when he put his hand down to lift himself, pain shot up his arm.

After returning to the lock up, he had pulled a dozen shotgun pellets from his arm and about twice that number from his thigh. He had sponged the wound with antiseptic liquid, but the flesh was red and swollen. He drank whiskey for the pain, but it had gone to his head and he had slept far longer than he intended: it was the afternoon of the next day now.

He rose slowly and painfully and walked across to the basin at the back of the lock-up. He went to splash water on his face, but stopped when he saw that his hands were covered in dried blood.

He scrubbed his hands raw trying to clean away Escobar's blood, but when he finished, there were still dark U-shapes around the edges of his fingernails. He went back and sat on the mattress, feeling light-headed. His thoughts wandered. . .

Gabriel Varela had left *La Legión* in 1986. He started work as a stunt rider that same summer, back when the yanqui actor, Doug Sampson, had been running the place. He did his first work off the books that same summer, helping Sampson to collect poker winnings from guys that were trying to welsh.

Varela had carried on like that for a number of years, working springs and summers as a stuntman at the theme park and doing occasional jobs for Sampson and his buddies. Most of it was straightforward muscle work – intimidation and collecting debts that couldn't be collected through regular channels.

Word spread quickly about Varela. He was smarter and more cautious than most of the other men working in the same field, and he had few vices: he had no appetite for cocaine, did not gamble, drank moderately and smoked only an occasional cigar. And he was focused, disciplined and utterly dispassionate.

Within eighteen months, he began doing so much of the other type of work that he gave up as a stuntman. After that, he kept himself private and secret. He rented an isolated rural property on the way to Granada, a place where he could stand on his balcony and see the snowy peaks of the Sierra Nevada. If people wanted to contact him, they could do so only through the personal ads in the newspaper, providing a telephone number which Varela would then phone.

It was a good system. It created a buffer between Varela and the world in which he moved. And it meant that people could not contact him with rush jobs. He had no interest in anything that might land him in prison.

Payment was always in cash.

At first he kept it in a sports holdall under his bed, but when he had accrued more than two million pesetas, he hired a security deposit box at a bank and left the money there. Each month he would bundle together the cash he had earned and bank it. Then he would take a pen, cross out the previous total on the piece of paper he kept in the box and write down the new total. It was his only record of the amount.

It was Doug Sampson who introduced him to Sixto Escobar and the other pricks from *Grupo La Flecha Rota*. That was when the serious money began to roll in.

He had no respect for any of the men for whom he worked – he had seen how crooked and corrupt their world was. He came to despise their fat, flushed, greedy faces. If that was what riches did for a man, Varela wanted no part of it.

And yet the prices they were prepared to pay were so ludicrous, he couldn't say 'no'. Sometimes he would return from a night's work with a wad of 10,000 peseta notes so thick, he could hardly wedge it into his pocket.

And so the money had accumulated in the bank vault.

When Esme was born, he began to spend the cash, buying the best-quality baby equipment money could buy. Later, once his relationship with the mother was over, he began giving her 80,000 pesetas each month so that she could care for Esme properly.

One day around the turn of the century he had gone to eat at a bar and overheard politicians talking on the television, discussing a new currency, the Euro. The food had turned to ash in his mouth as he realised his box of money, the fruit of more than a decade of illegal labour, now had a shelf-life. The new currency would be introduced on January 1st, 2002. People would have a year after that to get rid of their pesetas, which would then cease to be legal currency. Varela had accrued more than 20 million pesetas – around 120,000 euros in the new currency.

He managed to get his money converted into euros over the

course of 2002, exchanging small amounts every few weeks in order to avoid suspicion. Even so, it was the first time that he realised sitting on a large amount of undeclared cash was a bad idea. And he began to dream of using the cash to purchase something tangible, something that could provide Esme with a solid start in life. He was still wondering how to achieve that when, in 2005, the message appeared in the personal ads of *La Razón...*

All six of them were there next day when Varela went to the rendezvous point, the whole of *Grupo La Flecha Rota*: Gomez, Morales, Escobar, Yagüe, Phillips, Borja.

As always, Gomez had done the talking, wrapping everything in his cloying clouds of euphemism. *We've got a problem, Gabi, a loose cannon. He could bring us all down, Gabi. We need to find a permanent solution. You can name your price, Gabi.* Varela had said he would think about it overnight and come back to them.

He sat awake long into the night, considering what he should do. Men had asked Varela to kill before, but he had always refused. This time it suited his own needs. He could use these pricks to solve his problem.

Besides, what could happen? He didn't believe in concepts such as heaven and hell. And if there was a hell, he had dug his own grave a long time ago.

Next day, he went to a sports shop and bought a bright red kit bag. Then he went to the bank vault, took out 110,000 euros and loaded them into the kit bag. Afterwards he drove out to meet Escobar at Little Arizona.

'Got a price?' Escobar had said, puffing on one of the cheap cigars he liked.

'Yep.'

'How much?'

'I don't want you to pay me a goddamn thing,' Varela had said, hefting the kit bag up onto the desk and opening it so that Escobar's greedy little eyes could see the wads of banknotes inside.

'All I want is for you to sell me a house.'

12

B Y THE TIME Danny got to Lucia Borja's address, a television news team had already set up its satellite truck at the end of the road. Beyond it were two cars from the *Policia Nacional*. Uniformed officers were stretching incident tape across the road and around the walls of Lucia Borja's house. Dozens of people had gathered on the pavement. The air was filled with whispered speculation.

The case against Sixto Escobar was already strong. According to some of the residents Danny spoke to, no-one had seen Lucia Borja since Sunday evening, when Sixto Escobar had visited her house. People remembered the way his 4x4 had screeched to a halt outside the property and how poorly he had parked it.

Neighbours had heard raised voices around 20:00, a man's and a woman's coming from different parts of the house. The noise continued for about ten minutes. One woman claimed to have heard Sixto asking Lucia 'what the hell she had done'. Fifteen minutes later, Sixto had performed a hurried three-point turn and raced away in his car.

'And no-one thought of phoning the police?' Danny said. 'Or of checking up on Señora Borja?'

That question prompted a lot of embarrassed avoidance of eye contact.

'She wasn't a well-liked woman,' one of the neighbours murmured, as people drifted away.

Paco Pino had been talking to an ambulance man who had actually seen the body.

'She's had her head caved in with a golf club, by the looks of it. Anyway, she definitely died from blunt force trauma wounds to the head. Apparently, she's been dead for days. He said she was swollen and blue. Sounds like a classic crime of passion. And it explains why Escobar disappeared so suddenly, doesn't it? He came round here, lost his temper and finally did her in. Then he bolted.'

'It's the timing that bothers me,' Danny said. 'They'd been divorced four years. What prompted him to go round and cave her head in on that specific day? Do we know who found the body?'

'Some bloke.'

'You got a name for him yet?'

'I'm still working on it. But I got some shots of the guy as the police were taking him away.'

Paco fiddled with his camera. 'Here he is,' he said, showing Danny the digital screen. 'Looks a right *pijo*, doesn't he?'

Danny shielded the screen with his hand, squinting as he realised he recognised the man with the pink sports shirt and slicked back hair.

'I know him,' Danny said. 'His name's Nacho Yagüe. I spoke to him yesterday.'

'That's the lab boss's son, right?' Paco rubbed his hands together. 'Oh, this is great. I'm going to get onto *El País* now.'

They waited until the body bag containing Lucia Borja's

remains was stretchered out. By that time, there were two dozen reporters on the scene and news crews from all the major television stations were filming their straight-to-camera reports at the end of the road.

Danny and Paco walked to the closest bar. Danny sat at a table while Paco chatted on his mobile. When Paco stopped talking, he ordered two glasses of pacharán.

'Are we celebrating something?' Danny said, nodding towards his glass of the sticky red liqueur.

Paco rattled the ice in his own glass and smacked his lips.

'*El Pais* want another exclusive.'

'An exclusive? About what?'

Paco frowned. 'What the hell do you think? About Lucia Borja, Sixto Escobar and this hatchet man, Gabriel Varela. About the house Sixto sold him.'

Danny dropped his voice. 'You didn't tell them Varela's name, did you?'

'I don't remember. I think so, yes. Why, is it a problem?'

'Of course it's a problem. No-one else will have found out about that yet, and I don't want other people getting onto the trail. This is our story, Paco.'

'Jesus, but you're a difficult bloke sometimes, Danny. You've spent the last eighteen months whingeing that you've had nothing decent to write about. Now we've got a bona fide story and a national newspaper willing to buy it, and you're getting gun shy.'

'It's not that, Paco. I've a contact in the prison service that is going to look up details on this Gabriel Varela guy. I don't want to go off half-cocked. There's more to this than meets the eye.'

'Like what?'

'It all centres on the Bellavista urbanisation. That's the connection between all these guys. We know the Bellavista is right next to the town of Palomares, and we also know that Hector Castillo was studying the drift patterns of plutonium. And then, all of a sudden, he gets hired as a consultant by a development company.

'Iñaki Arroyo has said that a "consultant" was basically a catch-all description for people the developers had bribed. What if this Hector Castillo found a pocket of irradiated earth on the Bellavista and the developer bought him off? That would mean some of the houses on the Bellavista were built on contaminated land. And what if –'

Paco made frantic shushing noises. A reporter standing at the bar turned towards them.

'Danny, don't say things like that in a public place. Walls have ears.'

Danny looked at him askew, expecting the photographer to follow the comment up with his toothy grin.

Paco didn't smile.

'Jesus, you're serious, aren't you?' Danny said.

'Yes, I am.'

'What the hell's got in to you?'

Paco sighed in that way people do when circumstances have backed them into a corner.

'Because that story has already been done, Danny. And it ruined the journalist who wrote it. I've already tried to tell you that.'

It took Danny a moment to realise what Paco was talking about.

'You mean Eduardo Bolaño, don't you?'

'Yes.'

'You mean you lied when you said you didn't know what the story he printed on his webpage was about.'

'No, I didn't lie, damn it. I just didn't tell you everything, because Eduardo's story was blown out of the water. Totally.'

'Tell me what happened.'

'He wrote the exact same story you've just mentioned: he claimed the Bellavista had been built on contaminated land. But no-one would print it, because Sebastian Gomez had been throwing his weight around, threatening libel suits left, right and centre.

'In the end, Eduardo put up a website. But that was only up for a day or so. Thirty-six hours at most. Gomez took out an injunction and had the thing closed down. Then he came after Eduardo with a libel suit.'

'What happened?'

'Eduardo was wrong. Not only was there a scientific report to prove it, the residents' committee on the Bellavista paid for its own investigation and they came to the same conclusion.'

'You told me this Bolaño was a good journalist. What if he –'

'He *was* a good journalist. And "was" is the operative word, because he was just like you: driven, stubborn and always trying to right wrongs.'

'What are you trying to say?'

'Danny, the most dangerous lies are the ones we *want* to believe, aren't they? Eduardo's story was totally discredited and the damages he had to pay ruined him. He lost everything: his job, his house and, most importantly, his reputation. No-one in the media would touch him with a bargepole after that. And that's why he topped himself.'

The two men sat in silence, sipping their drinks. Paco's phone rang. He looked at the number on the screen.

'It's the news editor from *El País*. What shall I tell him? Are we going to do the story or not?'

Danny shook his head. 'There's something else here. And until I know what it is, I'm not giving away the stuff I've managed to find out so far. As soon as we go to print with this, other reporters are going to be chasing the story. I want this to be our baby.'

'*Your* baby, Danny. You want it to be yours.'

'What's that supposed to mean?'

'You know why I take pictures, Danny? And why you report stories? I hate to get down to brass tacks here, but we're in this to make money, aren't we? Don't you understand that? We're not policemen. We're not even private eyes. *Solving* all this shit isn't our problem.

'Sure, I'd like to win a Pulitzer Prize, have my picture in The New York Times and travel the world. But I've got a wife, two kids and a mortgage – a mortgage that I'm currently struggling to pay. That's my reality, Danny.' He jabbed a finger at his own chest. 'That's me, Paco Pino, love it or leave it. I can't go chasing round every time you get a hunch. And if you were honest with yourself, neither can you.'

Paco slammed a ten-euro note on the table.

'That's for the drinks. I'm not thirsty anymore.'

'Where are you going?'

'I'm going to do some fucking work, Danny. You know

what I mean by work, don't you? I mean getting things done, rather than sitting around building castles in the air.'

Danny said nothing. There was no talking to Paco when he was angry.

Paco paused in the doorway. 'And if you do decide to write something, don't you put my name on the byline. You're on your own now.'

13

Two plainclothes bastards from the *policia judicial* handled Nacho Yagüe's interrogation, one of them sitting back to listen while the other jumped in, suspicion and disbelief written large in their hard eyes as they fired questions at him.

How did Nacho know this Borja woman?

How long had he known her?

If this woman was a family friend, why hadn't he seen her for years beforehand?

One of them even intimated that Nacho was involved in the killing and asked him to explain his movements on Sunday, the day they said that Lucia had been killed.

But the worst question was the one they kept asking him: Why had he gone to her house on that particular afternoon? Didn't he just say he hadn't seen the woman for years?

How could he answer that? He'd gone to see Lucia intending to ask her why she'd argued with Nacho's father, and whether she had taken the water analysis results from the folder. That was the hardest part, trying to answer without dropping himself in it. He still had no idea what the link between his father's company and Lucia Borja was, but he perceived the dim outline of trouble all around him, like icebergs glimpsed through sea mist. His attempts at dissembling had put scowls on faces that Nacho hadn't believed could become any more unfriendly.

Nacho should have run as soon as he'd peered through the window at the back of Lucia's house. But the sight of the bloated blue-black corpse on the floor inside had made him cry out and by the time he'd stumbled down the path towards the gate, ashen-faced and gagging, a neighbour had already been peering through the gate at him, asking what on earth was wrong. Escape had no longer been an option.

The horrendous smell of the corpse was still with him. In the toilet at the police station, he had washed soapy water into his nostrils, but he could still taste the stench in his mouth and at the back of his throat.

Eventually the police officers withdrew from the interview room and spent long minutes talking outside in low voices. Nacho began to wonder whether they would arrest him. He hadn't wanted to involve his lawyer, but after three hours in the *comisaría de policía* he began to consider phoning her.

Suddenly the attitude of the police had changed. They brought Nacho coffee and a fresh packet of Marlboros. When they returned to the interview all of their questions were about Sixto Escobar. It took Nacho a few minutes to realise what was happening: they now suspected Escobar of the crime.

Nacho quickly became a veritable fountain of information, dredging up every scrap of gossip and innuendo he could about Escobar and his divorce from Lucia Borja. He even invented a nightclub altercation between Escobar and some Russian in an effort to persuade the police of the man's violent nature.

An hour later they let him go.

'But don't leave town, Señor Yagüe,' the big shaven-headed officer had said, catching Nacho's arm on the way down the steps. 'We've not finished with you, yet.'

Nacho's car was still parked outside Lucia Borja's house, but he realised he couldn't collect it now: the press were probably still at the murder scene. He would have to fetch it tomorrow.

He took a taxi across town to the laboratory. He needed to find some answers, some definitive information about how his father was linked to this whole rotten business, before the police could call him back for more questioning.

He walked rapidly across the car park and headed down into the basement of the laboratory. Kiko emerged from his office in a fug of black tobacco smoke, his expression especially hangdog. His bulbous eyes were red and his lank hair stood up as if he'd been rubbing it.

'I've found the information you wanted,' he said in a low voice. 'It was on a floppy disk. I've printed it all out.'

'And?'

Kiko led Nacho into his office. The small desk was covered in rolls and rolls of old-style green and white printout paper.

'According to this we carried out a series of bi-weekly tests on water drawn from boreholes in and around the Bellavista development, tap water that was being supplied for domestic use via this company, *Suministros La Flecha Rota*.

'We performed the standard potability test to determine the water's suitability for domestic use. Samples were taken from a number of different sources and tested for a wide range of contaminants: Antimony, Asbestos, Barium, Flou-'

'Just give me the short version, Kiko, that's what I pay you for. How does it affect us?'

'That's why I wanted to speak to you. All these results are absolutely fine,' Kiko said, indicating one pile of paper. 'But this pile over here are the tests that I mentioned before, the ones your father carried out in private in March 2005, without following the proper laboratory procedure and without allowing anyone else to see the results.

'Your father was subjecting the water samples to an entirely different process from that which you'd use for normal water testing: coprecipitation with ferric hydroxide, followed by electrodeposition and a –'

'Yes, but why?'

'That's what I'm worried about,' Kiko said. 'Because if the figures I'm about to show you are correct, then we have a very serious problem on our hands.'

14

Wednesday, 29th August, 2012

THE DAY OF Marsha and Danny's barbecue didn't start well.

At eight, a tearful Lourdes phoned Marsha to say that she was really sorry, but the family wouldn't be attending the barbecue. At 08:03, Marsha began poking Danny awake, demanding an explanation.

'Lourdes says you've had a falling-out with Paco.'

'Jesus, stop poking me, woman. I'm awake.'

'What's going on?'

Danny sat up in bed. 'We had an argument yesterday while we were working. But it was a minor thing. I didn't know Paco was going to throw his toys out of the pram.'

Marsha thrust Danny's mobile at him.

'Sort it out. Now,' she added, when Danny's head sank back to the pillow.

Danny went outside and sat in a plastic chair on the patio. He lit a cigarette and rubbed fingers through his tousled hair. He knew from past experience that, when Paco lost his temper, all that was normally required to rectify the situation was for Danny to apologise, whether the slight was real or imagined.

But the truth was, Danny could be just as proud and child-
ish as Paco, and part of him was tempted to leave things as
they were. It was Paco who had got the hump and stormed
off. If he wanted to miss out on a damned good feed-up, that
was his look out.

That train of thought was derailed when Danny saw the
way Marsha was watching him through the window.

He lifted the phone to his ear and said, 'Can you bring me
a fork and a bottle of olive oil?'

'What for?'

'To help with the massive lump of humble pie I'm about to
choke down.'

Ten minutes later he returned to her and said, 'Problem
solved: Paco, Lourdes and the two girls will be arriving at
18:00.'

'Thank you,' Marsha said with a smile, as she sliced peeled
potatoes to make a tortilla. Danny put his arms around her
and kissed her neck; then he allowed one hand to slip down
towards her buttocks, but Marsha giggled and broke away
from him.

'There's no time for any of that, Sonny Jim, I've far too
much to do. And so have you.'

After that, Danny took a cold shower – a *really* cold
shower – got dressed and drove to the covered market in town
to buy the food for the barbecue. Marsha had decided to hedge
her bets and buy both meat and fish, so Danny bought two
kilos of ribs and a half-kilo each of pork steaks, beef fillets and
pinchos. Then he went to the seafood stall and bought a kilo
of sardines, two kilos of mussels and a box of prawns. It cost
a fortune, but it was Andalusian tradition at this sort of thing

to prepare twice as much food as your guests could possibly hope to eat.

When he got back home, Marsha was frowning.

'You've had a phone call.'

'Who was it?'

'Her. She says it's important.'

'It always is.'

Danny decided he had enough on his plate already without adding his mother to the mix, so he didn't bother returning the call. Adriana Sanchez had other ideas. Five minutes later, Danny's phone rang. He let it ring. Five minutes later it rang again.

'I'd better get it,' he said. Marsha just shrugged.

'Danny,' Adriana Sanchez said when he answered. 'I had the *most* interesting conversation yesterday.'

Danny rolled his eyes. He recognised that sing-song tone in his mother's voice: it meant she knew something he'd rather she didn't.

'And what was that?' Danny said.

'Apparently, Doug Sampson had to chase some bothersome reporter away from his house with a rifle. Gave the poor chap quite a fright by the sounds of it.'

'What makes you think it was me?'

'English accent, blond curly hair and a car with one wheel in the wrecker's yard. Sound like anyone you know?'

'Look, Mum, I'm busy. You've had your fun. And, yes, he scared the hell out of me.'

'Don't take that tone, Danny, it makes you sound like a truculent teenager. Especially when I've called to help you out.'

'Help me how?'

'If you need to speak to Dougie, I can help you with that.'

'Do you know him?'

'Of course, I do.'

'This is *the* Doug Sampson, the American actor? '

'*Actor*? Have you ever seen one of his films?'

'How do you know him?'

'We're members of the same country club. Let's have lunch and I'll tell you all about it.'

'OK, when?'

'Why, now, of course.'

Danny looked at his watch.

'I can't. I'm busy.'

'Well, I'm off to Madrid this afternoon, so it's now or never.'

Danny rolled his eyes. It was always the same with his mother: her way or the highway.

'OK. I'll see you in twenty minutes, then.'

Marsha looked at him askance when she saw him sweep up his shoulder bag and notebook.

'I'm sorry,' Danny said, heading for the door. 'I'll be back as –'

'I'm not going to try to stop you going out, Danny. But I will say this. It is currently thirteen minutes to twelve, ante meridian. Our guests arrive at half-past five, post meridian. Remember that, please. I want you here shaved, showered and sober at least an hour before that.'

Danny and his mother met at one of the most expensive bars in Almería city, the type of place where you paid twice the price for half the amount. Business in this particular bar was booming. That didn't surprise Danny, because the truth of Spain's recession was that it hadn't affected everyone; it had only really hit as high as the professional middle classes. The people with real wealth still had it – and in many cases, were angling to make a killing from the recession. House prices had plummeted and rental properties were now where the smart money was going. After all, a huge percentage of the Spanish population would now never be able to obtain mortgages, so it made economic sense.

Adriana Sanchez swept in twenty minutes late and greeted the waiters by name. She was wearing her usual loose hippy clothing, topped off with a purple pashmina tied in a loose slip knot. She greeted Danny with a couple of air kisses, exuding a waft of expensive perfume.

Back in England, Adriana Sanchez had always spoken to Danny in Spanish; here, though, she always addressed him in English. Danny had noticed that she naturally gravitated towards the language those around her were least likely to understand.

She looked him up and down.

'What on earth are you wearing?' she said, looking at Danny's faded Iron Maiden T-shirt and frayed jeans. 'It looks like someone covered you in Velcro and rolled you through the donations bags outside an Oxfam.'

'Doug Sampson, Mother,' Danny said, ignoring the jibe. 'You said you know him.'

'I do indeed. He's a dear friend.'

'Do you really mean that? Because I've had experience of his way of dealing with unwanted guests, so I want to be absolutely certain before I go back.'

'Oh, under normal circumstances I would say you'd burnt

your bridges with him. But there's one very simple way to get Doug Sampson's attention. And you're already half way there.'

'And what's that?'

'Sixto Escobar. Lord, he hates that man with a passion. He claims Escobar stole that awful western park from him. And Sampson was no friend to Martyn Phillips, either. There was definite bad blood there about some development project. Say that you intend to stick it to either of those two, and I can assure you Dougie will be all ears.'

'OK, give him a bell.'

'Slow down, Danny. You're no fun when you're in a rush. Typical man. Let's have some eats first.'

They ordered beers, grilled sardines and broiled sea snail with garlic and parsley. Finally, forty minutes later, Adriana Sanchez deigned to rummage in her handbag, looking for her phone.

'Remember you owe me one,' she said as she fished out a hundred-euro note and tossed it at Danny. 'Here, the grub's on me.'

Adriana Sanchez walked outside. Danny watched her through the window as she waved a cigarette in the air and talked into her smartphone – a top-of-the-range model, Danny noticed. He didn't need to be able to hear her to know what she was saying: *Darling Dougie, it's been such a long time. Now listen, I need to crave a boon. . .*

Danny had worshipped his mother as a child, the way all children worship adults who break the rules. Not that she had been around that much: Danny's grandmother had raised him. It wasn't until adolescence that Danny had realised that his mother did not understand the distinction between nonconformity and blatant irresponsibility. It had taken her years to link Danny's childhood habit of spontaneously vomiting during days out to her habit of feeding him hamburgers, chips, Coca Cola, ice cream and whole bags of sweets in quick succession.

The waiter grimaced when Danny handed him the hundred-euro note. That, too, was typical of his mother: she was paying, but in the most inconvenient way possible. It brought another childhood experience to mind, one of the few occasions on which Danny had gone on holiday with his mother. That had been when she was with Marty, the American she'd ended up marrying.

Between their lovemaking, late nights and hangovers, little Danny had quickly proved a burden. He remembered one morning in particular. His mother had sleepily fished a fifty pound note out of her lover's wallet and told Danny to go and amuse himself. Nine-year-old Danny had tried to buy some sweets, but no-one would change such a large note. One shopkeeper had even accused him of having stolen the money. Danny ended up crying alone on the swings in the park, staring at his un-spendable money. He'd thought his mother had played a trick on him. . .

'There, what did I tell you?' Adriana Sanchez said triumphantly as she resumed her seat opposite him at the table. 'Dougie said "yes" as soon as I mentioned the fact you were investigating Sixto Escobar.'

'Did you mention it was me he took a pot shot at?'

'Of course I did.'

'And?'

'He said that if he'd wanted to hit you, he would have.

He's a crack shot, apparently. Learned it in the army, or something.'

'When does he want to meet up?'

'Why, now, of course.'

Danny looked at his watch. 'Jesus, I can't go now. I've got people coming round this afternoon.'

'He won't take kindly to being stood up, Danny. It's now or never, I'm afraid.'

Danny looked at his watch. It was a twenty minute drive to Níjar. He had time. Just.

Danny stood up to leave.

'If this old bastard shoots at me again, I'm going to blame you.'

Adriana Sanchez waved her hand dismissively.

'Don't be so dramatic, Danny. Now, remember that Sixto Escobar, Little Arizona and Martyn Phillips are all terribly sore subjects for poor Dougie.'

'So you want me to bring them up at every possible opportunity?'

'What a nasty, suspicious little mind you have sometimes,' Adriana Sanchez said, with the faintest of smiles.

Danny returned the smile. 'I wonder where I get that from.'

15

Fʀᴏᴍ ᴛʜᴇ ʟɪᴛᴛʟᴇ Danny could remember of Doug
Sampson's films, the actor had always spoken with a yawing
Texan accent, but when he greeted Danny at the gates of his
property, he spoke with a smooth, cultivated Mid-Atlantic ac-
cent, one of those that sounded neither wholly American nor
British.

Sampson had clearly dressed for the occasion: he wore designer jeans, cowboy boots and a denim shirt, with a carna-
tion tucked into the welt pocket on the shirt's breast. Sampson
must have been in his mid seventies, but he still moved fairly
gracefully.

As they approached the house, Danny noticed the property
looked a little rundown, an impression that was heightened by
the battered orange pick-up that was parked in the carport.

Sampson led Danny into the living room, which was decorated with faded posters depicting commercials for a cheap
brand of whisky Sampson had promoted in the eighties.

Danny doubted the man would get many commercials
now: not unless it was advertising the dangers of too many
Botox injections. Cosmetic surgery had left the skin on Sampson's face stretched so taut that most of his emotions went only
half-registered, like an actor trying to emote through the skin
of a snare drum. His eyes seemed fixed to register a permanent

expression of surprise and his hair was still dyed that awkward jet black colour.

'So, you're the young man I shot at the other day?' Sampson said, as Danny took a seat on the threadbare sofa.

'Yes.'

'I'm sorry about that. I've had a rough time of it with you boys, though. Adriana has vouched for you. She says you're investigating Sixto Escobar.'

'Among other things, yes.'

'How can I help?'

Danny took out the photo of Gabriel Varela, the one where he was tied to the wagon wheel.

'Do you remember this man?'

Sampson took the photo and hesitated. Then he opened a small case and took out a pair of glasses. Danny drew breath when he saw how thick the lenses were.

'I only need them for reading,' Sampson said defensively.

'What about taking pot shots at people in your garden? Do you need them for that? Because you weren't wearing the damned things the other day.'

Sampson looked at Danny. Then he laughed a deep throaty laugh. 'I like you, boy,' he said, switching to his onscreen accent. 'Ya'll got the same sassy mouth as your mother. Don't worry, I can still shoot a fly's ass off from fifty yards with a rifle. Now, do you want me to look at this photo or not?'

Sampson perched the glasses on the end of his nose and examined the photo. Then he looked up at Danny with renewed interest.

'Sure, I remember him. His name was Varela, Gabriel Varela. He was one of the stuntmen at my place.'

'How did you meet him?'

'He turned up at my theme park one day. He was an ex-serviceman, like me. I wanted to help him out. And he would do stuff the other guys were nervous about doing: the high falls, being dragged behind horses, that sort of thing. The tourists loved him.

'But I could tell he was different straight away. All the other stunt guys were what you'd expect, wannabe tough guys that were only in it for the tourist skirt. But Gabi wasn't like that. He hardly drank, didn't smoke and took everything seriously. And he was tough in that quiet, solid way meant you knew instantly not to mess with him. But why'd you ask about Gabi?'

Danny drew breath.

And then he told Sampson everything: that he thought Varela had placed Hector Castillo's body at the theme park and that Varela had abducted Martyn Phillips from a property on the Bellavista and burnt him alive.

Sampson's eyes narrowed when Danny mentioned the Bellavista and Martyn Phillips.

'Serves the asshole right. Goddamn thief.'

'So you think Varela was capable of killing a man?'

Sampson considered this. 'Well, you heard rumours. But then you always do about guys like Varela, don't you? But if you crossed him in any way, you'd have a big problem.'

'There was a message at the property that Phillips was abducted from: *Ahora te toca pagar. Now it's time to pay.* Do you think Varela was trying to blackmail him?'

Sampson shook his head.

'No-one would have had more dirt on them than Gabi. But blackmail? Not his style. Gabi wasn't a thief and he wasn't a liar. He was a dangerous bastard, but you always knew where you were with him. Having said that, I'll tell you one thing about him: he never let any slight go unpunished. It was a matter of honour with him.'

'And being an ex-legionnaire, I'd imagine he had a fairly inflexible code of honour.'

'Precisely.'

'Rumour has it that Varela was available for other types of work as well. Do you know anything about that?'

For a moment, Danny felt that Sampson's neutral expression became a little forced, but it was difficult to tell. Sampson looked at him carefully and shook his head.

'Can you think of any reason why Varela would have gone after Phillips?'

'Whatever the reason was,' Sampson said, rising, 'I'm going to raise a glass in Varela's honour. Will you join me, Mr Sanchez?'

Danny said no, he was driving, as Sampson got up and took a bottle of champagne from the fridge. He took a champagne flute from a cupboard and opened the bottle with a twist of his wrist. The cork popped out of the bottle.

Sampson poured himself a glass and sighed when he sipped it. He was about to say something, when one of the bedroom doors opened and a lean, forty-something Latin man with a neat pencil moustache emerged, his black hair tousled like he'd just woken up. He pulled a black silk kimono around him as his naked feet slapped on the tiled floor.

'Did I hear a cork pop?' he said in Spanish, as he sauntered towards the kitchen.

Sampson's face was half-registering a totally different

set of emotions now. He took the newcomer by the arm and hustled him into the kitchen. Danny pretended to be studying his notes as the two men maintained a whispered conversation. The newcomer shrugged and walked away, blowing Sampson a kiss as he went.

'My PA,' Sampson said without a hint of irony when he returned. 'He's working on some paperwork.'

Danny smiled and nodded. 'I've been told that you used to contact Varela by leaving messages in the personal ads of a newspaper. For the other type of work, I mean.'

Sampson's expression darkened. 'I already told you, I don't remember anything about that.'

'Really? My source seemed quite certain.'

'Then go ask him.'

Danny let Sampson sip his champagne. Then he said, 'What can you tell me about *Grupo La Flecha Rota*?'

Sampson stopped dead and for the first time, it was clear what emotion his face was registering. Danny wondered why the American had never been chosen to play villains, because the momentary malevolence that flashed in his eyes was Oscar-worthy.

'I can tell you that they are cheating bastards. They screwed me out of millions.'

'How?'

'I worked my butt off for that Bellavista project. You know how many goddamn hands I had to shake? How many asses I had to kiss? And do you know what I got paid? A flat fee. And that's what got me into so much money trouble. Hell, I'd borrowed thousands, and then they screwed me. That was why I had to sell my theme park to that goddamn sweat ball.'

'You're talking about Sixto Escobar now, I presume?'

'Yes. But he wasn't the worst of them.'

'Who was?'

'Sebastian Gomez and that cousin of his, Morales. You know how it is with lawyers. They lay it all on with roses and wine, when in actual fact they are wrapping you up in barbed wire. Do you know how much those bastards made? Millions, each one of them. And we're not talking pesetas, here. They were swimming in money by the end of it. And Gomez and Morales took the biggest slices of all. They used it to set up their investment fund. They let me do all the work, then stabbed me in the back.' He hit his chest with a fist. 'It was *my* money that got things going. Those other bastards didn't have shit to start out with. Hell, why do you think it was even called La Flecha Rota?'

'Because of the name of the theme park when you ran it. It was where you used to meet.'

Sampson nodded his head, impressed.

'Done your homework, haven't you, son? But do you know why I chose the name Broken Arrow?'

Danny shook his head. Sampson's upper lip moved in a taut approximation of a smile.

'So, you don't know everything then, do you?'

He rose, went to the sideboard and took out a box of black and white photos. He handed them to Danny, one by one. The first showed Sampson as a young man wearing a military uniform.

'That's in 1963, when I joined the United States Air Force. Here I am, three years later, on my first overseas posting,' he said, handing Danny a photograph that showed dozens of military tents pitched on a sandy expanse of coastline.

'Do you know what that is?' Sampson said. 'That's Camp Wilson. Seven hundred men housed in seventy-five tents, just outside the little town of Palomares.'

It took Danny a moment to realise what it was he was seeing.

'You were part of the clear-up operation after the Palomares Incident?'

'Yep. And you know what that operation was called? It was called Operation Broken Arrow. That's military code for an accident involving nuclear weapons. We weren't supposed to take photos on account of it all being classified, but I smuggled in a camera.'

Sampson sat back in his chair and sipped his drink.

'It's also how I got started in films. While I was here, I got to know a sergeant who knew a guy that worked for Sergio Leone's production company. Anyway, in June of '66 when he started filming *The Good, The Bad and The Ugly* here in Almería, I got some work as an extra.

'You know that scene where they blow up the bridge? I play a union sergeant in that bit. I had a few lines, but they didn't make the final cut. Still, I got my foot in the door and made some good contacts. When I left the air force in '67, I went straight into acting. Think about it: January 1966, I was shoveling radioactive dust into oil drums. Two years later, I was doing the Johnny Carson show. Only in America, eh?'

'Weren't you worried about contamination? From the clean-up operation, I mean.'

Sampson waved his hand dismissively. 'Listen, I stayed in contact with some of my buddies that were here and every one of them is in perfect health, apart from one who died in a car crash. Of course, we had suits and facemasks. The Guardia officers Franco sent to help us were picking the goddamn stuff up with their bare hands. I'd love to know what happened to those poor bastards.'

Danny would have asked more questions, but the alarm on his phone beeped to tell him he really needed to get going.

He stood up and shook Sampson's hand.

'Can I contact you again when I have more time?'

'Sure, thing, Mr Sanchez. As long as you're on Sixto Escobar's case, you can phone me as much as you want.'

～

As soon as Doug Sampson saw the gates close behind the reporter's car, he headed for the kitchen. Ricardo was slicing a lemon on the breakfast bar, the kimono flapping open around his lithe body.

'What the hell are you playing at?' Sampson said.

Ricardo put spread fingers to his chest. 'Playing? Moi?'

'You know what I mean: flouncing around the place in a kimono like a goddamned pansy.'

Ricardo laughed. 'If anyone's a pansy, it's you, sweetie: it's your kimono, after all.'

'That's not what I meant and you know it. That guy was a reporter.'

Ricardo's smile remained playful. He touched fingertips to Sampson's face. 'Dougie, the cat's been out of the bag for a long time now. I don't know why you can't just relax and enjoy it.' He tried to place a kiss on his lover's lips, but Sampson recoiled, so Ricardo gave him a please-yourself wave of the hand and pushed past him, carrying his pink gin towards the terrace.

The two men did not talk again until the evening, when they were drinking Lambrusco and watching the sunset from the balcony. Ricardo was chewing his lip, lost in thought.

'You lied to the reporter, didn't you?' he said.

Sampson smiled. 'How'd you know?'

'You've got a tell, same as everyone.'

'So what'd I lie about?'

'About the newspaper thing. You do remember which newspaper it was they used to leave the messages in, don't you?'

Sampson mimed applause. They drank in silence. Then Ricardo said, 'So which newspaper was it?'

'*La Razón*. We used to put something in about an opportunity for an ex-legionnaire. But what's it matter?'

Ricardo didn't answer that. Later that evening he took the battered pick-up and drove into town. An hour later, he returned with copies of *La Razón* from the last three days. He spread the newspapers out on the table in front of Sampson.

'Take a look at that,' he said, pointing to the personal ads.

The same message was printed in all three of the newspapers.

GENEROUS OPPORTUNITY FOR FORMER LEGIONNAIRE. Willing to discuss full compensation for outstanding amount, plus a bonus of twice the initial premium. Call 626 365 779

Sampson's mouth hung open. 'They're trying to contact Varela.'

'It's been in the paper every day for the last three days now.

Always the same message. But on the last two days, they are offering *four* times the initial premium. This Varela guy doesn't seem too bothered about his cash.'

'It's like I told the reporter. Blackmail isn't Varela's style.'

'Well, that's all the better for us, isn't it, honey?'

'What is?' For the first time, Sampson caught the pensive look in Ricardo's eyes. 'What are you thinking?'

Ricardo sat on Sampson's lap and put his arms around his neck. 'Doug, honey, if this Gabriel Varela doesn't want to collect the money they're offering, I sure as shit do. And I'm pretty sure I know how we can do it, too.'

16

Danny stopped on the way home and bought tubs of
ice cream and packets of Haribo. Marsha had invited six couples, all of whom had kids, and Danny felt like spoiling them a
little. As it was, even with the stop at the supermarket, he was
home well before four o'clock.

Marsha was having a siesta on the sofa when he got home,
but when she heard the rustle of the shopping bags, she raised
her head and gave him a smile. Danny hit the shower, washed,
then put on his smartest jeans and check shirt, the Ben Sherman
that Marsha had bought him for Christmas. Then he took a
bottle of *Mahou* beer from the fridge and sat down to wait for
their guests to arrive.

Danny's patio had a wind-down awning that gave pretty
good shade and, by five, a light breeze had risen, taking the
edge from the day's heat. Marsha had laid the outside table
with a purple cloth. Candles in small dishes were laid out in a
line down the centre of the table for after darkness fell.

Besides the meat and seafood, Marsha had prepared salad,
roasted peppers and Spanish omelette, a big thick cake of fried
potato, onion and egg. Another plate held slices of chorizo
sausage and jamón.

The guests began to arrive at six. Most were teachers
from the academy at which Marsha worked, along with their

spouses and children. Paco, Lourdes and the girls arrived later, carrying litre bottles of *San Miguel* and a bag of sardines.

The barbecue followed the usual Andaluz pattern when entertaining. Those who hadn't seen Danny's property were given the tour. Then everyone stood around chatting, while the children – a dozen of them, ranging from four- to eleven-year-olds, most of whom seemed to know each other – set off exploring the wild expanse of Danny's garden, accompanied by his dog, Lucky. After a half-hour of socialising, the first beers came out and people sat down and began to form conversational groups.

Danny lit the barbecue at seven-thirty and put the first round of meat on about eight. Men gathered at the barbecue, talking about the things Spanish men always do – football, Spain's economy, the housing market – while the women went inside and helped Marsha bring the tapas out to the table.

There was no formal beginning to the meal. People simply helped themselves to the plates of meat and seafood Danny kept bringing over to the table, and most ate from paper plates while standing up, the pace and volume of the conversation not flagging one iota. One and a half hours later later, their guests were still eating, although the rate at which the food was disappearing had slowed noticeably. Marsha and some of the other women went inside to prepare coffee. Lourdes insisted on doing the washing-up, so Marsha began to dry, while Paco and Danny stretched cling film over the mountains of food that remained.

After that, Danny took his bottle of Jameson Special Reserve outside, and the adults drank Irish coffee while the children continued to play. Night came on and Marsha lit the candles.

It had been a while since Danny had socialised with Paco like this. He'd forgotten what good company the photographer could be when he was relaxed, full of food and slightly merry. Danny and Paco retold some of their favourite anecdotes from working together: the time Paco had split his pants while climbing a drainpipe to photograph documents on the desk of a mayor and the time in Marbella when Sean Connery had told them both to fuck off. Then Danny told everyone what had happened on his first visit to Doug Sampson's house.

After that, the conversation turned to Palomares. One of the teachers from Marsha's academy had family there.

'You know there's a big piece of land out by the cemetery that the government had to buy because of the radiation levels there,' she said. 'It's supposed to be fenced off, but apparently there are lots of places where you can get in.'

'But who'd want to,' Danny said, 'if the ground is so contaminated?'

'Oh, that wouldn't be a problem,' Marsha said.

Danny looked at her. 'Why not?'

'If there is anything out there, it will be plutonium 239. That's an alpha-particle emitter.'

'And what does that mean? That they're not dangerous?'

'No, alpha radiation is the most dangerous there is. But the particles are very heavy, so they can't travel more than an inch or two in the air. And they can't pass through clothing or skin.'

'And how do you know all this?'

'After our chat the other day, I did a little reading on the subject of Palomares myself. Plus I did an OU science foundation course about six years ago. One of the modules was all about radioactivity.'

Paco laughed and slapped Danny on the back. 'She's not just a pretty face, is she?'

Danny was still looking at Marsha, smiling the little half-smile he always did when Marsha impressed him.

'No, she isn't,' he said. 'Not by a long shot.'

At ten, Paco drove into town to buy cigarettes and fetch more ice. When he returned, he was carrying a brown envelope.

'It's for you,' he said, handing it to Danny.

'Where did you find this?' Danny said, turning the package over in his hands. There was no postmark or stamps on it, just a printed sticker with the words 'F.A.O. Danny Sanchez'.

'It was on the ground in the driveway,' Paco said, unscrewing the top from a bottle of Beefeater gin.

Marsha was giggly drunk. She plucked the envelope from Danny's hands.

'Ooh, look, my boyfriend gets anonymous letters. I wonder what's inside,' she said, ripping it open.

The envelope contained a plastic case with a DVD inside. The words WATCH THIS were written on it in English. Danny wanted to leave it until later, but Marsha insisted on watching it immediately, so everyone gathered in the living room as Danny put the DVD in the machine.

The television screen showed nothing but a white blur at first; then the view cleared to show a sheet of newspaper, wavering about a metre from the camera, close enough for it to fill the whole of the screen.

Danny leant closer to see what newspaper it was, and had

just enough time to realise that the page turned towards the camera held the *El País* article he had written about Martyn Phillips's murder, before a knife blade pierced the top of the page. The blade slipped through the paper and slowly slid downwards, its edge parting the paper like a razor, smoothly and without tearing.

'I don't like this,' one of the children said.

The paper fell away, drifting to the floor in two parts and they saw a blur of motion as someone stepped aside.

The camera was static and showed someone's bedroom. There was a bed covered in purple paisley sheets and tasselled purple fabric was draped over the bedside lamps. A Dalí poster was tacked to the white wall above the headboard.

Danny frowned, wondering why it seemed so familiar, then Marsha whispered, 'Oh my God. That's my bedroom,' pointing at the screen. Danny felt the colour drain from his face as he realised she was right. Christ, it *was* Marsha's bedroom.

And then the screen suddenly filled with a head wearing a ski mask.

'I'm waiting for you, Marsha,' the face screamed in a voice abrasive as fingernails on a blackboard. 'I'm right here waiting for you, you fat fucking bitch. Here, watch this, this is for you.'

Then the figure turned and began pissing onto Marsha's bed.

PART III

VIVA LA MUERTE

1

'Do you think Mr Gomez will be long, now?' Tommy Shrike said to Emilio Morales in English.

Shrike spoke Spanish fluently, but he never bothered if he could help it. He'd seen the way Spaniards looked down their noses at the Puerto Rican lilt to his accent: it was the same way people looked at wetbacks in the States. Plus, none of these dumb spics could pronounce his surname properly. *SHREE-kay*, what the fuck was that?

Emilio Morales, looked up from behind his desk and said, 'Señor Gomez has important business which he must attend to. He has instructed us to wait here until he returns.'

Shrike was sitting the way he always did when he was with a client, the ankle of one leg resting on the knee of the other, his right arm dangling over the chair back like he didn't have a care in the world. It was a pose he had perfected over the many years he'd worked the private security racket, a pose that showed the rich bastards who hired him that, while they might have bought the temporary right to tell him what to do, Tommy Shrike was still his own boss.

Shrike looked at his Rolex: it was an hour since he'd dropped the package off at the reporter's house. The prick must have seen the contents by now. It was good that he'd had visitors – and even better that the frump of a girlfriend was present, too. With a bit of luck she'd have gotten a good look at the DVD's contents.

Shrike had filmed it earlier that afternoon. He'd taken real pleasure in soiling the bitch's bed. He hadn't planned on doing that, it had just sort of come to him on the spur of the moment. But then wasn't that what people paid Tommy Shrike for? He didn't just get the job done, he was creative about it, too.

Shrike had worked private security for sixteen years. As a younger man, he had gravitated towards the higher risk type of jobs, but at thirty-eight, Shrike had decided he'd had enough excitement. Guys he knew were out in Iraq, looking after diplomats and petrol execs, but Shrike didn't plan on taking a bullet for one of those idiots.

They were sitting in Morales's office, in a high-rise office block in the city centre. The office was big, the walls lined with leather-bound books and antiquities, everything gilt-edged and tastefully chosen to impress upon visitors the wealth and cultivation of the proprietor.

Everything, that was, except for the mobile on the desk.

That was one of those pay-as-you-go types you picked up for emergency calls, a crappy orange plastic thing. That intrigued Tommy. He'd seen Morales's eyes flicker towards it on a couple of occasions, as if he was waiting for the thing to start ringing.

Shrike sat back and considered what he knew of the situation.

Shrike had done work for Gomez before, but he'd only been working this job four days now. It all centred on this Varela guy. As far as Shrike had been able to make out, back in the day Varela had been employed in a similar capacity to

Shrike, a guy Gomez would call in to get things done on the QT.

Somehow, this Varela was linked to a public utility company Gomez and Morales had been involved with in the past. On the Monday of that week, the day before Shrike had chased the reporter away from the *ayuntamiento* in Las Jarapas, he and Gomez had spent the whole afternoon and most of the night going through the records in the council offices, removing any mention of this *Grupo La Flecha Rota* and its various offshoots from the council minutes, while the mayor looked on, pale and nervous.

Shrike had seen the way Gomez and Morales had been following the stories in the newspapers, too. First, Phillips's death – that had been when they'd brought Shrike in to guard them both – and then this business with Escobar and his ex-wife, the one that had been murdered.

Gomez had been playing his cards close to his chest, the way he always did. That was no skin off Shrike's nose. The more they told him, the more he could help. It was their dollar. If they wanted to keep him in the dark, then so be it.

It was gone midnight when Gomez bustled into the room, smelling of wine and garlic, his fat little face wreathed in sweat, damp patches underneath the arms of his short sleeve shirt. You'd think with all his money, the least he could do was make sure he looked good.

Gomez laid his briefcase on the desk and sat down opposite Shrike.

'How do things stand with the journalist, Mr Shrike?' Gomez said.

'I've taken steps along the lines we discussed.'

Gomez nodded. 'Good. But do you think that it will dissuade the reporter from pursuing the story?'

Shrike shrugged. 'You can never tell how people will react. It might do. Or perhaps it will put his back up and he'll dig his heels in more. The main thing is, it will give him something else to worry about for a while. That's why I went for his woman. You get a much better reaction that way. And that's what you seem to need right now, isn't it? Time to think. Time to regroup.'

Gomez and Morales exchanged a look that Shrike recognised: the two men shared a secret that scared them. And it had something to do with that orange cell-phone.

Shrike sat in silence while the two men whispered. They seemed to be disagreeing about something. Finally, Gomez made placatory gestures towards Morales and turned to face Shrike.

'Anyway,' Gomez said. 'A new situation has arisen. One that is potentially far more dangerous.'

Shrike sat forward in his chair.

'Dangerous how?'

'I have just spoken to a P.I. that I use. He has managed to locate Sixto Escobar.'

'And?'

'Escobar is dead. He'd been knifed. His bodyguard, too. It is definitely Varela who is doing this. The P.I. found these papers stuffed into Escobar's mouth,' Gomez said, showing them to Morales. Morales's face blanched as he looked through them.

Shrike said, 'So, what is Varela's beef with you guys?'

Gomez plucked the waxed ends of his moustache. 'A number of years ago, Señor Varela was imprisoned for a crime which was indirectly linked with services he had performed for my business associates and me. Although he had been paid well for his services over the years, we deemed it prudent to offer the man an additional stipend in order to compensate him for the inconvenience of his incarceration.'

'In other words, so he'd keep his yap shut, right?'

Gomez's chubby face puckered at the crudity of Shrike's language. 'Precisely. However, it now transpires that the full amount was not paid to him.'

'What happened?'

'The money was entrusted to a third party who neglected –'

'Sixto Escobar is what happened,' Morales said, slapping a hand on the table. 'I told you at the time not to give the money to him, Sebastian.'

'And I told you at the time of the benefits of deniability that were afforded to us by indirect contact with Varela.' He turned back towards Shrike. 'It now transpires that neither Sixto Escobar nor Martyn Phillips paid Varela the money that was owed him.'

Shrike said, 'How much was Varela short-changed?'

'There were five affected parties. We each agreed to pay ten thousand euros each. Of which only thirty thousand was paid.'

'Does Varela know you two paid up?'

'It's highly unlikely. The added complication is that Señor Varela seems to be in possession of certain documents that are highly damaging to us.'

'How did he get them?' Morales said.

Gomez shrugged. 'I have been reliably informed that Lucia Borja visited Varela in prison. I imagine she took them to him.'

'But how did she get them?' Morales said, still looking at the paperwork.

'There is only one way she could have. She must have gone to Florentino Yagüe and bullied him. You know how Florentino was towards the end, Emilio, the way his conscience pricked him. If she had applied pressure to the right spot, I'll warrant that Florentino crumbled in a matter of minutes.'

'Let me guess,' Shrike said. 'This has something to do with this *La Flecha Rota* thing that we spent hours removing from the council records.'

'Correct.'

'Well, as long as you've got me, you don't have to worry about Varela. I can guarantee your –'

Morales scoffed. 'Let me be perfectly frank, Señor Shrike. I cannot afford to be seen wandering the street accompanied by a bodyguard as if I were a common criminal. My only concern at this juncture is my investors. It is imperative I maintain their continued confidence. To do that, I need to avoid negative publicity of any kind. All other factors are either secondary or irrelevant.'

Shrike nearly lashed out against the contemptuous tone in Morales's voice. He counted to three, slowly and silently. Then he said, 'In that case I think you should pay this Varela what you owe him. Can you contact him?'

'We have only one way of contacting the man.'

'How?

'Through personal ads in the newspaper,' Gomez said.

Shrike stifled a laugh. Jesus, these bozos were too much. 'A newspaper?'

'It was a method we employed to contact him before the advent of mobile telephones and the internet. We have already placed advertisements on three separate days instructing him to contact us on this pre-paid mobile and offering to reimburse him for four times the amount that is owed.'

'And?'

'So far there has been no response.'

'Perhaps he's not seen the message in the newspaper?'

'That's unlikely. He knows it was our only method of contact. Why leave these documents with Escobar's body if he did not want to open a dialogue?'

Morales sat with his fingers meshed, tapping his thumbs together.

'From my recollection of the man, Varela never seemed overly concerned about money. Not once he had purchased that wretched house from Escobar.'

Gomez smiled. 'Emilio, *everyone* has their price. Besides, it is the only realistic option open to us.'

'Seems to me you have another option,' Shrike said, putting on his best tough guy face. 'You could pay me to make Varela go away.'

Morales looked at Shrike from above his glasses. Gomez shook his head.

'As Señor Morales has already outlined, we cannot afford any hint of a public scandal. Besides, you could fail. And then what would happen?'

Shrike could feel a vein throbbing in his temple, the vein that always started to throb when he was pissed about something. There was something about the kudos they gave this Varela guy. Shrike already hated him.

'You think he's better than me then?' he said through clenched teeth.

Gomez laughed. 'I have absolutely no idea. But Varela fights hard and he fights dirty. People who underestimate him normally discover that too late. But that's not what this is about. I intend to pay for the simple reason that –'

The sudden ring tone stopped him mid-sentence. Gomez looked at Morales as the orange mobile on the desk vibrated and pinged to say a text message had been received.

'You see, Emilio,' Gomez said with a smug smile, reaching for the phone.

2

FOR A MOMENT, no-one in Danny's living room moved. Everyone merely stood and stared at the television screen. And then chaos broke out.

Children bawled, shocked parents tried to comfort them and Marsha began to scream, while the ski-masked figure on the screen laughed hysterically, pissing onto Marsha's duvet. Danny could not find the remote control, so he ended up yanking the plug from the wall to silence the bastard. By that time, Marsha was outside, trembling and crying, while a gaggle of concerned party guests argued about how best to comfort her.

Paco came over to Danny and said in a terse whisper, 'What the fuck was that? Is that something to do with the story we've been covering? Because if it is, we are in deep –'

He stopped as Lourdes stepped back inside. She too was trembling – from anger.

'This is your fault,' she said, staring at Danny and Paco. 'Both of you. You've learned nothing from what happened before, did you? You should have stopped this when Danny got punched to the ground.'

Paco was going to speak to her, but she shrugged his arm

away. He told her they should go home, but she shook her head. 'I'm taking Marsha back to our house. You're going to Marsha's flat to help Danny clear up the mess.'

Within ten minutes, everyone was gone.

'I know who it must have been,' Danny said, but Paco held up a warning hand.

'Don't, Danny. I just don't want to hear it now.'

They drove to Marsha's flat in silence.

There was no damage inside apart from the slit newspaper page and the soiled duvet case. Danny stripped the sopping bedding and threw it away. The mattress would probably have to go, too, but he would let Marsha decide on that as the bed was the landlord's property.

Paco was close-lipped as they worked. Once they'd cleared things up at Marsha's flat, he refused Danny's offer of a lift home and left without saying goodbye.

Danny checked the door to the flat. Whoever it was had got in had done so without damaging the lock. As a piece of intimidation, it couldn't be faulted. He thought about Shrike. It must have been him.

The bastard.

Danny was about to drive to Paco's house in search of Marsha when she phoned him to say that she was staying in a hotel that night.

'I need time alone, Danny. I've got some difficult choices to make.'

Danny spent the whole journey home wondering what the hell those choices might involve.

Back home, he put the DVD on again and watched it through twice until he was certain he recognised the lean, muscular profile on the television screen: it was Tomás Shrike. Or someone very like him.

Next morning, he went to the hotel Marsha was staying at bright and early with the intention of driving her to the airport, but when he arrived she was in the process of checking out and already had a taxi waiting.

Danny drove to the airport anyway and waited for her outside. When Marsha's taxi pulled up she saw Danny and gave a thin smile. They embraced, but when Danny tried to kiss her she put a finger to his lips.

'Don't, Danny.'

'Why not?'

'Because I am absolutely bloody furious with you, that's why,' she said, in voice that was curiously flat. 'In fact, I'm so angry, I can't even *be* angry yet. It's one thing to spend your every waking hour chasing a story, Danny, to the exclusion of everything else in your life. That I can deal with. But when the story leads to someone breaking into my house – *my* house, Danny, not yours – and trying to intimidate us, I draw the line. What you've done goes beyond stupidity. I asked you whether this was going to be dangerous, and look what's happened. I wanted to see how far you would go if I didn't raise any objections. I think you've proved now how insane you are about pursuing your stories. I just . . . look, if this is how your life is going to be, I'm not sure I can be part of it. Not at the moment, anyway.'

'Jesus, what's that supposed to mean? You're going to dump me here in the fucking airport?'

Marsha wiped tears from her eyes. 'Look, there are things we need to talk about but this just isn't the moment. I'll phone you when I get to England and my head's a bit clearer. I've got a lot on my mind.'

When they parted, Marsha's eyes were wet with tears. Danny watched her go through a mist of his own tears.

After that, he went home and tidied the house. A plate of leftover barbecue meat had been on the table overnight and cats had gnawed the bones and distributed them all over the garden. He cleared up the mess and put out all the rubbish. Then he sat on the sofa and stared at the wall.

He considered getting drunk – God knows, there was enough leftover booze to keep him pissed for a week – but he knew that wouldn't help, so he spent an hour in his office, trying to write.

He couldn't concentrate.

His mind was racing. Part of him was sick with worry about what this whole business with Marsha meant. He smoked endless cigarettes, analysing and reanalysing what she'd said and how she'd said it and what the hidden meanings might have been, his mood pinging between reassurance and despair. Christ, he'd not felt such emotional upheaval since he was a teenager – some things about being in love never changed.

But part of him was still preoccupied with the story. And, although Danny took the full blame for what had happened to Marsha's flat, he also knew that he would carry on, that he would see this thing through. Even more so, now: backing down to pricks like Shrike and Gomez wasn't an option.

At ten o'clock Paco Pino phoned.

'I'm taking a week off, Danny,' he said in a strangely staccato voice, almost as if he were reading the words. It took

Danny a moment to realise why: Lourdes was listening. 'When I come back to work, I'm going to cover straightforward news stories, nothing more, nothing less. I don't care if I have to go back to doing wedding and baby photos, I can't stand the stress anymore. Is that clear, mate?'

At 10:30 Danny's phone rang again. The number began with 0049.

The chirpy German press agent from MWGP said she had organised an interview with Antonio Saez, as per Danny's request last week. 'I'm afraid three p.m. today is the only time he can manage before October, though,' she said. 'He's going on holiday.'

Danny gave a rueful smile. It was an old trick, to spring an interview on a journalist with only a few hours' warning.

Danny said yes, he'd be there at three and hung up.

He stared at the wall. An interview with Antonio Saez, Mr Congeniality himself.

Just what he needed.

~

The MGWP research facility was located in a rural area to the east of Almería city, close to the airport. The main buildings were at the centre of a huge piece of real estate filled with plastic greenhouses and rows of photovoltaic plates.

The main office was situated in a building of chrome and glass. The flags of Spain, Germany, Almería and the EU fluttered in the light breeze coming off the nearby sea. The foyer was open plan and had a fountain with a clump of rich foliage in its centre.

Danny told the receptionist that he had an appointment with Señor Saez.

'He's not back from lunch yet.'

Danny looked at his watch. He was fifteen minutes early. 'Will you tell me when he gets back?'

The receptionist gave a wry smile. 'Keep sitting there and you'll hear when he gets back, I promise you.'

Danny wondered what she meant as he sat on a couch and flicked through the trade magazines on the glass coffee table.

A few minutes later, the distant roar of an engine became audible. Even from a distance, you could tell it belonged to a powerful car. The sound gained in volume until it became a throaty roar that Danny could feel vibrating in the pit of his stomach. Seconds later, an ice-white 2-door coupé pulled into the car park. The driver parked close to the main office and let the engine idle for a few seconds, as if giving everyone the chance to hear it purr, then switched it off. Danny had never had any interest in cars, but he knew the engine produced the sort of sound that would have had Paco Pino cooing in admiration.

'Is that Señor Saez?' Danny said.

The secretary nodded.

'Nice car. How much do they pay these guys?'

She smiled sadly. 'I wouldn't know. But I think he bought it with some money he won on the lottery.'

'Lucky him. When did he have this bit of luck then?'

'Oh, a long time ago. He's had that car eight or nine years now.'

Antonio Saez was one of those middle-aged guys who wore his jeans hitched high and his shirt tucked in, the ensemble held together by a thick leather belt with a chunky silver buckle. Saez's harsh eyes were sandwiched either side of a ploughshare of a nose and his eyebrows were thick, dark and set in a permanent frown. Colour him blue and he could have done a passable imitation of the eagle from The Muppets.

Danny followed Saez up to a first storey office. Everything inside the office was either white, aqua blue or transparent. Saez angled the blinds to stop sunlight shining directly on the interior. Even so, the impression of being inside a freshly-sucked mint remained.

Danny took out his pen and notepad.

'Before we begin, I'd like to clear one thing up,' he said. 'Why did you phone Sebastian Gomez after we spoke the other day? I take it that was you?'

Saez hesitated a moment, then said, 'Yes, it was me. I phoned him to ask for confirmation of what you had told me about Hector's death.'

'So you're not in bed with Gomez, then? Figuratively speaking.'

'What a world you people live in,' Saez said, shaking his head. 'No, I am not in league with Señor Gomez. Nor with anyone else. Now, according to the information I've been sent from head office, you want to ask me about the report we published in April 2000. Here,' he said, tossing a thick report with laminated covers onto the table. 'Feel free to peruse it. I'll happily answer any questions you have,' he added with a smug smile.

Danny flicked through a few pages, which were thick with scientific notation and the type of dense academic prose that only an expert would understand. Danny returned Saez's smile as he turned to the front page and examined the details of the scientific team that had done the research for the report.

'Why isn't Hector Castillo mentioned here?' Danny said.

'Why should he be?'

'I have it on good authority that he was involved in taking measurements for this investigation.'

Saez shifted in his seat and fiddled with the knot in his tie, clearly considering how best to answer.

'Yes, you're quite correct,' he said, speaking slowly now, as if considering every syllable, 'in that Hector Castillo was in charge of a preliminary study into drift patterns of the pluto-nium dust at Palomares. Due to the explosions of the conven-tional charges in bombs numbers two and four, the plutonium was vapourised. Winds at the time spread contamination into a number of areas some distance from the actual places where the bombs fell to earth. It was a project that was joint-financed by the University of Almería and by CIEMAT, although the actual groundwork was undertaken by MWGP.'

'Were any readings taken in the municipality of Las Jarapas?'

'Yes. And in the Sierra Almagrera as well. As the title says, we were trying to establish whether plutonium had spread beyond the immediate areas of the accident.'

'And?'

'And we were pleased to say that it hadn't. Not to any significant degree, anyway.'

'And Hector helped establish this?'

'Yes.'

'Why isn't he mentioned, then?'

'As I said before, Hector worked on an earlier draft.'

'And what happened to that earlier draft?'

Saez shifted in his seat.

Danny smiled and said, 'If you want me to contact your head office and have them tell you to tell me, I'll happily do it. I've got the number here.'

Saez's frown deepened. 'All right, if you must know, Señor Castillo was in charge of taking more than 400 separate soil measurements with an instrument known as a FIDLER.'

'That's an unfortunate acronym. What does it stand for?'

'Field Instrument for the Detection of Low Energy Radiation. Señor Castillo's readings were to be used to help build a 3D radiometric map of the areas we were studying. However, once all the readings had been taken, it transpired that a problem had occurred with the software used to record the readings, which thereby invalidated all of Señor Castillo's work. So badly, in fact, that we had to take an entire slew of his readings again. Hector took responsibility for the mistake and asked that he be removed from the project, a request to which I readily acceded, given that he had cost us months of work.'

'When was this?'

'I really don't remember.'

'In which area did he take the erroneous readings?'

'Again, I do not recollect.'

'What about his consultancy work?'

'Consultancy work? You mean as in working for an outside company?'

'I'm unaware of the appellation being used for anything else,' Danny said.

Saez's eyes narrowed. 'I refuse to be drawn on Hector Castillo. Now, unless you have any more questions specifically related to the report, I am under no obligation to answer you. In which case, I'd like you to leave.'

Saez showed Danny to the door and closed it behind him without saying goodbye.

Danny went downstairs. Before he got into his car he noted the details of Saez's car, an Aston Martin Vanquish. Then he took a photo of the vehicle and texted a motor mechanic friend with the question, 'How much would this have cost ten years ago?'

Five minutes later the answer came back. 'Depends on mods. Between 100-140k euros.'

'So, you had a lottery win, did you?' Danny said, looking back towards Saez's office. 'Lucky old you.'

3

That afternoon, Danny met his prison contact, Esteban, at a bar opposite the port of Almería. The two men were drinking grape juice and eating razor clams. At least, Danny was on the grape juice. Esteban had the day off, so he had been ordering himself glasses of white wine. They were on the third round, now, and the table was cluttered with long, thin shells.

Work in prison administration clearly suited Esteban: he'd put on a stone since Danny last saw him, and the gaunt, hassled look he'd had when working as a guard was gone.

'So, Varela was in prison for perverting the course of justice?' Danny said as he looked through the two pages of information Esteban had provided, trying to decide whether it was worth the price he was going to have to pay: the food and drink were on Danny, which meant he was already 25 euros out of pocket.

'Yep,' Esteban said. 'Apparently, Varela had ties to a corrupt policeman and one of the services he offered was filing false police reports to help provide people with alibis; the policeman could falsify the paperwork so that it proved you were somewhere else when a crime was being committed. When the policeman got caught, Varela was one of the people he grassed up. Varela was put inside in 2007. Then in 2010 he requested a move to a prison in Cantabria.'

'And this is what Varela looks like now?' Danny said, looking at the printout of a passport photograph attached to the top sheet with a paperclip.

'That was taken last year.'

Danny examined the photo. You could tell the guy was a former legionnaire. He had one of those fuzzy beards the legionnaires grew, although his dark hair was shaved short. The skin that was visible on his face was pitted and scarred and a piece of his right earlobe was missing. His thick neck seemed to grow straight out of the muscles on his shoulder. Danny thought back to Jorge's description of the man: a boxer's physique but a bare-knuckle face. That was pretty much right on the nail. Not a bloke you'd want to get on the wrong side of.

'And what's this address here? Calle Eli Wallach, Number 27,' Danny said.

'Varela corresponded with that address nearly three hundred times during his incarceration.'

Danny looked at the five-number postcode.

'This property is in Las Jarapas. I'll bet it's on the Bellavista.' He thought about what Jorge Valenzuela had told him, about the house Sixto Escobar had sold to Varela. It had to be the same one.

The second sheet of paper held a list of library books that Varela had read. The man had a strange taste in literature. He'd borrowed Don Quixote three times in the first two years of his incarceration, interspersed with the sort of books you'd imagine a former soldier reading: thrillers, military memoirs, histories of the Second World War, books on self-improvement.

And then suddenly his tastes had changed.

After a certain date, Varela had begun to request books from other prisons, books with titles like Cancer Explained and The Biology of Cancer.

'What was his interest in cancer?' Danny said.

'Who knows with a morbid bastard like that?' Esteban said with a shrug. 'Plus, don't forget prison libraries aren't exactly filled with the latest best sellers. Most of them are made up from hand-outs donated by local institutions. Those medical textbooks probably came from a university. Having said that, though. . .'

Esteban motioned for Danny to hand him the info.

'Here it is,' he said, pointing at two dates on the bottom of the first page. 'There were two occasions when Varela was granted compassionate leave to visit a sick relative. Well, actually, he visited the person the first time. The second was to attend a funeral.'

'Who was it?'

'I couldn't access those sorts of details. It must have been a close relative, though. And he or she must have been seriously ill. They don't grant that sort of thing lightly.'

'Like someone with terminal cancer?'

'For example. Does that mean anything?'

Danny shrugged. The second page held a list of books Varela had requested, but to which he had been denied access. There were three titles. All three were related to radiation and its effects.

'Did you find anything about the visits he received?' Danny said.

'It's right there at the top of the second page. Varela only had four visits the whole time he was inside. Three from someone called Wilhemina Schmidt. And one from a Spanish lady, Lucia Borja.'

Esteban smiled when he saw Danny's reaction. 'Now that name *does* mean something.'

Danny wasn't listening. He was looking at the name on the page, hardly able to believe his eyes.

Lucia Borja had visited Varela in prison on May 7th, 2010.

Danny looked at the date. The very next day, Varela had requested a book entitled, *Radiation: What it is and what you need to know.*

That couldn't be a coincidence. What had Lucia Borja told him? And why had Lucia Borja driven all the way up to a prison in Cantabria to visit the man?

Esteban patted his stomach. 'This detective stuff is thirsty work. I reckon we should order one last round. What do you say, Danny?'

Danny was smiling as he reread the papers. 'You order whatever you want, *amigo mio.*'

4

T HERE WAS A guy back in Atlantic City who used to laugh
at Tommy Shrike and his clean-living ways. He used to sing
Tommy a song whenever their paths crossed in a bar or a strip-
joint: *'Don't drink, don't smoke, what do you?'*

One night, Tommy had bundled the guy into the boot of
a car and driven him out to the woods by Brigantine Boule-
vard. Then he had taken a claw hammer and a wood block
and showed the guy's fingers *exactly* what it was that Tommy
Shrike liked to do.

That had been twenty years ago, back when Tommy Shrike
had still gone by his father's surname, Finch.

Tommy Finch had come a long way since. He wasn't called
Finch anymore, for starters. Even as a kid, Tommy had always
thought the name sounded way too pussy, so when he got into
private security work he started looking for a badass substi-
tute. At first he considered obvious alternatives like Hawk,
Falcon or Kestrel, but decided they would make him sound
like an '80s TV star. Then he found an article in a magazine
about the shrike, the butcher-bird that made a kind of larder
by impaling insects and lizards on thorns.

He filed the deed poll papers the very same day.

Shrike had done it all in private security work: close-pro-
tection, mannyguarding, paparazzi management. He talked it

tough because he knew damn well he could walk it tough, too. Tommy had started out as a boxer, but since then he'd mixed in a lot of oriental shit: kick-boxing, muay thai, some penchak silat. Tommy was all about the heavy duty techniques: sweeps, locks, chokes, throws. He was fast, too: he could kick half the teeth out of a guy's head and still have time to break the prick's nose before he hit the ground.

Tommy knew that for a fact.

Sometimes, Tommy longed for the old days: bust a few heads, break some bones, get some blood on his fists again. He did some semi-pro cage fighting when the urge took him – twelve bouts undefeated, all 12 K.O.s – but it wasn't the same. You didn't get the same thrill. There was a ref to stop the fights just when things were getting interesting. Because it wasn't putting the other guy down that Tommy liked; it was standing over him afterwards, deciding which bits to break, that gave Shrike a real hard-on.

That was what pissed him off so much about this Varela guy. So what if this bloke was ex-Legión? Shrike had never reckoned much to soldiers. What sort of a faggot needed a dozen other guys with him to start a fight? It took a real man to do it Shrike's way, to go it alone. The intimation that Tommy couldn't take this Varela prick – kill him – had really got him pissed.

For starters, Varela didn't seem anywhere near as tough as he was supposed to be. The whole conversation on the orange mobile yesterday had been carried out via SMS, with Gomez and Morales giving Shrike instructions on what to write.

Varela had arranged for the money to be exchanged at 20.00 at an underpass in the centre of the city. Shrike had already been there to scope the place out. The underpass was a disaster for a handover: dark, deserted and full of shadows, and yet also overlooked by the terraces of about three different bars. Anyone standing around there would stick out like a sore thumb, and it was the perfect place for an ambush. If Varela didn't know that, he was just some rank amateur.

And yet he was going to walk away with eighty grand . . .

Tommy was in the basement of a bank on the Paseo de Almería, standing in the corridor outside the basement room that held the bank's security deposit boxes. The door was half ajar and through it he could see Morales and Gomez counting out half-inch-high stacks of fifty-euro notes from their respective boxes and stacking the money into a metal security briefcase.

Jesus, Tommy thought, there wasn't any justice in the world.

Ten minutes later, Gomez emerged with the briefcase. Shrike said, 'Do you want me to take that for you?'

Gomez shook the security chain that ran from his wrist to the briefcase. 'You'll get this tonight and not before.'

'Guess I'll have to wait, then,' Shrike said, falling in behind them. As the three men ascended the stairs, Shrike's narrowed eyes never left the shiny silver briefcase chained to the lawyer's wrist.

5

IN THE EARLY evening Danny drove back to the Bellavista.

Number 27 Calle Eli Wallach was on the western edge of the Bellavista estate, the side that faced inland. The houses there were smaller and terraced, their gardens overlooking swathes of parched earth and scruffy foliage.

The man who answered Danny's knocking was in his late fifties and sported that unbecoming combination of bare chest, shorts, sandals and socks that only British men deem suitable attire for hot weather.

He was initially suspicious when Danny enquired how long he had lived there and from whom he had bought the house, but eventually curiosity got the better of him; he introduced himself as George Yudmin and invited Danny inside. Danny cast an envious glance at the condensation forming on the side of George's can of Stella as he followed him into the garden.

A woman on a sun-lounger raised a sleepy head as Danny walked past and pulled a blue beach towel up to cover the cellulite dimples on her thighs. The sun-lounger was set out beside a swimming pool, but the pool was only half-full. Danny could see the bottom of the pool was covered with dark grit.

'It's a bloody disgrace,' Yudmin said when he saw where Danny was looking. 'I've been trying to fill the ruddy thing for three months now and that's all I've managed to get. The water supply here is hopeless. We're holding a protest this Saturday in Almería city, outside the government offices.'

Danny thought of Alan Neave and nodded to show he was already aware of it.

Yudmin got Danny a glass of iced tea and cracked open another can of Stella for himself. His wife came through to join them in the living room.

'What can you tell me about the people that lived here before you?' Danny said.

'There was a German woman. And her daughter.'

Danny thought about Wilhelmina Schmidt, the woman who had visited Varela in prison. He asked Yudmin if that was the woman's name. Yudmin nodded.

'Did you ever meet Mrs Schmidt?' Danny said.

'Just the once.'

'What was she like?'

'Very German. Dark, intense. She wasn't very friendly. But then she was under a lot of pressure.'

'Why's that?'

'Her daughter was desperately ill. In fact, I got the feeling they were selling the house to raise money for her treatment.'

'How old was the daughter?'

'Young. Perhaps nine or ten. It was difficult to tell as she was so ill, the poor little mite.'

'What was wrong with her?'

'She had stomach cancer.'

'And it had spread to her lungs and pancreas, as well,' Yudmin's wife added. 'The poor thing died shortly after we bought this place. That's what I heard anyway.'

'Heard from whom?'

'The estate agent who sold us the property.'

'Do you mind giving me the name of the estate agent?'

The couple exchanged awkward looks.

'I would do gladly, Mr Sanchez, but it won't do you any good. You see, she was murdered a few days ago. In fact, you wrote something about it on the Sureste News website.'

It took Danny a moment to realise what Yudmin meant.

'Do you mean to say that Lucia Borja sold you this house?'

'Yes, that's her. I mean, I thought she was a dreadful woman but, well, you wouldn't wish that on anyone.'

'Why didn't you like her?'

'First of all, a week before we were due to exchange contracts, she informed us we had to pay 40,000 euros in cash to avoid paying tax. Apparently, it's common practice out here. They even had a room set aside for us to go and count the ruddy money out. Absolute bloody madness.'

His wife nodded.

'And then, two days before the actual sale, we were going through some paperwork and this Borja woman suddenly rushed off and left us with one of her underlings.'

'Really?'

'Yes. It was when we were sorting out a difficulty that had arisen with the exchange of the deeds. When we came to actually buy the property, it turned out it didn't even belong to this Schmidt woman. It belonged to the daughter.'

'The ten-year-old?'

'The very same. Mrs Schmidt had the what's-its-name. . . the power to sign on her daughter's behalf and all that, but when we actually came to the deeds, it was all in the little girl's name.'

'Can you remember what she was called?'

'It was Maria something or other,' the wife said. 'I can go and find the paperwork if you think it's important.'

Danny said, yes, it was. 'If she was born in Spain, she would have had two surnames, the paternal one first, the maternal one second. I'd like to know what the other one was.'

The wife got up and began to rummage in cupboards.

'So, you think the sight of this girl's name on the deeds was what prompted the sudden change in Señora Borja?' Danny said.

Yudmin nodded.

'You should have seen the look on her face when she saw that. She was like the cat that got the cream. She just stopped mid-sentence. We were going through the paperwork and she suddenly got up and walked out. She didn't even come along to the signing of the deeds.'

'Yes, you're quite right Mr Sanchez,' Yudmin's wife said, coming back with the paperwork, 'she did have two surnames. Schmidt was the maternal surname.'

'What was the paternal surname?'

'Varela. María Esmerelda Varela Schmidt.'

6

GABRIEL VARELA STOOD in the darkness of the subterranean car park, waiting for Emilio Morales to emerge.

It was here that Varela had come to sign the paperwork for the house that Sixto Escobar had sold him. Morales had organised it so that the cash payment for the house would seem legitimate.

Varela had killed Hector Castillo the very next night. Gomez had set Castillo up with some bullshit excuse about meeting at a restaurant out by the beach, a restaurant with a nice dark alleyway right beside it.

Varela had killed the man quickly and quietly. He came at him from the front and hit him a single, well placed blow in the chest with his punch dagger, piercing his heart. He had caught Castillo as he fell and gently held his head as the man expired. Then he dragged the body by the heels to the end of the alleyway where Varela had parked, checked no one was looking, and then bundled the body into the boot, which he had covered with bin-liners.

Then he drove out to the Tabernas Desert, to the deep hole he had already dug. He wrapped the body in a linen shroud – he was determined to give it a decent burial – filled in the hole and rolled a big, flat boulder on the grave to hide signs of the freshly turned earth.

That night Varela had lain awake in bed considering what he had done. He was not a man given to brooding or worrying, and yet something about the matter bothered him. He knew that by killing he had crossed a line. There was no going back.

But there were to be no reprisals. The police organised searches, questioned colleagues and friends, but within a fortnight Hector Castillo's name had joined those of the thousands of other people that had disappeared in Spain no longer being investigated.

Varela had waited six months before he had had the house transferred into Esme's name. Esme and her mother moved in a week later.

It was the first time Varela had seen the mother smile in years, as she rushed from room to room with Esme in her arms, shouting, 'Look, liebling, all this is yours. Look what your Papa has bought you. It even has a swimming pool.'

After that, when he was arrested and put in prison it did not really bother him: he had taken care of Esme and, besides, he was used to life among liars and brutes. In some ways, prison was easier than life in *La Legión*. He did not really notice the walls and bars.

Not until Esme was diagnosed with cancer.

It was then that the full force of being caged hit him. He lay awake at night, staring at the strip light in the bare ceiling and wondering if this was punishment for his wickedness.

When her condition worsened, he told the mother, Wilhelmina, to sell the house and use the money to pay for private treatment. Wilhelmina's family had a flat in Cantabria, so she could live there with Esme. Varela applied for a prison transfer and the family relocated to the north of Spain.

Private medical bills had eaten through the 200,000 euros they got for the house. And still Esme's condition worsened. So much so, that one day they had put handcuffs on Varela and driven him to the hospital where Esme was being treated.

Varela had not recognised her at first. The disease had unpicked her, left her a shrivelled stick wrapped in white. But she had looked up at him that same way she always did, her eyes filled with love and utter faith in him, as if now that her Papá was there, he would make everything all right again.

How he had wept that night, alone in his cell, his face buried beneath his bolster so the prison guards would not see or hear him. He could not imagine a worse pain.

But then the Borja woman had come to the prison and told him the truth about what had caused Esme's illness, about *Suministros La Flecha Rota* and about what the bastards had allowed to happen.

After that, he had raged with an implacable inner fire, prowling up and down like an angry beast within a cage, prodded by the goads of his own conscience. He had wanted to kill every person he came across, but he knew he could not risk any action that might prolong his incarceration.

He thought about Castillo, and understood why Gomez and Escobar and all the others had wanted the man killed: Castillo had known. He had known and he had wanted to warn people.

And Varela had killed him.

That was the worst thing, the knowledge that the whole situation was partly Varela's fault. How had he ever thought to prosper by committing murder? He could see it now, that everything he'd ever touched had turned to shit, King Midas in reverse. Knowledge of his guilt was like a huge weight that dragged behind him: the rasp of its presence was everywhere he went . . .

Varela turned as he heard the sound of the metal gate opening. Headlight beams swept the concrete walls as Morales's big silver Jaguar came down the ramp and headed for his reserved parking space.

Varela came at the man from behind as he emerged from his car.

Morales's eyebrows rose in surprise, and terror spread across his gaunt face. His briefcase fell to the ground

'Gabriel . . .' he said, stepping backwards, fumbling with his mobile phone. Varela crossed the distance between them in two strides. Morales tried to defend himself and cried out for help. Varela pushed his flailing hands aside and broke the man's nose with his fist.

Morales sank to his knees, blood flowing between his fingers.

'You know why I'm here, don't you?' Varela said, holding a cable tie taut between his gloved hands.

Morales shook his head. 'Gabriel, we've paid. The money's all been paid.'

That stopped Varela dead. 'What do you mean?' he said. 'What money?'

Morales sputtered blood. He was crying now.

'We put the advert in the newspaper. You answered. On

the mobile. The money you wanted. We're paying at eight o'clock tonight. 80,000 euros.'

Varela lay the edge of his punch dagger horizontally across the man's larynx. 'Where? Tell me, quickly.'

7

A N EX-GIRLFRIEND ONCE told Tommy Shrike she could always tell when he was plotting something: apparently he licked his lips a lot, and he stopped blinking.

Tommy hadn't blinked for about three minutes now.

He was sitting in the driver's seat of his car with the metal security briefcase on his lap. His eyes flickered towards the clock on the dashboard.

19:43.

He was thinking about the same thing he'd been considering all day: was he seriously going to let this Varela prick walk away with eighty grand? Or should he keep the cash for himself?

But that meant he would have to silence Varela first. That way, Gomez and Morales would never know. It would seem like Varela had been paid and was satisfied.

Shrike had spent the morning rigging up a strangling wire, attaching wooden handles to each end. He needed to get enough pull on the wire for it to bite into the flesh around Varela's neck. That way, Varela could scrabble all he wanted, but there wouldn't be any way of getting purchase on the strangling wire.

Shrike had chosen the garrotte because he needed to do the deed quietly, but he also wanted it up close and personal.

He wanted to whisper his name into Varela's ear as he died: Tommy Shrike. Tommy Shrike.

Shrike knew a dozen ways to make the money disappear afterwards, to wash it clean and keep it for himself. Or he could use it to set himself up dealing. Eighty grand would buy six or seven decent bricks of coke. Cut it with glucose and you could easily double your money.

But before he did anything, he needed to check the money was all there. He didn't trust Morales, and he definitely didn't trust Gomez.

He took his bowie knife and hammer and cracked the briefcase open.

There.

It was open. There was no turning back now.

He checked through the wads of banknotes. It was all there, all eighty thousand.

Shrike ran his fingers around the inside of the briefcase, checking the lining. He paused when he found a bulge inside the lining. Shrike didn't need to slit it open to know that it was some form of GPS device.

He smiled. So, Gomez and Morales didn't trust him.

He left the GPS where it was for now. He'd figure out what to do with it once he'd dealt with Varela.

Shrike closed the briefcase and tossed it onto the back seat. Then he put his fingers to the wooden handles of the garrotte in his pocket.

'Time to walk the walk, Tommy boy,' he said softly as he started the car.

8

Danny was sitting in his car outside George Yudmin's house with the arthritic air-con system turned up to max, going over his notes.

A young girl named Varela had owned the house – had owned it since late 2005 – a house that had previously been sold for a ridiculously low price to Gabriel Varela. This Maria Esmerelda had to be Gabriel Varela's daughter. That same girl had died of cancer.

Danny had asked Yudmin to try to remember precisely when in 2010 Lucia Borja had noticed the girl's name on the deeds. Yudmin shrugged but his wife said, 'Yes, I remember. It was on May 4th.'

'Are you absolutely certain?'

She nodded. 'I remember because George always told that stupid Star Wars joke: May the Fourth be with you.'

May the fourth. That was three days before Borja had visited Varela in prison.

There could only be one explanation. Borja knew the girl was terminally ill. But practically as soon as she had realised the girl was related to Varela she had driven all the way across Spain to visit Varela in prison. Almería to Cantabria: that was a twelve-hour drive – twenty-four hours for the return trip.

Borja had told Varela something that had made him believe

his daughter's illness was linked to radiation. Danny knew that from the library books Varela had read in prison.

But in that case, why had Varela gone after Martyn Phillips? That part didn't add up. And where did Hector Castillo fit into the picture? Danny was missing something. The trouble was, he was out of his depth when it came to anything but the most rudimentary science. That meant he needed to find someone who did understand and could explain things to him.

He looked at his watch: it was nearly eight o'clock. There was still time to catch someone at the university.

Danny made a point of maintaining good relations with the press department at the University of Almería: you couldn't put a price on the amount of expert knowledge to which it gave him access. Danny phoned, explained what it was that he needed and stressed that it was important. The press officer got back to him ten minutes later and said that there was a Professor Aceveda on campus who could speak to him at nine, after he'd finished lecturing at the summer school the university ran.

Danny got in his car and drove south.

The UAL campus begins fifty metres from the coast. Students in some faculty buildings can look out of the window and see waves foaming on the rocky breakwaters.

Professor Cristiano Aceveda was around Danny's age and looked a little like the Richard Dreyfuss character in *Jaws*: he had the same neatly trimmed beard and glasses and wore the same formal/informal combination of shirt, tie and jeans.

They went to the café on the edge of the campus and ordered iced coffee. A wall-mounted television burbled in the background, tuned to the local news channel.

'I've been told you are looking for information on pluto-nium,' Aceveda said.

'Yes. Specifically in relation to the Palomares Incident. And to the possibility of there still being undiscovered plots of ir-radiated earth.'

The professor frowned and some of the amiability left his face.

'Is there something the matter?' Danny said.

'About two years ago, I had a visit from a gentleman who asked me questions along those exact same lines. When he didn't like my answers, he became angry and began ranting about all sorts of wild nonsense. He even accused me of lying and accepting bribes. I had to get security to eject him.' The professor looked at Danny over the top of his glasses. 'You wouldn't happen to be anything to do with that man, would you? His name was Margaux, Louis Margaux.'

That was the man Alan Neave had mentioned, the guy from the Bellavista Residents for Truth website. Danny shook his head.

'I know who you're talking about,' Danny said, 'and I've nothing to do with him. In fact, my interest here is purely back-ground research. I promise I won't quote you on anything. I just need help understanding what dangers are present in plu-tonium- contaminated soil.'

The professor sighed. He removed his glasses and cleaned the lenses on his shirt sleeve.

'OK. But first, I want it made perfectly clear that my answers will be totally unbiased and impartial. If you want the facts about Palomares and the plutonium there, I can give them to you, as far as we know them. But they may not be particularly newsworthy.'

Danny flipped his notepad open. 'How much of a health risk does plutonium- contaminated soil pose?'

'Well, this is the big question. On the one hand, plutonium is about as toxic a substance as you can get and has a half-life of 24,000 years. The plutonium Safety Exposure Limit for workers at nuclear plants in the USA was 500 billionths of a gram. Also, it's difficult to answer exactly where the risk begins, as it implies there is a cliff edge where at one concentration everything is fine, and then an increase causes a problem. In fact is it a continuous scale, with increasing risk.

'However, plutonium is primarily an alpha particle emitter. Since alpha particles are heavy – relatively speaking – they are easily stopped by the first thing they encounter. Clothing, a piece of paper, even human skin is sufficient to prevent alpha particles from entering the human body. Added to that, alpha particles can travel only a very short distance in air. Approximately 1.4 inches, if memory serves.'

'What about if they get inside the human body? Say from breathing in the dust.'

'That's a very different story. In the case of plutonium being inhaled or ingested, then it can cause significant damage as the internal organs would be attenuating the alpha particles. And the plutonium would settle on the surface of bones where it would affect newly dividing cells. Of course, the chances of inhaling or ingesting plutonium are thankfully miniscule. Unless you work in a nuclear facility, or someone slips it into your drink.'

'Could that have happened at Palomares? Could people

have inhaled it? Or ingested it?'

'There is no "could" about it, Mr Sanchez. It has *not* happened. That entire area has been subjected to the most stringent scrutiny, and the inhabitants of the village were carefully monitored. I'm afraid this is where my conversation with Señor Margaux became less amicable.'

'What about in Las Jarapas? Could people there have been affected?'

'Well, no, there was no scrutiny of the inhabitants of that municipality. But then again, there is no plutonium in that area. The university itself co-financed a study of the area at the turn of the century. Besides, even if there had been plutonium in the soil, it would have been spread over hundreds of metres. It would only really pose a threat if it were somehow concentrated in one place.'

'Concentrated?'

'Put all together. For example, the areas of Palomares that the Spanish government has been forced to expropriate and close off have a particularly high radiation count because the Americans dug trenches there and stored oil drums filled with radioactive earth in them, thereby concentrating an amount of plutonium that had previously been spread out over a wide area.'

'What about the groundwater? Could this stuff have seeped through into the groundwater?'

'No. In order to pose a real health threat, you'd have to have a concentration of contaminated soil flowing directly into an aquifer, something that in this case couldn't happen.'

'Say people had been exposed to irradiated soil. What would we be seeing?'

'Right, this is now pure speculation. I'll answer the question to satisfy your curiosity, but we are talking in purely hypothetical terms now, OK?'

Danny nodded.

Aceveda said, 'Well, in this purely hypothetical situation, you would be seeing a rash of lung cancer throughout the area. Possibly, some throat and mouth cancer, too. But the full effects would not be seen until maybe eight to twelve years after the original contamination. Before that, you would only get isolated cases. Children and the elderly are normally the most susceptible to developing cancers from this type of thing.

'However, it would be very difficult – *very* difficult – to pinpoint the cause of these illnesses as plutonium. While it is one of most harmful substances known to man, people with a vested interest can easily pay other scientists to say exactly the opposite – look at the example given by the tobacco industry. If legal action were brought, I think the best anyone could hope for would be to force an out-of-court settlement.'

Danny was jotting down notes while the television in the café burbled in the background. At that point, Aceveda began to explain in greater detail the way that alpha particles cause cancer, but Danny's attention began to wander. The news bulletin on the television was distracting him.

Danny could see the wall-mounted television screen over Aceveda's shoulder. As his eyes flickered towards the screen, he suddenly frowned, wondering why the hell Doug Sampson's face was spread across it.

He motioned to the bartender to turn the television up. Aceveda stopped talking and watched as the evening news bulletin blared out.

'. . . gun battle in the centre of Almería city. Reports that the American actor, Doug Sampson, was involved are yet to be confirmed, but the police have told us that two men have been killed and a third seriously injured.'

Danny's chair scraped on the floor as he stood.

'Sorry, professor,' he said. 'I've got to go.'

PART IV

SERPIENTE DE VERANO

March, 2005

'WHAT THE HELL *has happened?' Hector Castillo said, shaking his head as he looked through the sheets of laboratory analysis within the cardboard file. 'What have you done? These results can't possibly be right.'*

None of the other five men in the room responded; they stared glumly at the surface of the conference table, hoping someone else would reply. Sebastian Gomez broke the silence, his voice placatory.

'Hector, you're the scientist, that's why we're showing you this. What we need to know is what we're looking at and how serious a problem it might pose. According to what I understand, the current readings are only an infinitesimal amount over the safety level.'

Castillo sighed.

'As I've said three or four times now, when it comes to ingesting this stuff, the margins are infinitesimal. And the effect is cumulative. The more you ingest, the greater the risks. ¡Joder! look at this. The level is rising.' Castillo was rummaging through the pages of laboratory analysis faster now. 'But how could this be? Any one of these readings would have been immediately flagged by the regional government. You've got months of results here.'

Florentino Yagüe sat with his head bowed. Castillo turned towards him.

'We weren't looking for it,' Yagüe said. 'It's not something that would show up on normal testing.'

'But according to this you started these more rigorous tests

in September last year. Why has nothing been done since? Did you fake the readings, Florentino?'

Yagüe's lip trembled.

Again Gomez spoke. 'Florentino took the necessary steps to prevent undue panic from spreading. However, it now seems the problem is going to persist for the present time. So we need to decide how best to proceed.'

Emilio Morales said, 'Obviously, our primary objectives now must be to protect our investment and to firewall ourselves against possible legal action. With this in mind, I have drawn up a contingency plan should we have to cease trading and –'

'What the hell are you talking about?' Castillo said, his voice becoming shrill. 'Does that mean you're not going to warn people?'

The other five men exchanged nervous glances.

Gomez said, 'I feel going public with any of this information would be unwise at this juncture.'

'Go public?' Hector Castillo scrunched a wad of papers in his fist, waved them towards the other men. 'We all know. The information already is public, isn't it?'

There was more uncomfortable silence.

Castillo shook his head, unable to comprehend. 'Don't tell me you're seriously considering keeping a lid on this. We're talking about people's lives here. Why the hell wouldn't you want to tell people?'

'Señor Castillo, the financial and legal implications of this situation are potentially catastrophic,' Morales said.

'Besides, we are all implicated,' Sebastian Gomez said, looking pointedly towards Castillo.

It took Castillo a moment to realise what he meant.

'Is this problem something to do with the contaminated soil you removed? God, it is, isn't it?'

Gomez nodded his head.

'Which, I'm afraid, means it is your problem, too, Hector.'

'What was that? A threat?'

Gomez's smile was instant.

'Of course, it wasn't a threat. I am merely pointing out an aspect of the situation that perhaps you have failed to grasp properly. Anyway, we have still to establish whether this is a permanent problem. Who's to say the readings won't drop? It could happen, couldn't it? You said so yourself, Hector. And there is no evidence of crime here. Did anyone act with malice aforethought? Did anyone deliberately intend to harm anyone? Why should the members of this investment group face total ruin – and possible incarceration – for something that is really an Act of God?'

'I don't believe I'm hearing this.' Castillo was standing now, heading towards the door. 'That mine shaft flooded in 2001. That means people have been ingesting this crap for four years already. You're all mad. Mad.' The door slammed behind him.

Gomez turned to Martyn Phillips. 'Martyn, quickly, go after him and try to talk some sense into his head. We're facing total ruin here.'

Phillips hurried from the room, his face pale.

The silence in the room thickened; every man's face was shadowed. Phillips and Castillo could be heard outside the room, their muffled voices arguing. The scientist's shrill voice rose, suddenly. ' . . . go to the papers. I will. This is wrong, wrong, wrong.'

The voices faded.

'Well, gentlemen,' Sebastian Gomez said, vocalising the thought on everyone's mind, 'it seems we have a mutual problem.'

Sixto Escobar's face shone with beaded sweat. He scratched fingers through the damp mat of hair on his chest.

'I'll tell you one thing. I'm fucked if I let that prick's ethics bring us down. Fuck him. If he won't play ball. . .'

No-one spoke, but the shadow of something fluttered through the room: ties were straightened, collars loosened, hard looks exchanged.

'I can see we are of one mind,' Gomez said eventually. 'Let's try to make Hector see reason. And if not. . . well, I think we should contact Señor Varela and see if he can suggest a suitable solution.'

'And a reasonable price,' Escobar said.

1

GABRIEL VARELA SLUMPED forward against the steering wheel. The orange pick-up slewed across the road. Only one of Varela's hands controlled the vehicle. The other was pressed to the bullet wound in his inner thigh. He'd lost a lot of blood and was starting to show signs of hypovolemic shock: his heart raced, his breath came in gasps and his skin felt cold and clammy.

He'd been shot twice. One bullet had hit him below the left collarbone and passed through his shoulder. The other had hit him in his right inner thigh. The exit wound had torn a fist-sized chunk of fabric from the seat of his jeans.

It had all happened so fast. After speaking with Morales, Varela had knocked the bastard unconscious, tied his hands and feet and bundled him into the boot of Morales's own car. Then he had taken that vehicle and rushed across the city to where Morales had said the exchange of money was taking place, an underpass close to the railway sidings a half-mile along the line from the central station. Varela had parked Morales's car close by and walked the last hundred yards. He had arrived just in time to see a thin Latin man with a moustache pointing a gun at a lithe, muscled man in a white T-shirt holding a metal briefcase.

The muscled guy had said, 'Who the fuck are you?' in Spanish.

The other had motioned for him to hand over the brief-case. Muscles had taken two steps forward and kicked the gun from the other guy's hand with a sudden foot-swipe that had been almost too fast to see. Then he had wrapped something around the slim guy's neck and begun choking him.

That was when Varela had got involved.

He came from behind at the guy in the white T-shirt with his punch dagger, seeking to drop the biggest threat first, but the guy was way too fast. Varela had still been two yards away when the guy spun round and hit him with a kick in the centre of his chest.

It had been a long time since anyone had hit Gabriel Varela so hard. If it weren't for the bullet wounds, he would still be feeling the blow. It had shaken him right down to the marrow of his bones.

After that, white T-shirt had hit Varela with a flurry of blows, while the Latin guy fell to the ground, choking and flapping and clawing at his throat.

Varela felt a punch break his nose; another blow shattered some of his teeth. Varela kept on the guy, though, crowding him, pushing him back, parrying some blows, taking others while he positioned himself.

Varela had been hit a dozen times before he landed his first punch, a solid blow to the guy's midriff with his punch dagger. Varela put all his weight behind it and it lifted the guy off his feet, sent him flying backwards.

The guy twisted as he fell and landed on all fours like a cat, but then he sort of crumpled in on himself as blood began to leak from the hole Varela had punched in his midriff. Varela had been about to move in for the kill when the guy pulled out a pistol and fired four shots. One of the bullets hit Varela in the leg, and he stumbled forward as another shot hit his shoulder and he went down.

Then a car door slammed and a second set of gunshots began echoing off the concrete of the underpass, the bullets pinging against pillars, sounding impossibly loud. And then everything went suddenly quiet and Varela lifted himself painfully to his feet, leaking blood from his leg and his shoulder.

White T-shirt was unconscious; he had a bullet wound in his leg. The guy with the garrotte around his neck lay still, his face blue, eyes bulging. The newcomer was lying face down, with blood pooling around his head and the back of his skull blown away.

Varela had taken the metal briefcase from the floor. There was no way he could get back to his own car, so he climbed into the orange pick-up that the second shooter had emerged from and found the keys still in the ignition. . .

The moon hung low in a wide expanse of sky as he dragged himself from the pick- up and stumbled towards the door of his lock-up, one hand pressed to the wound in his thigh, the other dragging the metal briefcase behind him.

Once inside, he cut his trousers open and shone a torch on his leg to examine the wound. One look at the mangled mess told him he didn't have long.

He sighed and leant back against the wall. There was a summer storm brewing outside, you could feel the thickness in the air. Wind whistled through the crack in the ceiling, making the flaps of the cardboard boxes all around him flutter.

His work was unfinished. Still, he had not expected to catch them all. Therefore he had a contingency plan.

He took the briefcase, rested it on his lap and wiped the top clear with the sleeve of his jacket. Then he took a sheet of paper and wrote '*Utiliza esto, por favor*'. He took the folder that held the originals of the documents from the laboratory, the evidence of the bastards' crime, and placed the handwritten message on its cover. Then he weighted it down with the briefcase.

His hand trembled as he lifted the phone and began typing a text message, smearing blood on the plastic screen as he did so.

Gomez and Morales. The fuckers had to pay for what they'd done to Esme. There was only one person that could make that happen now.

2

I T TOOK DANNY ten minutes to get to the site of the gun battle. It was an underpass about a half-mile down from Almería's train station.

It was one of those stories that are just so perfect, you couldn't believe they were true. Doug Sampson – Wild West star of a hundred on-screen showdowns – had been shot dead in what seemed to have been a gun fight. Even better, early reports also indicated that Sampson been found with a pistol in his hand, and that he had actually begun the short but frenzied exchange of gunfire that had brought the evening traffic in the city centre to a standstill. Early radio reports claimed Sampson and another man had been killed, while a third man had been seriously injured and taken to hospital.

The underpass was like any place where there is only bare concrete: dim, drab and dirty. Pillars underneath it were wrapped with incident tape.

Danny was no expert, but even from a distance it was clear the fight had involved multiple guns.

The two bodies were dark lumps stretched out on the ground. They could only be seen clearly when one of the white-suited forensic officers moved behind to set out numbered plastic triangles beside the fallen bullet casings.

Already a dozen reporters had arrived. Danny approached

one of the older Spanish journalists, one he knew had a brother-in-law in the *policia nacional*.

'What's the score, Diego?' Danny said.

When Diego gave a non-committal shrug, Danny said, 'OK, play it your way, mate. But if one of those dead guys over there is Doug Sampson, it could be he's got relatives that want to talk. If I remember correctly, Diego, your English –' Danny switched to his best Speedy Gonzales accent – 'eez no so good.'

Diego chewed his lip. 'Which side is it that makes you such a ball-breaker,' he said, 'the Spanish or the English?'

Danny had his pen out. 'Quit insulting me and tell me what you've got.'

Diego steered Danny away from the other reporters. 'Keep it quiet, else you'll have all of them buzzing around.' He looked over Danny's shoulder. 'OK, I've got names on three of them. That's Doug Sampson over there,' he said, pointing across the road with his pen to illustrate each particular point. 'Sampson is dead from a bullet wound to the forehead. That one there is Ricardo Neymar. It seems he's got a garrotte wrapped around his neck. The injured man is Tomás . . . you pronounce it, Danny.'

'Shrike,' Danny said, relishing the sound of the name. 'How badly hurt is he?'

'He's been stabbed in the stomach, plus he took a bullet to the leg. He's in a bad way, but is expected to live.'

'So, what happened?'

'A witness saw this Shrike guy waiting in the darkness with a briefcase, one of those metal security ones. Then an orange pick-up pulled over and Ricardo Neymar got out. He went over to Shrike, started talking, but Shrike attacked him and began to strangle him. Then someone else got involved, a big guy in a military-looking jacket. He and Shrike started trading blows. Apparently, it was real Matrix-style, kung-fu shit. Then Sampson got out of the pick up and started blasting. After that no-one knows what the hell happened as all the witnesses hit the deck.'

'So, where's the guy in the military jacket? And where's the briefcase?'

'That's the real question, isn't it?' Diego said. 'Because, according to my brother-in-law, they definitely ain't here. So, when are you going to contact Sampson's family? You'll get me some quotes, won't you?'

Danny was making reassuring noises when his mobile pinged to indicate he'd received an SMS.

He looked at the screen.

There was an address in Almería city, and the words, VEN AHORA. G.V.

Ven ahora: come now.

3

THE SECOND TIME Danny pressed the intercom buzzer, Paco Pino's face appeared on the video screen. The image fisheyed as Paco leant closer to the upstairs camera. Paco sighed when he saw who it was.

'I know all about Doug Sampson and the gunfight, Danny. You'll have to cover it with –'

'Is Lourdes there?'

'No. She took the girls to her mother's house.'

'I need to show you something.'

Paco sighed again. 'How do I know I'm not going to like it?'

He buzzed Danny in.

Upstairs, Danny handed Paco his mobile.

'Here. I got this text message forty minutes ago.'

'G.V.?' Paco said. 'That means Gabriel Varela, doesn't it?'

'I think it does. Have you got Google Earth? I want to see where this address is.'

Paco typed in the address and the monitor filled with an image of train tracks and industrial buildings. The outlines of the buildings were barely visible until Paco enlarged the search, when a series of blurred rectangular boxes became visible; a smaller square building lay in front of them. It took Paco a moment to realise the implications of what he was seeing.

'Are you considering going there, Danny? It's a property right next to El Puche. That's a rough old part of town.' Paco looked at his watch. 'Especially at eleven o'clock at night.'

'I know. That's why I don't want to go alone.'

Realisation dawned on Paco's face.

'No way. This Varela guy's a psycho.' Paco crossed the room and picked up the telephone receiver. 'Call the police, Danny. Let them handle it.'

Danny shook his head. 'Varela was involved in a shootout tonight. And one of the guys that got shot was Gomez's security guy, Shrike. I don't think there's any danger for us. I've come this far. I want to know the truth. I'll go alone if I have to, but I'd prefer it if you had my back.'

Paco put the telephone receiver down. He sat heavily on the sofa. 'I love you like a brother, Danny, but you're a difficult bloke to *like* sometimes. You know that, don't you?'

Danny said nothing and waited. Nearly a minute of silence passed before Paco said, 'If I go with you – and that's still a big if, mind – will you agree to put this story to bed, no matter what we find?'

'Yes.'

'Don't try and give me your winning fucking smile, Danny.' Paco massaged his temples. 'All right, I'll go for the sole reason that if you went alone and something happened, I wouldn't be able to live with myself. But I think you're a bastard for putting me in this position in the first place.'

They didn't talk much after that. Both climbed into Danny's car.

It began raining when they were approaching the city of Almería, one of those sudden summer monsoons that happen in Spain sometimes. Lightning flashed, silhouetting mountain peaks on the horizon.

They were driving through an industrial park on the edge of the city, filled with factories and derelict business units. Most of the businesses seemed to have been closed down and many of the buildings had broken or boarded-up windows; their walls were covered with graffiti.

The address they sought was at the end of a street. The gate of the property was bent backwards and badly buckled. It looked like someone had driven through it.

Paco insisted Danny turn the car around and park it facing back towards the main road.

'In case we need to leave in a hurry,' he said, adjusting the camera strap around his neck.

The building had probably been used as a storage facility at one point, although it no longer seemed to be trading. The door of the wooden office flapped open in the wind and a painted sign advertising the facility's prices lay on the muddy floor.

There were two parallel rows of storage units set out like garages, the metal roller shutters that accessed each of the lock-ups facing each other. All of the shutters were closed.

Apart from the last one on the right.

An orange pick-up stood outside the lock-up; the driver's door was open and flapping in the wind.

Danny approached slowly, shouting out, 'Hello?' as he advanced.

The chain-link fence had been ripped apart. Only a few yards beyond it, the traffic roared past on one of the major roads that criss-crossed the city.

The lock-up was filled with stacks of plastic tubs and cardboard boxes. Part of the roof had collapsed and the wind whistled through the rectangular space.

Danny called out, 'Hello?' again.

Paco said, 'I don't like this.'

Danny froze as his torch beam flashed across the figure slumped at the back of the lock-up. He stepped back and clutched the wall.

'Varela? Is that you?' Danny said.

No answer.

Danny lit his torch again and used its beam to guide him between the piles of boxes.

Gabriel Varela sat with his legs out before him, his head bowed towards a mass of bloodied fabric and cotton in his lap. The floor beneath the man's legs was dark with pooled blood.

Danny touched his fingers to the man's face. He was cold.

'We've got to call the police, Danny,' Paco said. 'Don't step in the blood.'

There was a table beside Varela. A metal security briefcase lay on it. A fluttering scrap of paper and a cardboard folder protruded from one corner of the briefcase, pinned to the table-top by its weight.

Danny pulled the scrap of paper free and read the words scrawled on it in Spanish: *Use this, please.*

'Use this? Use what?' Danny said.

'He meant the briefcase,' Paco said. 'Let's look inside.'

Danny put a hand out to stop him. 'Careful. It could be a trap.'

'Make your mind up, Danny. An hour ago you were saying Varela didn't mean us any harm; now you're worried about booby traps. I say we look inside the case and see if there's something inside that is going to put an end to this whole shitty business.'

The outside of the case was sticky with smears of half-dried blood. Danny looked for something to wipe it clean. There was only Varela's clothing. He didn't much fancy touching that.

In the end he got a stick, threaded it through the handle of the case and lifted it down onto the floor.

Danny and Paco knelt in front of the briefcase. It looked like someone had already broken the thing open, as the metal of the briefcase was scored and scratched and the edges were bent outwards.

Danny flicked the clasps open and raised the lid.

His eyes widened as he looked down at the contents. Paco Pino's mouth gaped.

Then Paco spoke, the words separated by a two-beat pause. 'Fuck. Me.'

4

Sᴇʙᴀsᴛɪᴀɴ Gᴏᴍᴇᴢ ᴡᴀs on the phone to the P.I. he used. 'What the hell has happened? Where the hell is Shrike?' he hissed, his hand cupped around the mobile.

When he'd listened to the response, he said, 'Will he live? Really? He doesn't deserve to. I can't believe he has fucked this all up so badly. And where's Emilio? I need him to get on to his police contacts. I need to know what's happened. If he won't answer his telephone, go to his house. I don't care if you have to break a window to get in. Find him.'

Gomez poured himself a glass of Vichy Catalan and sipped it slowly, then ate a piece of Turkish Delight from the box on the table. It was all slipping away. ¡Joder! if the slightest whisper of his involvement in any of this went public, he would be ruined. Investors would melt away just when the fund was stretched to its limits.

The money. Where was the money? If the police found that, it would raise some awkward questions. And the case had a damned GPS device in it that could be traced back to who knows where. And the employees at the bank had seen him take the damned thing down to the security boxes. It wouldn't take a genius to work out how the wretched thing had been filled with money.

Television coverage was saying that Doug Sampson had

been involved. Yes, that made sense. The filthy catamite. He was the only other person that knew about the messages in the newspaper. It hadn't been Varela that had posted them, it was Sampson. He ate another piece of Turkish Delight. His head whirled. He needed protection now. He dabbed his brow with a perfumed handkerchief.

Gomez spent the next thirty minutes on the telephone, calling round every press contact he had, speaking to newspaper editors and the owners of radio stations, trying to put his own spin on things, reminding them about Sampson's murky past. He tried to sell the gun battle as a lovers' tiff, a bitch fight between queers that had gotten badly out of hand.

At ten, the P.I. phoned.

'The police have just pulled your cousin out of the boot of a car that was parked near to the scene of the shootout. His nose is broken and he had his hands and feet bound with cable ties.'

'OK, I'll deal with that,' Gomez said. 'Find out where the hell that briefcase of money has ended up. Until we find where that has gone, we can't really move.'

5

Friday, August 31st, 2012

DANNY SANCHEZ AND Paco Pino were still kneeling before the open briefcase. The wind howled through the crack in the ceiling. The edges of the thick wads of bank notes inside the briefcase fluttered. For the third time, Paco picked up one of the bundles of bank notes and stared at it open-mouthed. For the third time, Danny told him to put the money down.

'Why?' Paco said.

'It might blow away. Plus, I don't want you getting too attached to it.'

'I'm already very attached to my half, mate, don't you worry about that.'

Danny looked at his friend. He frowned when he saw the photographer was serious.

'Surely you realise we can't keep this money, Paco.'

'What the fuck are you saying? We're set up here for life. Or for the next few years, anyway. *¡Joder!* this will put a serious dent in my mortgage.'

'Are you nuts, Paco?' Danny said, his voice rising, as he saw Paco's expression.

'Me, nuts? You find God knows how many tens of thousands of euros and you don't want to keep it? What the hell's the problem?' Paco waved towards Varela's dead body. 'He doesn't need it any more, does he? For the first time, we're ahead of the game, *amigo*.'

'How do we explain where it came from?'

'I don't plan on explaining it. I plan on spending it.'

'And what are you going to spend it on?'

'A new car, for starters.'

'Paco, we don't know where this money came from, or what the hell it was for. If it's the proceeds of blackmail, keeping it could rebound on us. And what if it's drug money? What if it's marked or can be traced? How are you going to explain that to your bank when you use it to pay off your mortgage? And you know as well as I do, you can't pay more than 15,000 euros cash for anything, anyway.'

As he spoke, Danny closed the briefcase and shut the clasps, forcing Paco to withdraw his hands. But when he lifted the briefcase, Paco gripped the other side of it with both hands.

'Where are you off to with that?' said Paco, petulantly.

'Where? Anywhere but here. We've got a dead body and a briefcase filled with cash. How the hell do we explain that if the police turn up?'

Perhaps it was a trick of the light flickering outside, but Paco's eyes seemed lit with an ugly glow as each strengthened his grip on the case.

'I want my half, Danny.'

'Paco, let go.'

The storm outside was really raging now, the rain pounding down with monsoon force. The ruined house wheezed like a pair of bellows as the wind rushed through the broken roof and whistled out through the open shutter.

'I've been chasing around after you all week,' Paco said. 'Now, when something finally goes our way, you want to give it away.' Paco's voice dropped to a rapid, solicitous whisper, his eyes focused on the briefcase. 'Varela wanted us to use it. He said so on the piece of paper. He's giving us the money. Who cares where he got it from? We'll bury it, Danny. Somewhere only you and I will know where. And . . . and we'll only take it out a bit at a time. That way no-one –'

Danny tried to tug the briefcase away from Paco. Before he knew what was really happening, they were in a struggle, tugging the briefcase back and forth between them.

'I know what you're trying to do.' The light in Paco's eyes turned aggressive as he sneered the words. 'You want to keep it all for yourself. You want to trick me.'

The tug-of-war continued until Paco suddenly pushed as Danny yanked. Danny tumbled backwards, overturning the table upon which they had found the briefcase. Suddenly the room was filled with spiralling pieces of paper as the folder on the table-top fell and the wind caught its contents.

Danny leapt to his feet and rushed to regain his hold on the briefcase, but Paco swung a wild haymaker that caught him on the side of the head. Danny's ear exploded with pain. Both hands shot to his ear as Paco punched him again on the back of the head, knocking him to the ground.

Danny's face hit the ground a fraction before his hands. He tasted blood and dirt in his mouth. He lay still, groaning.

Paco stood in the centre of the room, staring into space, both hands clasping the briefcase to his chest.

'Take it, Paco,' Danny said, spitting blood and holding a hand up to indicate that he didn't want to fight. 'Take the fucking money. But it's nothing to do with me, all right?'

Paco Pino looked towards Danny as if seeing him for the first time. He opened his mouth to speak, but his lips moved without making any sound.

'My God,' he managed to say. 'What have I done to you, mate?'

The briefcase fell to the ground.

And then Paco Pino burst into tears.

He cried the way people unused to open displays of emotion did, a huge wave of emotion that flooded his face in seconds.

As Danny got slowly to his feet, Paco Pino grabbed him in a bear hug and held him there, blubbering on his shoulder.

The two men stayed that way, Danny watching over Paco's shoulders as pieces of paper fluttered and rushed across the floor, rising out through the opening at the front of the lock-up, over the fence and away into the traffic.

Danny was still there, locked between Paco's arm, when a sheet of paper fluttered and stuck to Danny's face.

He peeled it away and was about to screw it up when something made him stop. He smoothed out the crumpled paper and saw immediately what had caught his attention: the blue-white corporate logo of Florentino Yagüe Laboratories. The top of the page said, CLIENT: Suministros La Flecha Rota, Results of Bi-weekly Water Analysis, Sample taken, 12th April, 2002.

Below it was a long list of analysis results.

Danny pushed Paco away.

'This is just like the burnt paper I found at Martyn Phillips's house,' Danny said. 'Only this is an original.'

Danny looked around him. The cardboard folder still lay on the floor, next to the overturned table.

'Paco, where was that folder when we came in? Was it on the table?'

Paco sniffed. 'I think so. Underneath the briefcase. Why? What's the matter?' he said when he saw Danny's face fall.

'Varela's message, Paco. *Please use this*,' Danny said, rushing towards the front of the lock-up. 'He wasn't talking about the fucking money. He meant what was inside that folder.'

6

DANNY RUSHED OUTSIDE but it was already too late: the wind had taken the papers. Danny searched the whole area, but managed to retrieve only six sheets of paper that had become trapped against the fence outside the lock-up.

Paco stood with his rump against the bonnet of Danny's car, his head down, oblivious to the wind and rain, his big bald head dripping droplets of water.

'What are we going to do with the money, then?' he said, when Danny returned to the car, cursing. 'We can't just leave it here. And if we're not going to keep it, we should take it to the police.'

Danny shook his head. 'Chances are this money belongs to Gomez. It was his guy that had the briefcase. And perhaps he'll want this money back. This is the first chance I've got to make the bastard talk.'

Paco laughed bitterly. 'You've spent the last week trying to convince me this Gomez guy is only one step down from Beelzebub. And now we're just going to give his money back?'

'I'm sorry, Paco.'

'Take me home.'

They drove in silence. It was nearly three a.m. when Danny dropped Paco off, but all the lights were on in Paco's flat. When Paco got out of the car, he turned and bent to look inside.

'When you get home tonight, Danny, sleep on the sofa.'

'Why?'

Paco cast his eyes up towards the lighted window in his flat. 'Because, thanks to you, that's where I'm going to be sleeping tonight.'

Danny drove home, but he couldn't sleep. He sat up all night, smoking and thinking, with the director's commentary of *Alien* burbling softly on the TV in the background.

Suministros La Flecha Rota. That had to be the company that had supplied the tap water to the Bellavista, the one that had suddenly cut off the supply and left the inhabitants high and dry. Danny cursed the loss of the rest of the sheets of paper. The six sheets he had managed to retrieve contained analyses of water from between 2001 and 2004. He looked over the results. They meant absolutely nothing to him.

Still, he could get someone to check them later today. First, he needed somewhere safe to keep the money until he could confront Gomez. But where could he put it? He didn't want to leave the briefcase at his house, nor did he want to be driving around with it.

Danny took the briefcase and used cellophane to wrap pieces of cardboard around it to make a rectangular package, which he then wrapped in two sheets of leftover Christmas wrapping paper, the only material he could find that was big enough to cover it all.

At 08:00 he set off for the post office.

Twenty minutes later, the woman behind the post office counter looked at the diagonal lines of snowmen and sleigh bells on the parcel before her. Then her eyes strayed towards the calendar on the wall.

'This present is either very early, señor, or it's really, really late.'

Then she noticed that Danny was sending it to himself. She shook her head as if the foibles of foreigners would forever be beyond her.

Danny didn't care. Tomorrow a slip of paper would be delivered to his house informing him there was a parcel to collect. Anyone wanting it would require proof that he was Danny Sanchez and that he lived at the correct address. Until then, the parcel would be hidden among hundreds of others in the back of the postal depot.

At nine o'clock, Danny phoned Professor Aceveda.

'Do you know anything about water testing?' he said.

'A little. But it's not really my speciality.'

'Do you know if drinking water is tested for radioactivity?'

'OK,' Aceveda said, 'I see where you're going with this. The answer to your question is yes and no. Routine water testing is for gross alpha and gross beta particles. However, those gross measurements do not give any information of the isotopic composition of the sample, nor do they tell you the estimated radiation dose. And given the tone of our conversation last night, I think perhaps what you're really asking me is whether drinking water is tested for the presence of plutonium. In that case, I would have to say, no, not specifically.'

'So, it would be possible for the radiation in drinking water analysis results to be within acceptable levels, even if it contained plutonium?'

'Yes. But again, I have to say that the groundwater in Palomares was tested and there is no contamination.'

'What about in Las Jarapas?'

'Impossible. Even if there had been any contaminated soil there – which there wasn't – it would have been far too thinly spread to affect the groundwater.'

Afterwards, Danny drove across town to the premises of Laboratorios Florentino Yagüe S.L. When he got there, he asked to see Nacho Yagüe.

Yagüe paused on the stairs on his way down and rolled his eyes.

'What do you want?'

Danny showed him the crumpled, dirty pages of water analyses he'd retrieved from the lock-up. Yagüe blanched but insisted he knew nothing about them.

'It's important. This means something,' Danny said.

Yagüe blew air. 'Well, I'd have to look. But we lost a lot of stuff in a . . . well, the point is. . .'

Danny frowned. 'In my experience, meandering half-finished sentences are never a good sign, Señor Yagüe.'

Yagüe promised to phone Danny when – if – he had located the results. Danny left the laboratory thinking that he wouldn't hold his breath. Then he got on the phone to Alan Neave.

'Mr Neave, I want to ask about the water company that used to supply the Bellavista. Was it *Suministros La Flecha Rota*?'

Danny listened to Neave's response and said, 'In that case we need to talk. Are you busy now?'

Danny had reached Neave's house by eleven o'clock.

Alan Neave showed him into the front room. A number of other men and women from the residents' association were there, discussing paperwork. Danny did the rounds, shaking hands, but inwardly he was cursing: the more people you tried to interview at once, the less information you normally got.

'I believe you mentioned you had some documents from *Suministros La Flecha Rota*,' Neave said. 'Might I ask how you obtained them?' Danny handed him the six rain-wrinkled sheets of lab analysis.

'If I told you, you wouldn't believe me,' Danny said with an ironic smile.

'It's fascinating that you should have these,' Neave said, 'as we requested to see the results of the water analysis years ago and this wretched company would not even tell us which lab was testing the water.'

He handed them to another man, Tony, someone who had worked for a water company in the UK.

'How did they get away with that?' Danny said.

'This company seemed to have a lot of friends on the council. Practically every request we put in for paperwork was either lost or fudged.'

'Why did you request them?'

'One of our members was doing a tour of some of the industrial sites up in the mountains. He noticed that some of the mine shafts seemed to have been flooded and he was worried that residue from the mines might have been washed into the aquifer.'

'And had it been?'

'Not according to the data we managed to obtain. But it took us nearly a year to get any documentation from this company.'

'I spoke to an old man up in the mountains,' Danny said. 'He told me that a gold mine purchased by *Grupo La Flecha*

Rota has flooded on a number of occasions over the years.'

Neave nodded. 'Practically every time there was heavy rain. But we didn't know the mine belonged to *La Flecha Rota*. Can you prove that?'

Danny showed them the page he had ripped from the council minutes.

Neave showed this to the others; they looked at the scrumpled piece of paper, whispered among themselves and set it on the coffee table along with Danny's analysis results.

'What happened with the water supply then?' Danny said. 'When was it suddenly cut off?'

Neave said, 'Everything was fine at the start, although the water was a little gritty from 2001, which is the first time the mine shaft flooded. But in 2008, they suddenly cut off access. You would not believe the nightmare we've had here since. They jerry- rigged something from the pipeline that supplies the actual town, but that only supplied the houses on the side closest to Las Jarapas. The rest of the urbanisation was without a regular supply for eleven *months*. They gave us some cock-and-bull story about this *Suministros La Flecha Rota* having gone bust, but we didn't believe a word of it.'

'Why not?'

'You've got to be a special kind of idiot to have your water company go bust when you've an entire aquifer at your disposal, and a countrywide drought going on. And the whole thing was so rushed. Literally a week after the problems began, they started demolishing the bloody pumping station. There was no attempt to try to sell it on as a going concern. The whole thing was just shut down and they filled in all the boreholes.

'Anyway, they managed to get the supply going through

the existing pipelines, but fed from the main grid, the one that supplies the town. On the far side of the urbanisation, the water pressure is still so low it just dribbles out of the taps.'

Tony had finished looking through the sheets of water analysis.

'There is nothing untoward about these water results,' he said.

'Are you sure?'

'Absolutely. Everything is within perfectly acceptable parameters.'

Danny swore. Neave and the others exchanged looks.

'Were you expecting them to be otherwise, Mr Sanchez?'

'Look,' Danny said, 'this whole business centres on these water results.'

'Really? How?'

Then Danny told them about Varela, and the house he had purchased, and the cancer that Varela's daughter had suffered and about Lucia Borja's visit to Varela in the Cantabrian prison.

When Danny finished, no-one said anything, but there was much fidgeting. After a while, Neave said, 'Mr Sanchez, I fear there has been some misunderstanding. I invited you here because I was under the impression that you were going to cover our imminent court case, not begin to spread wild rumours.'

'What if these water results have been falsified?' Danny said, reclaiming the sheets of paper from the coffee table. 'Because if they have, you've got a serious problem. This water company was clearly skipping all the rules, and they had the council in their pockets.'

Neave drew himself up and looked around him for support. The other members of the residents' committee nodded their agreement. Neave went over to the attack.

'I have to say, your comments are most worrying, Mr Sanchez. Do you have evidence to support your speculation? Because most residents here have seen their properties lose about 40% of their value in less than thirty-six months. Wild rumours of this type could destroy what little value they still have. If you have any documentation to support your allegations, now is the time to show it to us.'

Danny's shoulders sagged.

The conversation meandered after that, but the members of the residents' committee continued to exchange silent looks. Danny left them to it.

He was walking back to his car when a big black saloon with tinted windows began ambling along the road beside him, its passenger door open.

'Mr Sanchez,' a voice said.

Danny stopped.

'I believe we need to speak,' the voice said.

Danny turned and squinted into the vehicle's dark interior. When he saw who was sitting sprawled across the leather seats, he stopped dead in his tracks.

It was Sebastian Gomez.

7

Danny CLIMBED INTO the back of the car. He pulled the door shut. The interior had that new car smell and was deliciously cool. The air con was a barely audible whisper.

'This is a surprise,' Danny said.

Gomez smiled. 'I know you've been very keen to speak with me for a number of days now.'

'How's Tommy Shrike doing? And what happened at the underpass?'

'I have no idea of whom or what you are talking,' Gomez said with a wry smile.

'How'd you know where to find me?'

'I've made a point of befriending a member of the residents' association here. He keeps me abreast of everything the association does.'

'I doubt "friend" is the right word.'

Gomez shrugged. 'Our association is mutually beneficial. What better definition of friendship is there?'

'So what am I doing here?'

'I want to show you something,' Gomez said, handing Danny a Tupperware box. Danny hesitated before taking it and pulling the lid off. Inside was a mass of ash, melted plastic and charred scraps of metal.

'Naturally, I expect a certain degree of loyalty from my employees. I would require you to sign a non-disclosure agreement, one that would prevent you from revealing anything that might prove harmful to either my business interests, or those of my associates.'

'Yeah, that figures,' Danny said.

'I don't know why you adopt such a scornful tone. Your friend, Señor Pino, seemed very open to the suggestion. I spoke to him before coming here. Anyway, I'm giving you until midday tomorrow. By then, I want either your signature on the non-disclosure contract, or I want my briefcase and its contents back.'

'Or what?'

The amiability dropped from Gomez's expression and was replaced by a hard, cold look.

'If you don't comply, I am going to tell the police that you have the money and that you were in league with Varela in a conspiracy to blackmail myself and Señor Morales. The police already know that Señor Morales was kidnapped. I will implicate you in that as well. And I will make certain that you come to serve a custodial sentence. Now get out of my car.'

8

Danny watched as Gomez's car drew away from the kerb. His nose wrinkled: his nostrils seemed full of Gomez's sickly eau de cologne.

Danny was angry with himself. For a split second he had actually, genuinely, considered Gomez's offer. And Gomez had seen it – and smiled, in an oily, complicit way, as if saying, 'Yes, we're all the same, aren't we?'

Still, Gomez had stopped bullying him and was now resorting to bribes. Danny must be doing something right. That was why he wanted to speak to the one person who'd still escaped him. Danny drove to the end of the street and began stopping passersby, asking if they knew where Louis Margaux lived.

The property was the last house at the corner of a street on the southern side of the estate, the part that overlooked the dried-up course of the River Almanzora. The glass to the side of the front door was cracked.

'Who is it?' a man's voice said when Danny knocked.

When Danny explained, Margaux said, 'A newspaper? Don't tell me those bastards from the neighbourhood association have sent you round?'

Danny laughed at that. 'Not exactly. If you'll just open the door, I'll happily explain everything you need to know.'

Louis Margaux was tall and gangly and had the distract-ed air of an academic. He wore a threadbare cardigan, smart trousers and yellow Crocs. His ploughshare of an Adam's apple jerked up and down as he spoke.

'What do you want then?'

'I've seen your website. I want to know what the informa-tion is that you can't publish.'

Margaux leant out of the door and looked up and down the street. 'These houses are built on contaminated soil,' he said.

'Why do you still live here, then?'

'I've got no choice, I can't shift the place. Besides, I want to stay here. I've got to warn people.'

Margaux opened the door wide and invited Danny through to the living room. The wall above the fireplace held a corkboard that was covered in newspaper cuttings. A list of dates had been fixed in the middle of the corkboard; pieces of string linked them to items of information. Danny saw his own article on the wall. There was also a newspaper photo of Hector Castillo circled in red marker pen.

Margaux saw where Danny was looking. 'This Hector Castillo bastard is where it all starts.'

'What do you mean?'

Margaux rummaged on a bookshelf loaded with piles of dog-eared books and folders filled with more clippings, until he withdrew a copy of the MWGP report that Antonio Saez had shown Danny. He opened it out at the page where the scientists involved were listed.

'Notice how on this report Hector Castillo isn't mentioned anywhere?' Margaux said.

'Yes, I know.'

'Look at this.'

He handed Danny a sheet of paper bearing the UGT letterhead. It said that Hector Castillo had been granted permission to access the site "in order to take scientific readings". 'Notice how he's described there as the head researcher?'

'Where did you get this?' Danny said.

'All in good time. But it proves that this Castillo was involved in looking for the irradiated soil that was here. And yet mysteriously, he ended up working for a development company. Strange coincidence, don't you think?'

'So what do you think happened?'

'They bought him. They paid him off, got him to keep quiet about the contaminated soil.'

'It's a very compelling theory, but it's worthless without proof.'

'You want proof? Come with me.'

Margaux led Danny through to a room at the back of the house. The walls were plastered with hundreds of black and white photos of a woman.

'That is Joleen, my wife,' Margaux said. He pointed to the photo at the top left of the rectangular montage. 'I took that first photo the day she was diagnosed with cancer. And then I took a photo every day for the next 382 days that she survived. This is where they began the chemo,' he said, pointing to a photo a quarter of the way down. 'This is when they told us it had metastazied. And this one here was when we learned it was terminal.

'It's like the disease dismantled her, don't you think? First it took her hair and her eyebrows. Then it took her smile. And finally, it took her. I keep this here to remind me, Mr Sanchez: my wife was murdered.'

Danny said nothing. Margaux stood, staring at the photos in silence. Then he reached down to the cupboard on the floor and withdrew a shoe box, which he opened carefully and held towards Danny. The box was filled with dusty grey-brown earth.

'Watch this,' Margaux said, as he withdrew a small hand-held Geiger counter and waved it over the contents.

Danny stepped backward as the Geiger counter sprang into life, emitting a rattling buzz, so fast it was almost a drone. Margaux smiled and moved the instrument closer to the earth. The Geiger counter howled.

'Don't worry,' Marguax said. 'Plutonium gives off alpha emitting particles. They can't travel far through air. But you said you wanted to see proof. Well, this soil sample was taken at the start, before construction work on the Bellavista began.'

'Where did you get it?'

'When my wife became ill, I started looking into this whole business about the contaminated soil. And I found that a Spanish journalist had tried to cover this story right back when the Bellavista was being built.'

'Eduardo Bolaño? Did you know him?'

Margaux's eyes widened. 'I'm impressed that you've heard of him, Mr Sanchez. No, I never met Bolaño. But when I began investigating, after Joleen died, I spoke to Bolaño's widow and she let me have all his research.'

'Did you show this to the residents' association?'

Margaux scoffed. 'You mean Neave and his cronies? You won't get any sense out of them. Neave sank his entire pension into a second property here on the Bellavista, expecting to make a quick buck, but he got caught out by the downturn in the Spanish economy. Now, all he's worried about is getting shot of the property all his money is tied up in. It's the same story for most of the bloody people in the residents' association.'

'We need to get more information,' Danny said. 'We need to convince them.'

Margaux said, 'I don't think that's going to be possible unless we can see the first draft of the MWGP report, the one where Hector Castillo's readings were supposedly wrong. The problem is, the guy who screwed poor Eduardo Bolaño is still working at MWGP. He was the one that gave Bolaño that soil sample I showed you, but the bastard later recanted on his testimony and left Bolaño exposed to the libel action.'

'What's his name?' Danny said.

'It was a man named Antonio Saez. He's a research scientist at the company.'

Danny picked up his shoulder bag. 'Come with me. I think I know how we can get hold of that first report.'

9

At one o'clock, Danny drew up outside the offices of MWGP. Inside the building he asked to speak to Antonio Saez.

Saez made him wait five minutes. When he came down the stairs, the man's expression was more than usually severe.

'What do you want? I've answered as many of your damned questions as I've a mind –'

'Eduardo Bolaño,' Danny said, speaking quietly but clearly. 'Do you remember him?'

Saez's face fell. It took him a moment to recover. By then, Danny was saying, 'I had a good look at your car the other day. An Aston Martin Vanquisher. That's a nice motor, isn't it? They're about 100 grand new, aren't they?'

'What possible business is it of yours what I drive?'

Danny smiled: he had put Saez immediately on his guard.

'Rumour has it you had a lottery win.'

'I want you to leave, now.'

'Strange, I'm willing to bet that that "lottery" win happened round about the same time you recanted on your testimony to Eduardo Bolaño. What happened? Did Sebastian Gomez get to you? Or were you only ever using Bolaño to pressure Gomez into coughing up a bribe?'

Saez gripped Danny's arm and pulled him away from the secretary.

'You're playing a dangerous game, Señor Sanchez.'

'It's no game,' Danny said, pushing Saez's hand away, 'but, of course, you'll have all the relevant paperwork relating to your lottery win, won't you? To show to the police, I mean, when I give them your name.'

'You're mad,' Saez said.

'Think about it, Señor Saez. Four people are dead now because of this mess, maybe more. If I give the police your name, they'll be all over your affairs like a rash. Especially when I tell them the amount of pay-offs and bribes the people responsible were throwing around at the time.'

Saez stopped. When he turned, he was shaking with anger, although his face was pale. His lip trembled. For a moment, Danny thought the slender scientist was going to take a swing at him. Then something inside Saez seemed to snap. His shoulders sagged. He moved closer to Danny and hissed, 'What do you want from me? Is this some cheap blackmail scam, because if –'

'I want to see Hector Castillo's report. The first one, the one he prepared on the drift patterns from the Palomares accident.'

'Why?'

'Because I'm willing to bet that first report shows there *was* radioactive soil in the municipality of Las Jarapas, right slap bang in the middle of where the Bellavista urbanisation was being built. That was why Castillo fudged the results, wasn't it? The developers bought him.'

Saez said nothing, but his expression had become defensive. Saez led Danny upstairs to his office and told him to wait. Ten minutes later he returned with a pen drive.

'This contains a PDF of the first report. Before I give it to you, I want you to promise me that you won't drag my name into this business. If there was any malfeasance, it was Castillo's, not mine. I only discovered what had happened later on. And, let me assure you, the results of the second report were correct. There *is* no contaminated soil on the Bellavista. Make of that what you will.'

Louis Margaux was waiting for Danny at a nearby roadside cafeteria. He looked up expectantly when Danny returned.

'There you are,' Danny said. He turned the laptop towards him.

'What is this?' Margaux said, but he'd already guessed. 'It can't be,' he said as he began flicking through the pages. Danny was smiling, too; Margaux's child-like excitement was infectious.

'I'm glad you like it,' Danny said. 'Now, can you tell me what the hell it all means?'

Margaux had his own copy of the report open on his lap. He began flicking through it, comparing the maps and tables it contained with their counterparts on the computer screen.

'Here,' he said. 'Look at this diagram. This is the map of the Bellavista. This one from the original report shows three considerable pockets of radiation slap bang in the centre of the Bellavista.'

'So there was irradiated earth on the Bellavista?'

'According to this, yes.'

'So, why did the second report show there was no contaminated soil?'

'Simple. They lied.'

Danny shook his head. 'Don't forget the residents' association commissioned their own report. They wouldn't have lied.'

Margaux didn't seem convinced. He sat back in his chair.

'What about this?' Danny said. 'What if this first report *was* right and there was irradiated earth all over the very centre of the development. So, they had to bribe Castillo, and get him to fudge the results. But that still left them with the problem of the contaminated soil. What if they got rid of it somehow? What if they did the same as the Americans? What if they dug up the contaminated earth, put it in oil drums and shipped it off somewhere else?'

Margaux scoffed.

'How the hell would they have done that? Look at the amount of earth that would be. You'd need to dig down at least 50 centimetres. You're talking about hundreds of cubic metres of earth. That's dozens of lorry loads. And if they buried it, they would have needed a mighty big hole.'

Danny could see the logic of that. He went outside, lit a cigarette and considered the matter.

There was no moment of sudden revelation. The answer dawned on Danny in slow stages as he smoked.

He started by thinking about what Margaux had said, about needing a bloody big hole. His thoughts went naturally to the abandoned gold mine in the mountains above the Bellavista, the mine that was purchased by a development company that showed no interest in developing the place. Christ, he realised, it wasn't the land in which they had been interested. It was the damned mine shaft.

After that everything fell into place.

The dates fitted. At around the same time Castillo had

fudged the figures, the developers had bought the mine. And at the same moment, they had closed down the whole development and brought in cheap immigrant labour to work through the night. Danny thought about the old man he had met up in the mountains and the lorries that had been thundering up to the mine every night for a week. They had put the contaminated soil in barrels and dumped it down the mine shaft.

Then Danny thought about what Professor Aceveda had told him, of the dangers of concentrating the contaminated soil in one place. The mine shaft had flooded God knows how many times. And every time, the Bellavista residents had found black grit in their water.

And then his thoughts turned to Martyn Phillips's house on the Bellavista, to his empty swimming pool and the garden he had allowed to wither away, to the carafes of mineral water in his house. The cynical bastard. He had known that it wasn't the soil that was contaminated. It was the water. He'd sat there and protected himself, while all around him people's children were drinking and bathing in the damned stuff. And that explained the health checks Phillips had had, the sudden hypochondria.

Small wonder the man had turned to drink, especially when his wife's foundation was a constant reminder of what they had done. And, of course, he had wanted to prioritise giving aid to sick children from the Bellavista: the bastard had known it was his damned fault.

Lucia Borja had told Varela and it was the reason that he'd gone after Phillips and the other members of *Suministros La Flecha Rota*. Varela's daughter lived on the estate. She was exposed to the contaminated water. And she died of cancer.

Danny was willing to bet the papers that had blown away at the lock-up proved that the water was contaminated.

And that must have been why the water company ceased trading so abruptly. Every time the mine shaft flooded, more of the contaminated soil would have been washed into the aquifer. Sooner or later, they would have realised that they couldn't hide it any longer and that was when they decided to wind the company up.

Danny tossed his cigarette to the floor. He took his laptop back.

'Sorry, Mr Margaux,' Danny said, 'I'll have to email you this file. I've got some writing to do.'

10

D ANNY WROTE THE story in two hours, sitting in his boxer shorts, chain-smoking. He stuck to the facts he could prove.

He started with Hector Castillo and the fudged report on
the contaminated soil. He then mentioned the strange labour
dispute that had occurred on the Bellavista, the presence of the
immigrant workers and the purchase of the abandoned mine.
He quoted the old man, mentioning the numbers of lorries that
he had seen going up to the mine. After that, Danny developed
the theme of *Suministros La Flecha Rota* and the way in which
it had suddenly ceased trading. Finally, he dealt with Lucia
Borja, her grievance with Sixto Escobar and Sebastian Gomez
and how she had used Gabriel Varela in order to achieve her
vengeance. The completed article was roughly 2,400 words
long.

When he'd finished he attached the file to an email and sent
it to Paco Pino with a message saying, *Make sure you bloody
read the article this time. I want both our names to go on this.
And fuck Sebastian Gomez's offer.*

Then he set off for Paco Pino's house.

His mobile rang continuously while he was driving, but
Danny didn't respond. He wanted to discuss this face to face
with Paco.

'I know what you're going to say,' Paco said when he let

Danny inside his flat, 'but no one is going to print this. Not without proof.'

'I've got proof.'

'Let me see it.'

Danny took out the sheet of paper he had ripped from the council minutes and the six wrinkled pages of water analysis results. Paco's nose creased as he regarded the scrappy, torn edge of the council minutes and the spatters of rain and mud on the lab results.

'This is it?'

'This is all I have at the moment. But once we publish, it will flush out more details, I'm sure of it.'

'And these water analyses show the water to be contaminated with plutonium?'

'No. But I –'

Paco shook his head. 'Then we don't have it.'

'So, what do you want to do? Accept Gomez's offer? Is that your price, Paco? Forty grand? This prick has spent his entire life buying people. And now you're going to let him buy us?'

Paco sank his head into his hands. He stayed that way for a long time, sighing. Then he said, 'I'm sick of this, Danny. This isn't the way I work. Do you know what I dream of? A fucking nine-to-five job. You're obsessed. And I just don't understand anything any more. If you want to go on a crusade, fine, but don't expect me to go trailing around after you. I'm tired and I'm fat and I'm. . . I just don't have this obsession that drives you.'

'If this is about you belting me, that's water under –'

'No. This is about you. Look at what happened to Marsha. And *still* you want to continue?'

'Paco, just help me get to speak to a news editor. I'll do the rest.'

They spent two hours on the phone. Danny quickly realised he was on a hiding to nothing. Gomez had been busy. News editors were either instantly dismissive of the story, or quick to point out the holes. *Not without solid proof* was the mantra Danny heard repeated. The problem was, they were right: Danny didn't have the story. Not the sort of nailed down, watertight story he should have had. And it was his fault. That stupid briefcase full of money had turned their heads, made them unaware of what was really important.

Eventually, a news editor at *El Mundo* agreed to look at the story. Twenty minutes later, she asked to speak to Danny via Skype.

The Spanish woman's face and upper body filled the screen as she sat behind her desk, looking through the printouts of the documents Danny had emailed. After a minute of silence, she looked up, adjusted her glasses and shook her head.

'The story you want to write, Mr Sanchez, I'm afraid you don't have it. What you have is a lot of supposition – albeit very credible – and conjecture. But you need more hard information. I can't possibly consider publishing this as it is at the moment. We would be opening ourselves up to all sorts of expensive litigation.

'But the story here about this Hector Castillo fellow, the contaminated soil and the possible cover up is interesting. I'd be willing to run with that. This other thread about the removal of the soil, the mine and the contaminated water is a no-go until you obtain more proof.'

Danny was getting angry now, angry the way he always

got when he knew the other person was right and he didn't want them to be.

'Don't you understand?' Danny said. 'Thousands of people have been exposed to this water. They need to be warned.'

'I agree,' she said, 'but where's your proof, Mr Sanchez? Even if you were able to obtain documents from the local health centre proving an especially high incidence of cancer among residents of the Bellavista, it still wouldn't be enough. People get cancer all the time.

'If you are really this concerned, I'm afraid you will have to find another method of disseminating your information. Of course, you're welcome to try it with other publications, but I can guarantee they'll say the same thing: You don't have the story. With something like this, it's got to be cast-iron, 110% infallible. There is always the internet, but I really wouldn't advise it. Not against a man like Sebastian Gomez. If you libel him, he will ruin you and there are specialists now who can trace ISP addresses no matter how well-disguised they are.'

The woman said goodbye.

After that, Danny phoned Alan Neave, and asked the residents' association to help disseminate the news, but Neave cut him off when Danny began to explain.

'You want to tell people about this . . . *theory* without the slightest proof? Do you know what it will do to house prices? You'll single-handedly wipe this whole estate off the map. You won't be able to give the houses away. I'm sorry, Mr Sanchez, but I have been sorely misled about your intentions in pursuing this story, and I would appreciate it if you didn't call me any more.'

Danny went outside and joined Paco on the balcony, shaking his head.

'Right,' Paco said, 'let me see if I've got this straight. We've wasted an entire week on a story no newspaper will print, that we daren't publish on the internet and that we can't even give away to the fucking residents' association that represents the affected people? What do you suggest we do now, then, Danny? Go round knocking on people's doors trying to tell them that maybe, about four years ago their tap water was contaminated? Because, let me tell you, if I had someone turn up out of the blue like that, I wouldn't pay them much attention.'

Danny said nothing.

Paco lit a cigarette and said, 'We've no choice, Danny. We're going to have to give Gomez his money back. Tempting though forty grand is, I won't be beholden to that bastard for the rest of my life. How much did it cost to post the briefcase to yourself?'

'More than thirty euros.'

'Well,' said Paco in a flat voice, 'when you pick it up, tomorrow, you can at least reimburse yourself before you give it back. Because we are going to have to give it back, aren't we? There's nothing else we can do with it.' He shook his head. 'It sticks in my craw that we have to give it back to the bastard, though – especially after all the shit he's put us through. I wish we could throw the whole lot of it away. Or at least give it to a charity.'

Danny sat down heavily. The two men sat in silence until Paco rose and suddenly bellowed, 'Fuck it!' and kicked the chair across the balcony. Then he picked up a pile of papers that was on the coffee table and tossed them over the rail of the balcony. The wind caught the paper, sent it flapping in a hundred different directions as it fell towards the ground.

Paco turned, expecting admonishment from Danny, but Danny was lost in thought.

'What is it?' Paco said as Danny stood and rushed to the balcony, leaning over to watch the pages as they fluttered back and forth across the pavement below.

When Danny turned he was smiling.

'Can you get hold of a good-quality video camera and a tripod, Paco?'

'Probably. Why?'

'I've had an idea.'

11

Saturday, September 1st, 2012

S EBASTIAN GOMEZ WAS at the window of his office, high up on the sixth floor. He had one of the best views in the city here, looking out over the port away to his left and the governmental buildings and the Palace of Justice to his right.

Those busybodies from the Bellavista residents' association were holding their wretched protest meeting about the water supply today. Still, it was good that their attention was focused on the poor service, not on looking into why *Suministros La Flecha Rota* had so suddenly ceased trading.

It was in 2008 that the men behind *Grupo La Flecha Rota* had finally decided that the level of plutonium in the tap water had become too high. By that time, guilt had caused Florentino Yagüe and Martyn Phillips to unravel; Yague had sought solace in religion; Phillips, in the bottle. And they'd both got involved in that stupid charity Phillips's wife ran. Gomez had told them it was a stupid idea, that it might draw unwanted attention to them all; people had noticed that the mine shafts in the mountains were flooding and were beginning to ask questions about the water quality.

That was why they had decided to wind *Suministros La Flecha Rota* up and call it quits.

What had happened with the water was unfortunate, but Gomez felt no compunction. There was no malice intended. The simple fact of the matter was, by the time the contamination in the water had been detected, people had been ingesting it for more than three years. The company was already culpable, so it was better to ride it out and hope the problem went away.

No, they'd made sound business decisions all the way down the line. If he could go back, he would change things – of course he would. But the fact was, he was not culpable. And besides, the actual cause of cancer could be attributed to so many things.

He could hear the sound of chanting and whistles and the occasional crackle of a voice speaking through a megaphone. He pulled the blinds aside and looked away down the street in an effort to see what was happening, but the only thing visible was a group of *policia local* officers chatting in the street. The demonstration was taking place somewhere around the corner, outside the offices of the regional government.

Gomez let the blind fall back into place and looked at his watch: 09:40. The journalist had until midday.

He was feeling more than usually pleased with himself.

Things were starting to level out.

Varela was dead. Phillips and Escobar, too. And the Borja bitch. Morales was recovering in hospital. Gomez had spoken to him the night before and told him what to tell the police: that he remembered nothing at all about what had happened and had no idea who his kidnapper was. In fact, he should say that he hadn't even seen the guy's face, that he'd been attacked

from behind and bundled into the boot before he even knew
what was happening.

It was a plausible story. After all, Emilio Morales was a
wealthy man: a kidnap and ransom demand was not so far-
fetched.

Shrike was in custody, charged with the murder of Ricardo
Neymar. Shrike had tried to double cross them and he had
paid the price. Gomez would see to it that he learned to regret
that mistake.

There was just the situation with the journalist to sort out
now.

He had the contracts ready on the desk in front of him: one
for Danny Sanchez, the other for the photographer, Paco Pino.
It was based on a special watertight non-disclosure agreement
that Gomez himself had originally drawn up for employees of
a tobacco company years back.

Gomez had checked the newspapers carefully that
morning. There was not a whisper of the truth printed in any
of them. He'd done a good job of nipping the story in the
bud the day before. There wasn't really any way the journalist
could publish the story now.

He got up from his desk and went back to the window.
The hubbub in the street below had changed. He'd been listening to faint echoes of chanted slogans coming up through the
high-rise canyons in the city centre for the last half-an-hour,
but the sound was different now. It sounded less structured
somehow, and reminded him less of a protest meeting and
more of a football match.

Gomez pulled the blind to one side and angled his head so
he could look down along the street.

Blinding sunlight reflected from the glass-fronted building opposite, but he thought he saw movement at the end of the street where the protest was taking place. He squinted. There were people there now. He shielded his eyes, unsure of what he was seeing. It looked as if the people there were running in all directions at once.

As he watched, a man ran past on the opposite side of the street, bent double, chasing a scrap of paper along the street. Then Gomez saw another man. This one ran with his hands crossed in front of his chest, protecting something stuffed down the front of his jacket. He frowned when he saw that the police officers were also chasing scraps of paper; at that moment his secretary buzzed him to say that a Señor Sanchez was there to see him.

Gomez told her to send him up and sat down behind his desk, wondering why he suddenly felt so uneasy.

12

DANNY PUSHED THE office door open without knocking. He was damned if he would show Gomez any courtesy.

The lawyer was sitting behind an antique desk. Sunlight shone through the blinds, reflecting on the desk's polished veneer and his lacquered hair.

Gomez smiled sadly when he saw the briefcase in Danny's right hand. He motioned towards a chair on the other side of the desk and invited Danny to sit.

'I must say, strange though it might sound, that I'm rather disappointed to see you've brought my money back,' Gomez said, nodding towards the briefcase.

Danny placed it on the desk. When Gomez reached for it, Danny pulled it back slightly.

'Before I return this, I'd like to tell you what I think happened. Just for my own peace of mind.'

Gomez leant back in his chair, his fingertips steepled.

'You must think me a fool.'

'Was it your idea to dump the irradiated soil into the mine shaft?'

'I have no idea what you are talking about,' Gomez said, with a note of irritation.

'When did you discover the water had been contaminated?' Danny said. 'That was why you had Hector Castillo

343

killed, wasn't it? He wanted to warn people, didn't he? But that would have opened you all up to hundreds of lawsuits. Far simpler to keep schtum and hope the problem went away, wasn't it? But it didn't, did it? Because every time the rains came, the mine shaft flooded and more of the contaminated soil went into the aquifer.'

'I really don't have time to listen to your wild allegations, Señor Sanchez. I'm afraid that is for you to prove. Because if you publish one word of any of this, we will be seeing each other in court, I can promise you that. Do you know what the concept of onus probandi is, Señor Sanchez? The necessity of proof always lies with the person who lays charges.'

'You've got to be a heartless son-of-a-bitch to keep a thing like that quiet just to protect your fucking money.'

Gomez waved his hand in a gesture of contempt and reached for the briefcase. A faint smile creased Gomez's lips as he turned the briefcase towards him. When he popped the clasps and opened the lid his smile disappeared.

'I'm a man with scant appreciation for practical jokes, Señor Sanchez,' he said, turning the empty briefcase around on the desktop. 'Where is my money?'

'It's outside.'

'Outside where?'

'In the street.'

Gomez's brows creased. 'In the street. How?'

'About ten minutes ago, I went in to the government building up the street and rode the elevator to the roof. You know which building I mean, don't you? The building where about a hundred of the poor bastards you poisoned are currently holding a demonstration trying to get a decent supply of water.

'When I got to the roof, I took your briefcase, opened it out and tipped the whole lot off the top of the building. Of course, that wasn't the only thing I tipped out. There were also 200 leaflets I had printed up explaining exactly what went on with the water at the Bellavista, and exactly who was responsible. It made a quite a shower, I can tell you. A real tickertape parade.'

Gomez scoffed. Then he caught the look on Danny's face, and he started to blink rapidly. Danny's smile grew as the colour drained from Gomez's face; he knew what the bastard was probably thinking: Gomez was remembering the sudden commotion outside. He must have heard it: the crowd's sudden roar as it realised it was raining bank notes had been deafening.

'You'd be surprised how far the wind can take bank notes from eight stories up. They'll be picking up fifty-euro notes all the way from here to the port.'

Gomez stood. 'You bastard. I'll ruin you.'

'You're welcome to try,' Danny said, standing also. 'But first you've got to prove it was me that wrote the leaflets and tipped your money away.' Danny wiggled his fingers. 'Because you won't find any prints on the briefcase. I wiped it clean last night and checked it under a UV light. And that means that, for once, the onus probandi is on you, pal. Have a nice day.'

13

Footage of the shower of money drifting down from the top of the government building made news programmes all over the world in the next thirty-six hours. It was the sort of quirky story television networks lapped up.

Danny had waited until the end of the protest before he tipped the money away. He had to be sure the other television cameras had packed up and gone before he emptied the briefcase. How else could he be certain that Paco Pino was the only one filming? He needn't have worried, though, as the protest had attracted very little attention from the Spanish media.

The exclusive footage Paco filmed from the roof of a building across the street showed the whole sequence of events: the fluttering mass of brown notes as it spread upon the wind, twisting and coiling like paper starlings; the reaction of the protestors as the mass of paper drifted down among them and began to settle on the pavement; and then the bedlam as the people at the protest march realised there were hundreds of fifty-euro notes blowing around their feet.

By the end of the first day, Danny and Paco had sold the story in seventeen different countries; they picked up another twelve sales the following morning. All in all, they earned more than seventeen thousand euros.

But the money was only the start of it. The next day, attention began to focus on the leaflets that had fluttered to earth along with the money. It was Danny's article, printed on both sides of a sheet of A4. The headline read: COMPANY SUPPLIED RADIOACTIVE WATER. Danny had not signed it.

On the Sunday Alan Neave appeared on a Spanish television news programme announcing that the residents' association would be looking into the claims that water contaminated with radioactive soil had been supplied to houses on the Bellavista urbanisation.

The first thing the association did was to arrange blood, urine and faeces tests for anyone who thought they might have ingested contaminated water. So many came forward, they had to queue up all day outside the Bellavista's community centre.

The association determined that in the last decade, thirty-six people had died of cancer-related deaths on the Bellavista, and a further forty-three were suffering from various manifestations of the disease.

The association also asked for donations to pay for an investigation. Within two days, they had managed to gather 4,000 euros. Specialists were sent down the mine shaft to photograph what lay at the bottom. The grainy, black and white images they took showed hundreds of battered and broken oil drums.

Meanwhile, Sebastian Gomez had not been idle. By Monday, he had hired scientific experts who presented an impressive dossier of evidence gathered from practically every nuclear facility in the world that operated close to residential areas showing that, while plutonium was carcinogenic, the dilutive effect of large amounts of water was sufficient to nullify its toxic properties. However, by that time, pressure had begun to build and public outcry had begun to be directed towards the two remaining board members of *Suministros La Flecha Rota*.

Gomez was egged as he walked to his car one day and the word *asesinos* – murderers – was scrawled in red paint across the front of the building where the investment group had its offices. And as the story began to gather pace in the Spanish and UK media, a veritable flock of lawyers descended on the Bellavista.

Now that the story was out, Danny was able to begin selling parts of it to the Spanish and British media. First, he wrote a big story on Gabriel Varela and the man's quest for vengeance. Then he concentrated on trying to prove that *Suministros La Flecha Rota* had knowingly supplied the contaminated water.

Danny suggested to the residents' association that they campaign in order to have the boreholes and wells used by *Suministros La Flecha Rota* reopened and the water tested, but Alan Neave pointed out that, even if the water was found to be contaminated now, it would not prove contamination in the past. Danny used this quote in an article he published for Sureste News, entitled *Association leader fears proof of contamination "impossible" to obtain*.

Danny got the call the day after his article appeared. The Spanish man who phoned refused to give his name. He asked to meet Danny that afternoon in a car park underneath a shopping centre.

He arrived thirty minutes early. He parked and walked to the place where they'd arranged to meet, the furthest, darkest corner of the subterranean car park. Fans whirred on the wall and Danny could smell the fast food restaurants in the mall upstairs.

The man waiting for him was small and painfully thin and had a hump-back. His eyes bulged from skin so pale that it was almost albino and his hair was lank.

The man wasted no time. He handed Danny a brown envelope. 'That's what you need for your story,' he said.

'Who are you?'

He shook his head. 'No names,' he said. 'Suffice to say that I worked for Laboratorios Florentino Yagüe for more than thirty years.'

'Why are you doing this?'

He considered the question, red bulbous eyes turned towards the unpainted concrete above them. 'I want to do what's right. Florentino Yagüe was a good man. I think that is why he kept these results, so that one day the truth would be known. But he was weak.'

Then the little man walked away into the darkness.

Danny did not follow. He waited for the man to leave, walked to a bar and ordered coffee. Then he opened the envelope. Inside, was a thick wad of papers, bearing the letterhead of Laboratorios Florentino Yagüe, S.L. The papers held a full run-down of all the water analysis results the laboratory had undertaken for *Suministros La Flecha Rota* between 1999 and 2009.

A post-it note attached to the top page read, *My employer's son thinks he has destroyed all the evidence of the water analyses, but I made copies before I handed him the floppy disks.*

From September, 2004 onwards someone had highlighted the results for something called Alpha Radiological Contaminants.

Danny looked through the documents, smiling.

14

T HE NEXT DAY he spoke to Marsha on the telephone.

'I saw the news,' Marsha said. 'About the Bellavista, I mean. Was the money anything to do with you?'

She listened as Danny explained. Then she said, 'What will happen now?'

'Now?' Danny's eyes were fixed on the wall. 'Now it will get mired for years in the Spanish legal system while the case is batted back and forth from one court to the other. The lawyers will turn it upside down and inside out and make it so that everyone involved is sick to the back teeth of the whole mess. Look at that business with the toxic olive oil in Madrid. More than 300 people died, but it still took the Supreme Court eight years to find the distributors of the oil guilty. This is going to be even more complex.'

Marsha sighed. 'I guess you won, then.'

'No, I haven't. Not if I've lost you.'

Marsha said nothing.

'You're supposed to say "But you haven't lost me, Danny".'

Marsha sniffed.

'I'm sorry, Danny. I've been doing some thinking during the last few days. . .'

Danny felt like he'd been punched in the gut.

'And?' he said.

'I need more from a partner than you're able to give. I need stability. I need normality. And I'm not going to get that from you. Not while you carry on working the way that you do.'

'Are you asking me to choose between you and the job?'

'No,' Marsha said. 'Because that wouldn't be any decision at all for you, would it, Danny? The job is who you are. I'm just an appendage to that.'

'So what are you saying?'

Marsha drew a deep breath.

'I'm truly sorry, Danny, but I think it's over between us.'

THE END

ACKNOWLEDGEMENTS

I HAVE THANKED THE same people in all my books, but I never tire of repeating my gratitude.

Jen and Chris are my publishers and I can't express my thanks enough for giving my work a platform. Linda first signed me to Salt and, together with Jim, helped weed out the myriad mistakes and inconsistencies in my English.

Dad, Mum, Louise, Richard, Helen, Russell, Dean, Lauren, without your support none of this would be possible.

My friends all know who they are, but I love them all and will never tire of showing my appreciation for their presence in my life.

A mi familia española: Loli, Mari Carmen, Inesita, Fran, y todos los demás que me cuidaban durante los 13 años que viví en su bonito país.

Broken Arrow required a great deal of research. The following people's help was invaluable:

Professor John Cassella from the Department of Forensic Science and Crime Science at Staffordshire University gave me some fantastically useful information on the effects of desert soil on dead bodies. His expertise really helped to shape the whole storyline with Hector Castillo.

Jeff Bickel from the Department of Nuclear Engineering at

the University of California, Berkeley, gave me information on plutonium and helped to really nail down the details of that part of the storyline.

Judith Gregory is a chemist and the wife of a good friend. She was tireless in tracking down the information I needed about water testing and, without her help, the book would have been a shambles from a scientific standpoint.

Photographer Mark Beltran helped to make Paco Pino sound solidly professional. Anything technical involving Paco and his cameras is actually Mark speaking. He also put some work my way back when I was really struggling financially, so I owe him and Richard a double thanks.